THE GLACIER BAY MURDERS

Trilogy Christian Publishers
A Wholly Owned Subsidiary of Trinity Broadcasting Network
2442 Michelle Drive
Tustin, CA 92780

For information, address Trilogy Christian Publishing
Rights Department, 2442 Michelle Drive, Tustin, Ca 92780.
Trilogy Christian Publishing/ TBN and colophon are trademarks of Trinity Broadcasting Network.
For information about special discounts for bulk purchases, please contact Trilogy Christian Publishing.

10 9 8 7 6 5 4 3 2 1
Library of Congress Cataloging-in-Publication Data is available.
ISBN 979-8-89333-259-9
ISBN 979-8-89333-260-5 (ebook)

www.donaldsheagley.com

Book 2 in The Hunter Kingsley Series

THE GLACIER BAY MURDERS

DONALD SHEAGLEY

Also by Donald Sheagley

MURDER IN THE NORTH ATLANTIC

A tale of greed, jealousy, betrayal, and murder, followed by an investigation initiated by retired Secret Service agent Hunter Kingsley. Kingsley is a Christian believer and also becomes a suspect as the investigation heats up. The Columbo-style inverted murder mystery will keep you engaged and wondering what will happen next, all the way to the last sentence.

Dedicated to my wife, Peggy, for all that she had to put up with during the writing and publication process, but also because she discovered a major snag in the story and helped with the resolution. I also dedicate this novel to Peggy simply because I love her.

CHAPTER 1

In 1976, the bicentennial year for the United States, Napa Valley, California, was put on the map as a result of what has become known as the Judgement of Paris. On May 24th of that year, Steven Spurrier, an Englishman who ran a wine shop and wine school in Paris, arranged and hosted a blind taste test of six top California Cabernets and Chardonnays against four French Bordeauxs and four French white Burgundies. The judges were among the best wine tasters in France, and, to everyone's surprise, they chose a California wine over the French for both the red and white flights. The movie "Bottle Shock" is a fairly accurate portrayal of this event. The Judgement of Paris ended an era in which it was thought that fine wine only came from Europe and started a vineyard and real estate boom in Napa Valley and the surrounding areas.

The 1976 wine-tasting event in Paris was not only a catalyst to the explosion of wineries in Northern California but also to wineries in other states in the United States and in other countries, such as Australia, South Africa, and South America. This 1976 wine industry watershed event curtailed the aloofness and snobbery the Europeans, particularly the French, had about their wines. But now, years later, according to some, it's Napa Valley and California wineries in general that display the aloofness and snobbery once only possessed by the Europeans.

Maybe it's inevitable that success breeds contempt. Maybe that's just the fallen human nature at work. California wineries are certainly successful. A good eighty percent of the wines exported from the United States come from California. But gone are the days when you could take a leisurely drive through Napa Valley and stop at a few friendly wineries for free wine tasting. Now, the roads are crowded, the restaurants have a waiting line, and most of the wineries have lost their down-home friendliness and charm. And no charge wine tasting in California is long since gone. It can cost upwards of seventy-five dollars at some Napa wineries just to sample a few swigs of wine.

Napa wineries have become big business. The wines are still excellent, but for a relaxing day of wine tasting, go elsewhere. And, with big business enterprises also comes a need to protect the interests of that business. Thus, a few years after the 1976 Judgement of Paris, the consortium known as Protect California Wine (PCW) was formed.

CHAPTER 2

More recently, in light of the dominance of California wines in the domestic market, some of the wine producers in other states have started to promote their wines more aggressively and sometimes in direct opposition to California wines. For example, the Verde Valley Wine Growers Association of Arizona sometimes dares you to compare some of their wines to the best of Napa Valley. The majority of Golden State wine producers are not afraid of competition with other states, as many of them believe a little friendly competition is good for the wine industry in general. However, a not-too-insignificant number of California wine producers are concerned that as wineries from other states gain more and more recognition, it will start to chip away at the dominance California wineries presently enjoy. With this concern in mind, a splinter group from the PCW recently emerged.

This splinter group has no official name but refers to themselves as simply "the group." In fact, the group is not official in any way, and the PCW has no official knowledge of it. In the meetings thus far, the group has discussed and formulated plans to identify and target certain out-of-state wineries with derogatory disinformation about their growing, harvesting, and production practices. For example, the group has discussed the possibility of manufacturing some kind of official report to the effect that, say, a certain out-of-state wine-growing region has been found to have toxic soil, and wine produced from grapes grown in that area could be detrimental to one's health. Underhanded, for sure, but why not—we are now in the disinformation age.

On Wednesday, March 15th (ironically, the ides of March), the group called an emergency meeting. Word of the meeting was announced via coded text messages and was held at a certain member's winery after hours. The members don't use their real names at the meetings. They use code names, like fraternity and sorority nicknames. Basically, members of the group do about everything they can to maintain anonymity. When you are contemplating quasi-criminal activity, anonymity is important.

The emergency meeting took place at the wine-tasting room of a not-so-well-known vineyard in upper Napa Valley at 8:30 p.m. All the workers and employees of the vineyard had long since left for home. The owners of the winery, code-named Shultz and Sandy, had three bottles of Merlot and three bottles of Chardonnay open on the counter for group members to enjoy during the meeting, and the opening salute. Even though the group has had only a few meetings to date, the members already have a wine glass salute they open and close with. With raised glasses, the meeting opened with: "We salute you, California, land of the vine. May you always prosper, and things will be fine."

Jeep (not his real name), the leader of the group, is a no-nonsense individual and got right to the point. "Fellow vintners, I have just learned some troubling news that, if true, could have a serious adverse impact on our California wine industry. My wife and I heard this yesterday from friends of ours, Hector and Paula Veracruz, who live in New Mexico. Hector and Paula are friends with a couple by the name of Scott and Catalina Poncetran. The Poncetrans live in Albuquerque and put together and host what they call a wine lovers cruise on an ocean-going cruise ship every year. They have been doing this for thirteen years now and normally have one or two winemakers on board who are allowed to bring some of their wines on the ship for wine-tasting presentations. Usually, these winemakers are from New Mexico and sometimes from Arizona, but never from California. That's fine. We don't care if their little group of loyal wine drinkers want to cruise and drink New Mexico wine. But this year, the Poncetrans have a more ambitious agenda.

"This year, according to our friends, Hector and Paula, who, by the way, are going on this year's upcoming wine lovers cruise to Alaska with the Poncetrans, there are going to be four different winemakers on board presenting their wines. And, one of the vintners is a California winemaker—a California winemaker from Napa Valley. Ed and Joyce Cooling, who own and help operate Los Amigos Cellars just a few miles from here, are the California representatives."

"Well, that's good," said Darth (not his real name.) "That's good, isn't it? So, this wine lovers cruise couple is going to finally include a California vintner. And Los Amigos Cellars put out some decent award-winning wines. So, what's the problem? I don't see a problem."

"Yeah," Dingo (not his real name) said. "I don't see a problem either. This Poncetran couple has finally seen the light and has included a California winemaker on their cruise. Bravo."

"Well," Jeep said, "there is a potential problem—a big potential problem. Let me explain. Normally, according to my New Mexico friends, Hector and Paula, the Poncetrans have a wine-tasting presentation by each of the winemakers on board the ship one at a time. And the Poncetrans are going to do that—four different vintners—four different and separate presentations. But, on the last sea day, the day before the ship docks in Vancouver, British Columbia, and everyone disembarks, the Poncetrans are apparently planning a blind taste test of wines from the four different vintners. That is, California wines are going to be pitted against wines from three other states. Probably against the best wines the other states have to offer."

"Okay," Dog Bite (not his real name) said, "maybe a few of the wine enthusiasts prefer one of the other state's wine over the California wine. That's just a preference by a few amateur individuals. If they prefer a non-California wine over any of our fine California wines, then they just don't have an educated palate. That's a reflection of their lack of education and sophistication. We can't help that."

"True," Jeep said, "if that were all there was to it. But my friends say that this blind taste test the Poncentrans have planned is going to be a big deal. They are apparently planning on having reputable, official wine-tasting judges do the tasting, not the people in the wine lovers group. And, there will supposedly be publicity. There is going to be at least one reporter in attendance."

"That sounds like the Judgement of Paris," Ted Bundy (not his real name) said.

"That's exactly what I'm afraid of," Jeep said. "I'm afraid that the Poncetrans are trying to reenact the Judgement of Paris. Only this time, I fear, it might become known as the Judgement of California."

CHAPTER 3

"Oh my," Ted Bundy said, "we can't let that happen. We have to stop this. Just like in Paris in 1976, if some upstart winery in another state has a wine that is judged superior to one of our California wines, and there is enough publicity, it could result in a big chink in the armor of our wine industry."

"I agree with Ted," Forklift (not his real name) said. "I don't know Scott and Catalina Poncetran, and I've never heard of their wine lovers cruises, but I think we have to take this situation seriously. The winemakers in France didn't take the boys from California seriously in 1976, and they paid the price. But, on the other hand, I don't think we should jump to conclusions. Can we find out more about the Poncetrans and their intentions with this blind wine-tasting event? And, no offense, Jeep, but how reliable is your source of information—your friends in New Mexico?"

"No offense taken," Jeep said. "Our friends in New Mexico are very forthright and honest about things and told my wife and me the information as a matter of conversation. Our friends, Hector and Paula Veracruz, are going on the wine lovers cruise to Alaska, but they are unaware that we, as California vintners, would have any concern over this blind wine-tasting test. I don't want to spook them with our concern so that they clam up. I want them to feel free to mention things about the Poncetrans and their intentions."

"Do we know, besides our California vintner, who the other three vintners are who will be participating in the wine-tasting event?" Ted Bundy asked.

"Yes, we do," responded Jeep. "I already mentioned the California representative, Ed and Joyce Cooling of Los Amigos Cellars here in Napa Valley. Then, there is Tony and Maryanne Black of Black's Smuggler Winery in Bosque, New Mexico. Jim and Linda Perdon own and manage Leapfrog Vineyards in Camp Verde, Arizona. And then, there is Jay and Roxanne Patterson of Silver Leaf Vineyards of Lincoln, Nebraska."

"Nebraska!" exclaimed Dog Bite. "You gotta be kidding me! They make wine in Nebraska?"

"Yes, they do," replied Shultz. "I did a little research. The first post-prohibition Nebraska winery, Cuthills Vineyards Winery, opened in 1994. Silver Leaf Vineyards opened in 1997 and are the second largest of the Nebraska wine producers and supposedly make some very good wines."

"Well, I'll be," replied Dog Bite. "I guess everybody wants to get into the act."

"That is the problem we are discussing," said Jeep. "Since this wine lovers cruise leaves on April 29th, about six weeks from today, if we are going to try to stop this Judgement of California wine taste test, we must arrange for something as soon as possible."

"But, wait a minute," Dingo said. "We seem to be assuming that one of these upstart wineries is going to win first place against our Napa Valley wines. That is something I don't think is very likely. I hate to sound uppity, but could you imagine a wine from Nebraska taking first place over a Napa Valley wine?"

"I agree," said Jeep. "One of our Napa Valley wines losing to an upstart Nebraska wine is not very likely. But remember, it is not just Nebraska the California wines are competing against. It is also Arizona and New Mexico. Let's just say that six different California wines are going to compete against six different wines from New Mexico, six from Arizona, and six from Nebraska. It's not unreasonable that one of those eighteen wines could win first place over one of the six California wines. Gentlemen—can you imagine the repercussions to the California wine industry if an Arizona or New Mexico wine won a superior taste test over a Napa Valley wine? Or, God forbid, a Nebraska wine taste tested superior over a California wine. California would be the laughingstock of the country—maybe even the world. Gentlemen—who agrees with me that we can't let this Judgement of California wine taste test of the Poncetrans take place?"

All the men agreed—Shultz, Darth, Dingo, Dog Bite, Ted Bundy, Forklift, and, obviously, Jeep. All the men agreed that, somehow, the Poncetran's wine taste test must not take place. Jeep and Shultz said the two of them would look into different ways the cruise ship wine test could be canceled, and then they would call for another meeting in a few days. When the seven men returned home, they told their wives that, at the meeting that "didn't really take place," progress was made on a possible solution to a problem that their wives were better off not knowing anything about.

CHAPTER 4

Sunday, March 19
Shultz and Sandy's Vineyard
Follow-Up Meeting

"Thank you, gentlemen, for showing up and being prompt," Jeep said. "It was another busy weekend here in the valley, and I'm sure we're all tired, so I'll try to make our meeting as brief as possible. Dog Bite texted me and said he would be a few minutes late, but let's get started, and I'll catch him up later if need be." Jeep raised his wine glass, and the rest followed suit. "We salute you, California, land of the vine. May you always prosper, and things will be fine."

Jeep continued, "Just to recap—this last Wednesday, the seven of us had an emergency meeting to discuss what could be the Judgement of California and how to stop it. Schultz and I said we would look into different things we might be able to do about the situation. Well, without delving into the convoluted way… Dog Bite. Thanks for coming. Pour yourself a glass. You didn't miss a thing."

Jeep again went on, "Without getting into the convoluted details of how Schultz and I learned about and then got a hold of this guy—well, I think we have a solution to our problem. That is, I think we found a guy who can persuade the wine lovers cruise people, Scott and Catalina Poncetran, not to go through with this big wine-tasting judgment they are planning on having on May 9th during their Alaska cruise.

"This guy—and Schultz was instrumental in finding out about this guy. It's one of those things where a guy knows a guy who knows a guy who knows a guy who fixes things—who takes care of problems for people. Not mafia. Not a criminal, per se. A guy who has associates, and they tackle problems, in not necessarily a totally above-board way, but usually without violence and outright criminal activity. Like, sort of a 'Mission Impossible' scenario."

"So, who is this guy, and what does he propose to do?" asked Darth.

"He didn't tell us his actual name," Jeep said. "He said it's better that way—at least for now. He just said to think of him as 'available'; available for the job. So, we started calling him Mr. Available."

"Okay," Darth said, "so how does Mr. Available think he is going to fix our problem?"

"He threw out some ideas," Jeep said, "but he said that it's better that we don't know the details. He said a lot of this kind of work is ad-lib. You have a plan, but that plan often disintegrates right at the get-go, and then you just make it up as you go along."

"Did he give you any idea at all of what he might do?" asked Forklift.

"He said, off the top of his head, that if he and his associates could keep the wine of the different winegrowers from getting on the ship, the problem would be solved. No wine—no wine to taste test—end of story."

"Hey, I like that idea," Ted Bundy said. "That is neat and clean. No wine for the taste test means the big, bad blind taste test never happens. No wine, no worries."

"I like that idea too," Dingo said. "So how did he say he would do this?"

"He didn't say," Schultz said. "He said if he started giving too many details, then we might try to do it ourselves. Plus, he said, he was just thinking off the top of his head, and he might come up with some even better ways to achieve the results we're looking for."

"Well," Dog Bite said, "even if we thought we could pull it off ourselves, I think we should have a third party, like this guy and his cohorts, do the dirty deed."

"Yes," Dingo said. "We need to keep arms-length from any kind of nefarious activity. Besides, we're busy running our wineries. I sure couldn't take the time off to get involved in some escapade."

"Okay, what do you guys think?" Jeep asked. "Time is of the essence here. We don't have a lot of time to shop around. Schultz and I came away with a favorable impression of Mr. Available. He seems like a no-nonsense, can-do guy. Should we hire him?"

"I'm inclined to go with him," Ted Bundy said.

"Did you and Schultz meet him in person," Darth asked, "or was this all over the phone or the internet?"

"We meet him in person," Jeep said. "He's a big guy and looks like he could take care of a lot of stuff by himself. He is not local. He is from out of the area, maybe Las Vegas. When we got a hold of him, he said he happened to be in our area on business. He said he doesn't divulge any information about past clients, but he did say that the Pick-n-Save market that was going to be built down by the junction is now not going to be built, and that was his doing."

"All right," Dog Bite said, "I'm willing to go along with hiring this guy, but what's it going to cost us? Did you discuss price with him?"

"Yeah, I'll go along," Forklift said, "as long as it doesn't cost too much."

"In rough figures," Schultz said, "the guy thought it might be between ten to twenty thousand, depending on if he had to go on the cruise or not. He said he might be persuaded to take part of the payment in wine. I think he sees this as a fairly easy job."

"I'm in," Dingo said.

Darth and Ted Bundy also agreed to give Mr. Available a go at it.

"Excellent," Jeep said. "Schultz and I will set it up with Mr. Available. And, one other thing which I think will put our minds at ease even more. Schultz and Sandy are going on the cruise with the wine lovers group. They received their reservation confirmation yesterday. It will be a vacation for them, and Schultz will be there to also make sure our mission gets accomplished."

"Good for you, Schultz," Dog Bite said. "It will be good having one of us on the spot."

Everyone else chimed in with thanks and agreement. Glasses were raised, and, "We salute you, California, land of the vine. May you always prosper, and things will be fine," closed out the meeting.

CHAPTER 5

Saturday, April 29
Vancouver, British Columbia, Canada
On Board the Alaskan Princess

The Alaskan Princess is one of the smaller ships in the Princess Cruise Lines fleet of twenty ships. It is the newest ship in the fleet and, as the name implies, was designed primarily for cruising the passageways and smaller ports of Alaska. It can also safely sail in closer to the glaciers than the larger ships.

At 1630 hours (4:30 p.m.), the ship's public address system came alive. "Good afternoon. This is Captain Horatio Bustamante. As we pull away from our berth, on behalf of Princess Cruises and the crew of the magnificent Alaskan Princess, I want to welcome you all on board. We have a fantastic itinerary planned, and, with any luck with the weather, we will see some spectacular scenery.

"We are at sea tomorrow and the next day. On Tuesday, May 2nd, we will cruise the Hubbard Glacier. Wednesday, we will spend the day at Icy Strait Point. Thursday, we will be at Juneau all day. Friday, we will spend the day at Skagway. Saturday, May 6th, we will cruise Glacier Bay National Park. Sunday, we will be at Sitka, and Monday, at Ketchikan. Tuesday, May 9th is a sea day, and Wednesday, May 10th, we arrive back at Vancouver at 0730 hours or 7:30 a.m.

"Again, welcome aboard, and may we all have a very pleasant journey. I will now turn it over to our cruise director, Lenny Coleman."

"Greetings everyone! This is your cruise director, Lenny Coleman. If any of you have sailed on the Ocean Princess in the last few years, you may remember me. I was cruise director on that fine ship for seven years. I recently transferred to the Alaskan Princess for a change of scenery. And scenery is what we are going to see. We are in store for a very scenic and fun-filled voyage.

"And, speaking of fun, please join me and some of the other cruise staff for our sail-away party just getting underway on deck fourteen, the Lido deck by the pool. Yes, it's a little chilly outside, but I believe we have a hardy group of people on board for this first voyage of the Alaska cruise season—so—let the hardy party, and let's party hardy! Besides, to help with our sail-away party, there are complimentary Alaskan Moose drinks available while they last. The drink is an Alaskan Princess original. I had a sample earlier today, and I guarantee it will warm the cockles of your heart. So, again, welcome aboard—and let's go party!"

CHAPTER 6

Stateroom C 232
Balcony Cabin of Hunter and Susan Kingsley

"So, Susie Quizie, do you feel like going up and partying hearty?"

"You know I do, Hunter, but let me finish unpacking and putting things away. I'm almost done. I hope I've brought enough warm clothes. I'm starting to have second thoughts about going on this early-season cruise instead of waiting until late June or July when it's warmer. And also, there's a greater chance of fog on these early cruises. It's going to be terrible if we cruise into Glacier Bay and can't even see the glacier because of fog."

"Yeah, it might be a little foggier in the mornings than it would be in July, but we'll be all right. Besides, the main reason we're on this cruise is because our friends, Scott and Catalina, chose this Alaska trip as this year's wine lovers cruise. And the reason they chose this cruise is exactly because it is an early season cruise and thus less expensive than one in June or July. Scott and Catalina wanted it to be more affordable so more people could go.

"And it worked. I think this wine lovers cruise of close to one hundred people is the largest group they've ever had. So, don't worry about the possibility of a little fog and cold weather. It's a wine lovers cruise. It will be great fun even if we don't get to see all the sights."

"I know, Hunter. I know all of that. I was just venting. And I know we're on this cruise because we wanted to finally go on one of Scott and Catalina's wine lovers cruises."

"Good. That's settled. We are going to have a great time no matter what. We are with our good friends, and they brought wine."

"Yes, we'll have a great time as long as there's not another murder on board like on our last cruise."

"Well, fat chance of that. Let's go topside and join the sail-away party."

CHAPTER 7

Stateroom C 232

Hunter and Susan Kingsley returned to their cabin right after the sail-away party.

"Oh, look, Hunter—there is a red light blinking on the phone." Susan walked over to the phone. "There's a message. It says we have a message."

"Okay. Play the message."

Twenty seconds later, Susan put the phone receiver down. "It was Catalina. She said to come to their cabin as soon as we can. It's cabin C 755—the Glacier Bay cabin, on deck ten, the same as our deck, but at the very rear of the ship."

"Okay."

"And Hunter."

"Yes."

"There was an urgency in her voice."

"Really. Well, let's go."

CHAPTER 8

Suite C 755
Suite of Scott and Catalina Poncetran

Hunter knocked on the C 755 cabin door. Catalina opened the door, and Hunter and Susan stepped in. "Wow," Hunter said. "You have got to be kidding me! This is a suite, isn't it? It has to be a full-blown suite. You have a living room and a separate bedroom. A wet bar. A big TV."

"And another wall-mounted TV in the bedroom," Catalina said.

"Good to see you," Susan said as she gave Catalina and then Scott a hello hug.

Hunter then gave Catalina and Scott a hug. "Sorry I got a little carried away, but this is really slick. You have so much room."

"Yes," Scott said, "and we have a good-sized balcony looking out at the propeller wake with access from two different sliders."

"This is an upgrade from Princess," Catalina said. "Princess was very kind to us this time. It's the first time we've ever had a suite on any of our cruises. We are really going to enjoy this."

"You guys deserve it," Susan said, "with all the hard work you two have put into these wine lovers cruises through the years."

"Well, thank you," Catalina said. "You're right. These cruises are a lot of work, but we thoroughly enjoy it. And we're so glad our retired Secret Service agent and his wife are with us. Not only because we're good friends and we enjoy doing things with you guys but also because we need your help. We think someone is trying to harass us."

"Yeah," Scott continued, "it's probably nothing, but a couple of things have happened that make us wonder."

"Like what?" Hunter asked.

"Well," Scott said, "a week before we were to leave for the cruise, we received an email from Princess saying that their policy had changed and they were not going to let our vintners bring their wine on board."

"That kind of ruins the whole idea of the wine lovers cruise, doesn't it?" Hunter asked.

"It certainly hampers it," Scott said. "We can still do our wine tastings and have our different winemakers on board, but we would have to use the ship's wines."

"Couldn't Princess just order wines from your winemakers," Susan asked, "and then they could still present their own wines."

"That's something that could be looked into," Catalina said, "but we'd need more than the one-week notice we received. However, fortunately, we looked into it, and it turned out to be a bogus email."

"That's right," Scott said, "we contacted Princess immediately, and they said they never sent such an email. They said nothing had changed, and we still had their special permission to allow our winemakers to bring their selected wines on board for our private wine tastings as we have always done."

"I bet that was a relief," Sue said. "But if Princess didn't send that email, who did—and why? Do you guys have any idea?"

"No," Catalina said, "and we didn't have time to delve into it. With the cruise only a week away, we had a lot of other things to do."

"So," Hunter said, "this bogus email is very curious. Did you happen to make a paper copy of it, and did you bring it with you?"

"Yes, and yes," Scott said.

Catalina went to the upper right-hand desk drawer, pulled out the copy of the email, and handed it to Hunter. Hunter and Susan looked it over. Hunter asked Catalina if they had any paper copies of legitimate emails from Princess to use for comparison purposes. They did. Hunter and Susan did a comparison observation, and then Hunter spoke up.

"It's just like the old days in identifying counterfeit money. The best way is to compare the suspect counterfeit bill with the one you know is real. You look at the details and note anything that is different in the suspect bill from the legitimate bill of the same denomination. And you compare the quality of the printing and the quality and thickness of the paper and so forth.

"It's the same with other things—suspect emails, suspect jewelry, suspect handbags. A good way to identify a fake when you're not an expert is to compare the suspect item to the real."

"And, as we know," Susan said, "in a similar way, we test what people say the Bible says with what it actually says. We look up the passage that people are quoting or paraphrasing and read what it actually says, including the context in which it was said."

"So," Hunter continued, "just a few quick observations about your fake email. The fake email did not come from the official Princess email address. It is not their domain name. It came from a Gmail address and not from princess.com.

"The Princess logo on the fake looks the same as the legit Princess logo, but by comparing the two, we see that the suspect logo image is not quite as sharp and distinct. It looks a little fuzzy and washed out. It's most likely a photocopy of the real Princess logo.

"And, it goes on. But I'm telling you stuff you guys probably already know. When you saw the email, you suspected it right away, correct?"

"That's right," Catalina said. "As soon as I saw it, I knew it didn't look right. I showed it to Scott, and he had the same impression. The overall look of it didn't seem quite right, no doubt because of the different little things you started to point out."

"But also," Scott added, "what the email said didn't seem kosher. It didn't make sense. We have a very good relationship with Princess, and we know they wouldn't come out of left field like that and blindside us—and at such a late date."

"Yes," Catalina said. "They wouldn't abruptly change an established procedure we've had with them for fourteen years. They would at least give us a heads-up well in advance. Not one week before the cruise."

"Absolutely," Hunter said. "You guys did well in immediately questioning something like this that comes at you out of the blue and out of the ordinary. That is always a good test—does it make sense—does it fit the ordinary scheme of things?

"Well, enough of that. The real question is why. Why would somebody send an email like this trying to impersonate Princess Cruise Lines to get you to not bring your four winemakers' wine on board?"

"And who?" Susan asked.

CHAPTER 9

"Who indeed," Hunter said. "Why and who? Why—and who? I think we have to concentrate on the why first. If we can answer the why, that may indicate the who."

"Before we go any further," Scott said, "let me add another little incident to this mystery. I haven't told Catalina this yet because, at the time, I didn't think much of it. Now it looks like the two events could very well be connected."

"What's the other event?" Catalina asked.

"This morning, I went to the dockside warehouse across the way from our ship where our winemakers' wine was housed. I needed to sign that our wine was all there before they loaded it on board. The arrangement was for them to forklift the pallets of wine onto our ship at about ten o'clock. I arrived at about nine twenty, and as I was beginning to take inventory, a gentleman pulled up on a fork-lift and was lining up to forklift the pallets of wine. I told him he was early and I needed to inventory and sign off on the wine first.

"He waved some paperwork at me and said he had orders to take the wine over to Customs. I told him that the wine had already cleared Customs, and I had the paperwork to prove it. The guy just ignored me despite my protests and proceeded with his attempt to take the wine. At that point, believe it or not, the Royal Canadian Mounted Police showed up."

"No way," Hunter said.

"On horses?" Susan asked.

"Scott, are you making this up?" Catalina asked.

"It's true," Scott said. "It was only one officer—and he was driving an SUV. This RCMP officer happened to be patrolling nearby and apparently saw the commotion between the forklift guy and me and stopped. The officer got out of his vehicle and started walking toward us. The forklift guy glanced down at his paperwork, said it was his mistake, and drove off in his forklift."

"So," Susan questioned, "the Royal Canadian Mounted Police patrol the cruise ship terminal and port area?"

"He said they do. He said a few years ago they got pulled off because of 'defund the police' and so forth, but just recently, they got put back on along with Border Security and Port Authority Police. He said it may sound impressive, but each agency only has a few officers, and crime—smuggling, theft, drug trafficking, and so forth has decreased but is still a problem."

"Well," Sue said, "he sure came to your rescue in the nick of time. And I still can't get the picture of him riding a horse at a full gallop to your rescue out of my mind."

"Yeah," Catalina said, "it was before my time, but Sargent Preston of the Yukon comes to mind."

"Connect the dots," Hunter said. "We have two dots—your bogus email saying you can't bring your wine on board the ship, and now apparently someone trying to steal your wine."

"Yeah," Scott said. "This morning's incident makes sense by itself—stealing wine. Those two pallets of premium wines add up to a small fortune. And, as the RCMP officer stated, pilfering and theft in the port area are rampant, with all the goods and merchandise going in and out. But couple that with the bogus email, and what do you get?"

"Someone is trying to get the wine," Catalina said. "All the wine shipments from our four vintners had arrived in Vancouver and were together in the warehouse well over a week ago. The fake email came afterward. Maybe the emailer and this morning's forklift guy are the same person or people. Maybe the emailer thought that if we believed the email, we would just try to dump the wine since we couldn't take it on board. Maybe they thought they could show up and volunteer to take it off our hands."

"Maybe," Hunter said. "I've been sitting here thinking. It's certainly possible that this person or these people just want the two pallets of expensive wine. But let me tweak it a bit. What if it's not so much that they want the wine, but they just don't want you and Scott to have it? What if they don't want you, Mr. and Mrs. Wine Lovers Cruisers, to have your wines—the wines from your vintners—on board the ship? Let's think about that."

"You couldn't have your wine tastings," Susan said. "If you don't have your wines on board—the four winemakers who are with you—you said one from New Mexico, one from Arizona, one from Nebraska, and one from California—they could not present their wines. So the wine lovers cruise would be a flop. Someone is trying to ruin your reputation. Maybe a rival wine group or promoter."

"That could be," Hunter said. "Any other thoughts?"

"Maybe it's just a prank," Catalina said. "Someone's playing a joke."

"No," Scott said. "There is something more than that going on here, don't you think, Hunter?"

"Yes. I definitely believe there is something more sinister going on here. More sinister than a simple prank. The good thing is the wine is on board and secure, and we're underway. The wine is secure, isn't it, Scott?"

"It's put away. I assume it's secure."

"Assume?"

"You're right. We shouldn't assume anything. Maybe I'd better go talk with Alex Lapierre, the head wine steward, and see where it is stored and give him a heads up on what has happened."

"Good idea," Hunter said. "Why don't I go with you—but we

shouldn't say too much to Alex—he's in a great position to help facilitate a wine heist. We should talk to ship security also. Everyone's a suspect, but we have to trust someone. Do you ladies mind hanging out for a bit while Scott and I take care of this? It shouldn't take long."

"We'll be fine, won't we, Catalina?"

Catalina agreed, and Hunter and Scott went off on their little mission.

CHAPTER 10

Sunday, April 30, 11:00 a.m.
The Charthouse Restaurant

After attending the eight-thirty non-denominational church service with Hunter and Susan Kingsley, Scott and Catalina Poncetran went directly to the Charthouse restaurant to make sure things were being set up properly for their eleven o'clock wine event.

The Charthouse is one of the main restaurants on the ship and is exclusive to the Alaskan Princess. It is located on deck six at the aft end. Its main feature is the giant picture window structure at the back of the restaurant that looks out at the ocean and the turbulent water the ship's propellers create.

This is the first meeting of the entire group of wine lovers cruisers since boarding the ship yesterday afternoon. Wine tasting with appetizers followed by lunch is the agenda. The restaurant is open to others, but the rear section next to the picture window is reserved for the wine lovers group. The wine-tasting presentation is going to feature Tony and Maryanne Black with wines from their Black's Smuggler Winery in Bosque, New Mexico, sixty miles south of Albuquerque.

Two minutes after eleven, Scott Poncetran stood up from his table, walked up to the table display of Black's Smuggler wines, and addressed the gathering of one hundred and one guests. Scott, just under six feet tall with greying medium-length slicked-back hair, always seemed to be dressed a cut above the people he was with but with a bit of flamboyancy. That is, he usually wore creased dress slacks, a collared shirt, leather shoes, but with funky socks, colorful suspenders, and a noticeable tie. Often, when addressing groups, he wore an article of clothing or even a full-blown costume befitting the occasion. Today, he was wearing silver sparkle loafers, blue/green socks with depictions of little swimming fish, gray slacks, red suspenders, and an open black collared shirt imprinted with pictures of bottles of wine next to wine glasses. To top it all off, he was sporting a black bowler hat. Quite the showman.

Scott rang a small golden bell to quiet the group and garner their attention. "Welcome everyone to our fourteenth annual wine lovers cruise and our second trip to Alaska. This is the largest wine lovers group Catalina and I have ever had, and we thank you all for booking your trip with us. Besides what the ship has to offer, we have a number of events planned just for you guys—just for our fantastic wine lovers group.

"The first planned event is this wine-tasting luncheon with the wines of vintners—winemakers Tony and Maryanne Black, whom I will introduce in a moment. We have an unprecedented four winemakers on board this cruise. Thus, we will have three more wine tastings featuring our three remaining vintners. We have reserved the tables you are seated at for our nightly dining in this remarkable dining room for a 5:30 seating. And we have a very special event planned for our last sea day on Tuesday, May 9th. Also, in amongst these planned events may pop up a few impromptu gatherings. The planned events are all listed with the times and locations in the materials you were given in your wine lovers welcome aboard package. If you misplaced your event sheet, or you just need another copy, see the lovely Catalina." Scott pointed to his wife as she smiled and waved.

"Before we get started with our wine tasting, I want to read to you why wine is much healthier for you than water. A number of you have heard this already as I read it at the beginning of all of our cruises, but it is a good reminder of one of the reasons we drink wine." Scott pulled a well-worn sheet of paper from his leather folder and began to read.

"In wine, there is wisdom. In beer, there is freedom. But in water, there is bacteria. In a number of carefully controlled trials, scientists have demonstrated that if we drink one liter of water each day, after a year, we will have absorbed more than one kilo of E-Coli, which is the bacteria found in feces. In other words, we will have consumed over one kilo of poop. However, we do not run that risk when drinking wine or beer or other forms of liquor because alcohol has to go through a purification process of boiling, filtering, and/or fermenting. So, remember, water equals poop, and wine equals health. Therefore, it is better to drink wine and talk stupid than to drink water and be full of poop."

After the chuckles and laughter had subsided, Scott continued. "Now I want to introduce your winemakers and host for this wine-tasting event, Tony and Maryanne Black of Black's Smuggler Winery in Bosque, New Mexico. Tony and Maryanne, would you stand up for a second." A round of applause ensued, after which the couple sat back down. "Catalina and I have been to their winery a number of times, as have some of you. If you have never had the pleasure of sampling any of their wines, I believe you're in for a real treat. So, Tony, would you come up to the front next to your wines? And before you start the wine-tasting, tell us a little bit about yourself and your winery.

"As Tony is making his way up here, I want to mention a little-known fact, and that is that New Mexico is the oldest wine area in the United States, dating back to 1629, well before the first vineyards in California, or any other state."

Ed, from Los Amigos Cellars in Napa Valley, California, leaned over and said to his wife, Joyce, "Do you get the feeling we're being set up?"

"Oh, I don't know, Ed. Scott quite naturally promotes New Mexico and New Mexico wines because that is where he lives, and he has a lot of friends in the wine industry there."

"True, but I still have an uneasy feeling about this big wine-tasting event Scott mentioned coming up on May 9th. Maybe Grady Flanigan is right about some sort of reenactment of the Judgement of Paris, but this time, our California wines take the fall."

"Well, we'll see. If it will make you feel any better, I'll talk to Catalina about it privately as soon as I get a chance. I think she will level with me."

"Okay. I think that's a good idea."

CHAPTER 11

Tony Black took the floor and stood in front of the display table containing the five wines everyone was about to sample from his Black's Smuggler Winery. The display was tastefully done with a backdrop of large mounted photographs of scenes taken from around the winery, small crates in front of the photographs with plastic grape bunches overflowing the tops of the crates, and the five bottles of wine in a semicircle in front of the grapes.

Tony began. "I inherited the land from my parents on which they used to grow alfalfa. I used to help my dad work the land and, at some point, became interested in viticulture and started studying winemaking. At first, I planted a few rows of Brianna and St. Vincent wine grapes. Since then, we have added several other varieties of grapes. My wife and I, along with two co-workers, do all the work. We are very much a family-owned and operated winery.

"We will never try to compete with the much larger wineries, most of which are in California, except in the category of taste. That is, we could never compete in the volume of wine produced, but we certainly can compete in the area of taste and enjoyment of the wine. Remember, wine is not consumed by the gulp but by the sip. Black's Smuggler is striving to win over your taste buds, and we certainly can compete with the big boys in that area. Quantity does not in any way ensure better taste. The individual taste experience is where we are trying to excel."

In the audience, California winemaker Joyce leaned over to her husband Ed and whispered, "I feel it now. I think you may be right. I feel we are being set up. We are Goliath from California, and little David is taking us on."

Tony continued. "So, in light of what I just said, we brought five of what Maryanne and I consider at present to be our best wines. In front of you are the five." On the tables in front of each wine lovers cruise participant were five pre-poured glasses of Black's Smuggler wine sitting on an eight-and-a-half by ten-and-a-half paper placemat with the title, "James Suckling's Great Wines of the World." The wines were arranged in a semi-circle, which mirrored the semi-circle of wine bottles on the display table next to Tony Black.

Tony proceeded. "We will start the wine tasting with the glass on your left, which is our Sauvignon Blanc. I will use a simple four-step method to evaluate each wine—namely, look, smell, taste, and think or conclude. This is review for most of you, so I won't go into any detail. First, we look." Terry tilted his glass and held it up to the light. "Of course, we are checking the color, the opacity, and viscosity, that is, the wine legs." Tony swirled his glass. "The prominence of legs in a glass generally indicates alcohol content and thus a richer texture and fuller body. I do see definite legs with this wine, but not as prominent as with some of our red wines.

"Next, we smell." Tony swirled his glass again and stuck his nose down in the glass as far as he could. He took two short sniffs and one longer one before pulling his nose back out of the glass. "What aromas do you detect?" Someone said apple. Another person said green apple. A third person said peach or apricot. A fourth person said she detected a hint of roasted nuts and vanilla. "Good. A few others have detected the nut and vanilla in the past, but it is a very subtle aroma. You must have a good nose.

"Now we taste. Our tongues can detect salty, sour, sweet, and bitter. Our tongues can also perceive the texture of the wine by, so to speak, touching it. We can also detect tannin with our tongue, which is that sand-paper drying sensation we can find in red wines. And, some of you more sophisticated wine lovers will want to swish your sip of wine in order to get all of your taste receptors into play." Tony swirled his glass of wine once again, took a quick sniff, then took a swig of the almost clear nectar into his mouth, followed by swishing motions. He then savored the liquid in his mouth for a few seconds before slowly swallowing.

"Finally, we think—that is, we evaluate our encounter with the wine. Did we like it, or did we not? Why? Which foods do we think the wine would pair nicely with? And so forth."

Scott commented. "Feel free to take notes or write comments on your James Suckling placemat. By the way, if you're not familiar with James Suckling, he is an internationally known wine and cigar critic. Okay, Tony, back to you."

"Now, let's go through our ritual with the next wine, which we see is some sort of rose. We know this by the color, which is somewhere between a white and a hearty red."

Tony led the group through the rest of the wine tasting, after which lunch was promptly served. Before the party broke up, Tony and Scott received a departing round of applause and

Scott reminded everyone that tomorrow, May 1st, there would be another winetasting and lunch in Sabatini's restaurant starting at eleven o'clock, this time featuring Jim and Linda Perdon and wines from their Leapfrog Vineyards in Camp Verde, Arizona.

CHAPTER 12

Hunter and Susan Kingsley stayed back as the rest of the one hundred and one wine lovers began shuffling out of the Charthouse dining room. Scott and Tony were talking with Alex Lapierre, the ship's sommelier, with each enjoying a glass of their favorite of the five Black's Smuggler wines from the presentation. As the area cleared, Scott spotted Hunter and Susan still seated at their table. He motioned them over to join in. Susan told Hunter to join them if he wanted but said she was going to try to meet up with Catalina. Catalina looked like she was through talking with the head waiter and was about to leave. Hunter jumped up and joined the trio of wine aficionados.

Susan joined Catalina, and they walked out of the Charthouse together. They walked up the stairs to deck seven, the Promenade deck, and entered the photo gallery. As they entered the gallery, Joyce Cooling of Los Amigos Winery in California greeted Catalina as she and Susan approached. Catalina introduced Susan to Joyce, after which Joyce asked if she could talk with Catalina privately about a concern she and her husband had. Susan told Catalina to go ahead and she would see her later at dinner. Catalina then suggested that she and Joyce go to the Wheelhouse Bar, a little further forward on the Promenade deck, as it usually wasn't crowded in the afternoons and, therefore, should be a somewhat private place to talk.

The Wheelhouse Bar is reminiscent of a bygone era of ocean-going vessels with its dark wood flooring, ceilings, and walls and brass artifacts and sailing apparatus. The bar has a warm and cozy feel to it with its nooks and alcoves and inviting atmosphere.

After a short walk, Catalina and Joyce entered the bar, walked past the large wooden ship steering wheel, and found an alcove with a comfortable-looking semi-circular built-in seating area with a small table—perfect for four and just as accommodating for two. The waitress came right away, and the two ladies both ordered iced tea. They had had enough wine for the afternoon.

Catalina started. "I am so glad you and Ed were finally able to join our wine lovers cruise. I know we had asked you before, but it was right around the time of your harvest in the early fall, and you, of course, could not come. We finally got you, though. This cruise is well before your grape harvest."

"Yes, Ed and I are so glad that we could join you and Scott this time. This should be good for us. And I don't think you have ever had winemakers from California on any of your cruises before. Am I right about that?"

"You are. You and Ed are the only California vintners we know as friends. I suppose we could have invited California winemakers we don't know to participate, but we have always had winemakers on our cruises that we already knew beforehand as friends. Scott and I have never put much effort into trying to make our cruises some enormous event. We don't make a lot of money at it but do it mostly for the fun and enjoyment of being with good friends. I guess we also do it because it helps give us, especially Scott, credence for our other wine-related endeavors. Scott does a lot of wine hosting and events for the New Mexico wine industry."

"That's sort of what I wanted to talk to you about, Catalina. At the wine tasting we just had—well—I don't know quite how to put this—but it seemed to Ed and me that Scott and Tony were talking New Mexico wines up a little too much. Like, when it comes time for Ed and me to present our California wines, the enthusiasm won't be there."

"No, I don't think that's true. We love your wines, and we often include a bottle from your winery at the wine gatherings we have at our home." Catalina thought for a moment. "You know, Scott is enthusiastic about New Mexico wines as that is his self-appointed job—to promote New Mexico and New Mexico wines. And Tony Black—that's just him—he loves his vineyard and winery, and he can't seem to talk it up enough."

"You're right, Catalina. When it comes our turn to present, we'll be enthusiastic also. We have some very good wines."

"You do. You produce some excellent wines."

"Another thing Ed and I were wondering about—concerned about—is the event on May 9th. I know you and Scott said it would be another wine-tasting but with wines from all four of us wine-makers. Is it going to be some sort of contest? Are the wines from the four of us winemakers going to be compared to each other?"

"In a manner of speaking, they are. We have four different sommeliers on board, in addition to Alex, the ship's sommelier, who helped with Tony's presentation. So, at our May 9th event, Scott and I thought it would be interesting for the group to see an actual wine rating or judgment take place. We thought it would be interesting for our group to watch the judges go through their routine or ritual as they rate the wines, like they do at state and county fairs and other wine competitions. We even had ribbons with medals made up to award the wines that get enough points to rate a bronze, silver, gold, or double gold. Scott knows more about the rating system because he does occasionally get a chance to be a judge at some of the New Mexico wine events. And I know that your winery has produced some award-winning wines."

"Yes. Last year, our Capriccio red blend—60 percent Cabernet Sauvignon, 21 percent Merlot, 9 percent Malbec, 6 percent Petit Verdot, and 4 percent Cabernet Franc—won a gold. And two years before that, our Capstone red blend actually won a double gold. We've also won a few silvers and bronzes over the years. We don't enter our wines in a lot of competitions, but we almost always participate in the San Francisco International Wine Competition and the California State Fair Wine Competition, along with a smattering of smaller local competitions."

"See," Catalina said, "you don't have anything to worry about. It's just a fun little exercise for our group of wine lovers. And, if any of the wines win any medals—that will hopefully mean something. That's why Scott and I wanted to do it up right with reputable wine judges and so forth. We even have two free-lance wine reporters on board, so there may even be some publicity involved."

"Oh, that should be fun."

"Yes, Scott and I think so. Since we have that last sea day just before we get to Vancouver and depart, we wanted to do something fun involving all four of you winemakers at the same time. We didn't want to say too much about it as we wanted to build up a little suspense and make it a bit of a surprise."

"Well, it does sound like a good way to get the four of us winemakers together in kind of a grand finale at the end of the cruise. Thanks for hearing me out about my concerns—our concerns. You have eased my mind. I am so happy that Ed and I were finally able to get away from our winery and join you and Scott on one of your wine cruises."

"Oh, us too. We are glad you are finally with us. We are here to have fun. Our group this year, for some reason, is a lot bigger than normal, so there are a lot of people we don't know very well. But our core group—the ones who cruise with us almost every year—is a lot of fun. I hope you and Ed have a great time and make lots of friends and are able to join us again."

"I hope so. Thanks again, Catalina. I am going to run along as I have a massage coming up shortly that I am really looking forward to."

"Good for you, Joyce. See you at dinner."

CHAPTER 13

At the restaurant, the four wine enthusiasts, Scott, Tony, Alex, and Hunter, finished their wines. Alex had to get back to his other duties and departed. Tony also left to catch up with his wife, Maryanne, who asked Tony to meet her at the casino when he was finished with his wine. That left Hunter and Scott.

"If you have a few minutes, Scott, I'd like to talk to you about something out of earshot of anyone else."

"Okay. I don't have anything I have to do right now. You seem a bit serious. How private a conversation does this have to be?"

"It's just between you and me. I don't want anyone else to hear. Let's go to my cabin. Sue shouldn't be there as she had something at one o'clock she wanted to go to, and it's a little after one now."

"Boy, you are serious."

"I want to avoid the possibility of even a waitress or bartender overhearing any of our conversation."

"Secret stuff, huh? Well, lead the way."

Hunter and Scott walked out of the restaurant, up the stairs to the Promenade deck, and forward to the mid-ship Panoramic lifts. They rode the elevator up to deck ten, then walked forward along the port corridor to cabin C 232. Hunter inserted his key card and opened the door. Hunter and Scott walked past the bathroom, then the queen bed, and Hunter motioned for Scott to have a seat on the sofa. Hunter pulled the chair out from under the desk across from the sofa, turned it around, and sat facing Scott. Hunter offered Scott something to drink, and Scott declined.

"Scott, I've given some more thought to the two strange incidents involving the winemaker's wines you brought on board—the two incidents you and Catalina related to Sue and me last night."

"Yes. Did you come up with anything new?"

"Maybe. I see your format. Each of the four winemakers is going to present a wine-tasting with the wines from their wineries. Today's presentation with Tony went just fine. I don't see how anyone would have a problem with that format."

"No one ever has in the fourteen years we have been doing this."

"We brought up the possibility that someone, maybe a rival, might be trying to discredit your wine lovers cruises, but I think that is quite a remote possibility. I think someone is concerned about your May 9th event. Just between you and me, explain exactly what you and Catalina have planned. It's a wine-tasting involving all four of the winemakers, but give me the details on how everybody is going to taste test and, I guess, compare the different wines."

"Sure, I can give you the details. The May 9th event will be a blind wine tasting of flights or groupings of wines—four in each flight—one from each of our four winemakers, in a comparison taste test. The wine pours will come from numbered bottles with the labels completely covered up. Thus, the blind part of the comparison taste test."

"So, each person will rate for themselves which of the four wines in each flight they liked best and on down the line to which they liked the least. Will you have enough of the wines left for everyone to do this?"

"Not for everyone. The one hundred and one wine lovers are not going to perform the taste tests. The blind taste tests will be performed by five professional wine judges. Our wine lovers cruisers will watch the proceedings and will witness and enjoy seeing professional wine judges in action. Most have never witnessed a professional wine judgment and should really enjoy the event."

"You have these professional wine judges on board?"

"Yes, we do."

"Who are they?"

"You already know one—Alex Lapierre—the ship's sommelier. The other four are sommeliers from four different upscale restaurants from the four different states our winemakers represent—New Mexico, Arizona, California, and Nebraska.

"Amy Christine is from the Anasazi restaurant in Santa Fe, New Mexico. Brian Downey is from Lon's at the Hermosa Inn in Paradise Valley, Arizona. Reggie Narito is from the Grange restaurant in downtown Sacramento, California. And Nickolas Paris is from the Au Courant restaurant in Omaha, Nebraska."

"So, at the May 9th wine-tasting event, the one hundred and one wine lovers are not going to get to taste any wine?"

"There will not be enough wine for the one hundred and one to mimic the five flights of four wines the five professionals will taste test, but they will each have a glass of wine in front of them. Their previously poured glass of wine will have a number written on the glass of wine's doily, which indicates which one of the twenty bottles of wine their glass was poured from. The number on the doily, of course, will correspond to the same one through twenty bottles of wine the sommeliers will taste test. So, while the sommeliers at the front table are evaluating and scoring the twenty samples of unknown wines, the one hundred and one wine lovers are to try to ascertain which one of the twenty wines they have before them. It will test their pallet's memory as they have previously tasted all the wines during the four wine presentations before the May 9th event."

"Very interesting," Hunter said. "That sounds like a lot of fun. I've never witnessed a professional wine evaluation."

"Most people haven't."

"But I do see a potential problem that the taste test by the sommeliers might cause."

CHAPTER 14

"So what is the potential problem you see, Hunter?" "Winners and losers. There's going to be winners and losers."

"No, not really," Scott replied. "The sommeliers are going to judge each wine using the wine industry recognized one hundred point scale. The sommeliers will judge each of the twenty wines on things like color, aroma, and flavor, including more technical things like sugars, acids, tannins, and volatile acidity. The points the five judges or evaluators give a particular wine will be added up and divided by five for an average. Thus, each of the twenty wines will be awarded the average of the points given by the five sommeliers. Wines that score high enough will win a medal.

"The industry recognized point break down for a medal is: seventy to seventy-nine points for a bronze medal, eighty to eighty-nine points for a silver, ninety to ninety-five points for a gold, and ninety-six plus points for a double gold medal. Catalina and I have the medals. We had them made up. They say, for example, 'Wine Lovers Judgement at Sea Wine Competition Double Gold.'"

"Do each of the twenty wines win a medal?" Hunter asked.

"Very unlikely. It all depends on the score. The sommeliers do a number of wine competitions each year and are adept at rating and scoring wines. Although our four vintners brought their premium wines—no lower quality table wines—a wine has to be pretty darn good to win a medal, especially a gold or double gold."

"So, Scott, you're not a full-fledged sommelier, but you are a recognized wine expert and also participate in a few wine competitions each year as a judge yourself."

"Yes."

"And I bet you have sampled all twenty wines sometime before the cruise."

"I have."

"What do you think the chances are of any of the wines winning any medals?"

"Good. I didn't do any formal evaluations when I tasted the wines, but I believe maybe two or three bronze or silvers are possible, and maybe even a gold or double gold. Maybe even two."

"Okay. Let me ask you this. Winning medals is one thing. The wines are being judged and scored as to the qualities they possess, but are not directly being compared one to another."

"Essentially, yes."

"However, the wines are also arranged in flights. Five flights with a similar wine from each of the four vineyards in each flight."

"Right."

"So, in each flight, one of the four wines is going to score higher than the other three—unless there is a tie score with at least two of the higher scoring wines."

"Yes, that's true."

"So, again, my point. The wines are being compared to each other within each flight. There's going to be winners and losers. Any time you have winners and losers, there's the possibility of some people being upset."

"Well, okay. I can see that."

"So, what if the California wine scores the highest in all five of the flights?"

"A sweep. Expected."

"What if a New Mexico or an Arizona wine scores the highest—wins—in one or two of the flights?"

"Unexpected."

"What if a Nebraska wine would come out on top in one of the five flights? What if it scored higher than the California wine—or the Arizona or New Mexico wine?"

"Very unexpected."

"What if a New Mexico wine, an Arizona wine, and a Nebraska wine each win in at least one of the five flights?"

"With the right publicity, that would be a boon to the non-California wine industry and a chink in the armor of the California wine producers."

"What are the chances of any of the three non-California wines winning in any of the five flights of comparable wines?"

"Very good."

"Well, there you have it. I think someone knows or has guessed you and Catalina might be doing something like this, and they want to stop you. Someone who wants to protect California's wine reputation and they don't want it to be put to the test.

"What about your California vintners? Do they know that their wines are going to be compared with other wines, and are they on board with that?"

"Ed and Joyce Cooling? Yes, they know basically what we have planned for May 9th, and they are agreeable to it. They were a little apprehensive at one point, but they have agreed to participate."

"Okay. I guess that probably puts them in the clear. If they were concerned enough about what might happen, all they would have to do is not participate."

"Right," Scott said. "If they don't want their wines to be judged, all they have to do is say no."

"I'm surprised they haven't bowed out. Since they are expected to easily win, why put it to the test? Let people's assumption prevail. Rest on your laurels."

"But their wines could win a medal or two. Medal-winning wines always bolster a winemaker's prestige and reputation. And withdrawing from a competition usually indicates fear of losing."

"Okay. I can see that. So that seems to rule Ed and Joyce out of wanting to stop your blind wine taste testing. Did you or Catalina tell anyone else connected with California wine production about the particulars of your May 9th event?"

"No. Other than our four participating vintners, we told no one. Oh—wait a minute—we did tell Hector and Paula Veracruz. I forgot about them. They are good friends who live near us in Albuquerque, and they used to live in Napa Valley. In the early planning stages of this cruise, Catalina and I bounced some of the ideas we had for a grand finale event off of them. At that early stage of planning, we didn't ask them to keep our ideas to themselves. I think they still have a few friends back in Napa who are in the wine industry. Hector and Paula are on board. They are part of our group of wine cruisers. You and I could talk to them if you want."

"Possibly. Maybe at dinner tonight. If we do, I don't want to accuse them of anything. Now, one more thing, Scott."

"Yes?"

"A few months ago, Susan and I were talking with you and Catalina on the phone. At one point, we started talking about one of your favorite subjects, wine, and you suggested we watch the movie 'Bottle Shock.' We did, and later, I read up on the so-called Judgement of Paris the movie depicts. It looks to me like you are trying to reenact the Judgement of Paris on May 9th, but with a twist. You have five reputable sommeliers as judges. You have wines from four prestigious wineries. All you need is a reporter or two to report the event."

"We have two reporters with us on the ship."

"Really! You have two reporters to report the wine-tasting event? Then you and Catalina are going for the big kahuna. To put it in wine competition terms, you are going for a double gold in publicity. You are going after wine giant California. You are hoping that one, or two, or three of your non-California wines will take down California Goliath—or at least wound him."

"Well, you're partially right. However, it's not so much that we're trying to take down California wines. That would never happen. The California wine industry is way too big. What Catalina and I are hoping to show or prove or bring attention to is the fact that other states produce some excellent wines that are every bit as good and worthy as California wines. And, if California were to get a bit of a bloody nose in the process, well, maybe they deserve it. Maybe California vintners, in general, have become a little too smug and uppity.

"And I'm not talking about our friends Ed and Joyce Cooling of Los Amigos Cellars in Napa Valley, as they are the nicest people you would ever want to meet. I'm just saying, in general, we have often detected a hint of snobbery with California vintners. Just try telling a California wine producer that you have tasted some very good wines from New Mexico or Nebraska and see what kind of reaction you get."

"Yeah, I can imagine," Hunter said.

"But the way Catalina and I see it, no matter what the results of our blind wine-tasting event turn out to be, everybody wins. If any of the New Mexico, Arizona, or Nebraska wines win any medals or any of the taste test flights, they get some well-deserved national recognition. And, maybe California winemakers become a little less smug and recognize vintners from other states as brothers and sisters in the trade. Even if California takes any kind of hit at all, it won't be much of one. It would be like Goliath getting a hang nail. Like I said, maybe it would humble them just enough to take a little of the aloofness some California vintners, especially some of the Napa Valley wine producers, seem to have. That would be a good thing. At any rate, Ed and Joyce have some excellent wines, and they will have a good chance of winning a medal or two and most or all of the flights."

"The way you put it, Scott, it sounds close to win-win for everybody."

"I think so. And also, besides maybe our non-California wineries getting recognition, so does our wine lovers cruises, Princess Cruise Lines, and the four restaurants our sommeliers are from."

"Well, you've sold me on this big wine-tasting event on the ninth, but whoever is trying to stop you and Catalina from having it probably haven't changed their minds. So, we still have to figure out who it is and deal with them."

"Right," Scott said. "I'm glad you're now clued in on what Catalina and I want to do and hope to accomplish at our big event—and that you're on board with it."

"I am. And I know you want to maintain the surprise element to it as best you can, so I'll keep our discussion to myself."

"It's okay to tell Sue. She's not a gossiper."

"Thanks for that."

Scott and Hunter stood up and shook hands. Scott told Hunter he would see him at dinner later today, then walked out of Hunter's cabin door and turned right.

CHAPTER 15

As Scott left Hunter's cabin, he checked his watch. It was almost three-thirty—two hours before five-thirty dinner. Why not go back to the cabin, he thought, and relax a bit... Maybe read a few more chapters in the novel he was reading by John Grisham... Maybe take a nap. As he entered his suite, he saw that Catalina was not there—no surprise—and he saw the room phone message light was blinking. He walked over to the phone and played the message. A voice he did not recognize told him to meet his wife at the medical center on deck four. Oh no, he thought. What's happened to Catalina? Is she sick? Has she had an accident?

Scott hung up the phone and immediately left the suite. He walked as fast as he could to the mid-ship elevators and rode the one on the left down to deck four. As he got off the elevator, he was suddenly grabbed from behind by a large and powerful person who placed a wet rag over Scott's nose and mouth. Scott thought it was chloroform he smelled, and he started feeling woozy and had trouble breathing as the rag was tightly pressed against his nose and mouth. The person started dragging Scott backward out of the small elevator lobby in front of the medical center and around the corner. As this was taking place, Scott heard a male voice next to his left ear say, "Back off, mister. Cancel the blind wine test. Cancel the May 9th wine tasting or else bad things..." Scott lost consciousness.

CHAPTER 16

About an hour later, Scott started to regain consciousness. It was pitch black except for a very small sliver of light coming in from under a door. Scott crawled over to the door and clawed his way up until he was standing. Still holding onto the door, he found the door knob, then fumbled for the light switch on the wall. He found it and turned on the light. He was in some sort of utility closet.

Scott turned the light off and cracked open the door. He could see a bland, non-descript hallway with linoleum flooring. Definitely not a passenger area. He didn't see anybody in the hallway, so he slipped out of the janitor's closet, went to his right, walked a few steps, turned right again, and found himself back in the small lobby area with the elevator bank on the one side, and the door to the medical clinic on the other side.

Scott looked at his watch. Four-fifty. He took the elevator up to deck ten and walked back to his suite. As he entered the cabin, Catalina said, "Hey, Scott. It's about time to get ready for dinner."

"Yep."

Catalina looked at her husband a little closer and said, "Are you all right? You look a little disheveled—seem a little spacy. What have you been up to?"

"Oh, I took care of a few things. I am starting to get hungry for dinner."

"It won't be long. Since it's only the second night, let's get there a little early again and make sure everything is set up for our group."

"Right. I'm going to do a quick clean up, change shirts, and I'll be good to go."

"Good," Catalina said. "I'm almost ready."

***

Dinner went well for everyone. At the end, Scott made a reminder announcement to the wine lovers group to be at Sabatini's specialty restaurant tomorrow for a special lunch and the second wine-tasting event featuring wines from Jim and Linda Perdon's Leapfrog Vineyards in Camp Verde, Arizona. Scott had Jim and Linda stand up, and Jim told the group that he and Linda were looking forward to presenting their wines tomorrow. There was applause, after which people started getting up to leave. Scott walked over to Hunter, who was still seated, leaned down, and whispered in his ear, "I need to talk to you."

CHAPTER 17

The way Scott said it, Hunter knew Scott didn't want their wives to hear what he had to discuss. Hunter then leaned over to Susan and said that he and Scott would meet her and Catalina in the Crooners Lounge in about fifteen minutes. Hunter then stood up, and he and Scott made their way out of the dining room, up one flight of stairs to the Photo Gallery and to a set of doors that took them outside to the starboard side of the Promenade deck.

No one was in sight, so they walked over to the railing, leaned on it, and looked out to sea. It was chilly for sure, but the mist on their faces and the salt air felt good. Scott turned up the collar of his sports jacket and tightened his tie. Hunter turned up the collar of his shirt and buttoned the top button. It was a relatively clear night. As their eyes adjusted to the subdued outside lighting, stars, a few at a time, started appearing in the sky.

Hunter turned to Scott. "So, what's up, my friend?"

"I was abducted just a little bit ago."

"Abducted? Are you serious? You were taken by force somewhere?"

"Yes. After I left your cabin this afternoon, I went back to mine to read, or take a nap, or both, and the phone message light was blinking. I played the message, and a male voice said to meet Catalina in the medical facility. I thought something might have happened to her, so I left immediately and rushed down there. As soon as I got off the elevator across from the medical center, I was grabbed from behind by someone big and beefy. A rag soaked in something—I think chloroform—was forcefully held over my nose and mouth, and he started dragging me backward. He then started whispering in my ear and said, 'Back off, mister. Cancel the blind wine taste test. Cancel the May 9th wine tasting or else bad things…' and that's all I remember hearing."

"Which ear?"

"Which ear?"

"In which ear did the male voice whisper these things?"

"Is that important?"

"Maybe not. It might help indicate whether this big beefy guy was left-handed or right-handed."

"Oh, okay."

"And it probably wasn't chloroform. Chloroform doesn't work that quickly."

"It was the left ear—I'm pretty sure it was the left ear."

"Okay, then your abductor was probably right-handed."

"Well, anyway, when I woke up, about an hour later, I found myself in a janitor's closet, around the corner and down the hall from the small lobby area between the mid-ship elevators and the medical center."

"That's interesting. That's a crew-only area, plus the security office is also in that hallway. At least that's where it was on the Ocean Princess Susan and I were on a couple of years ago. I'll have to check that out. I take it you didn't see the person who grabbed you."

"Nope. All I saw were black sleeves and black gloves and a soiled-looking rag."

"Did you see anyone else?"

"No."

"This certainly ups the ante. Things have suddenly gotten a lot more serious."

"I agree," Scott said, "but I think we need to continue to keep this low-key. That's why I didn't even want to tell Catalina about this. She might panic and want to shut everything down, including our wine tastings. And that may, as we mentioned before, be exactly what these people, whoever they are, want. They either want to ruin our wine lovers cruise reputation—maybe they're rivals in the business—or they are concerned about the blind taste test on May 9th. No. I take that back. We now definitely know they are concerned about the May 9th event. They don't want that to happen—for whatever reason—the male voice told me so this afternoon."

"Exactly."

"Well, I haven't checked on our wine since our wine-tasting luncheon today. Let's do that before we meet up with our ladies at the Crooners Lounge."

"Yes, let's do that," Hunter said. "Lead the way."

***

At the guest wine storage area adjacent to the Charthouse kitchen, Scott and Hunter asked to speak with sommelier Alex Lapierre. They were told he was out on the floor. Scott said not to bother him and to let them speak to any of the wine stewards. After a couple of minutes, wine steward Emilio Suarez presented himself.

"How may I be of assistance to you?" Emilio asked.

"Mr. Kingsley and I are checking on our winemaker's wine. We wanted to make sure it's all here and that nothing unusual has happened today regarding it."

"Funny you should ask. Earlier today—maybe around two-thirty—a man I did not recognize as one of our kitchen or wine crew, but in one of our uniforms, had a cart and started to load your wine onto it. I told him that the wine was not part of the ship's supply and it needed to stay here. I offered to check with my supervisor about the matter, but he said it was all right and left."

"Did you tell your supervisor about this?" Scott asked.

"I didn't, but I will."

"That would be good. Thanks for setting that guy straight."

"You're welcome."

"What did that gentleman look like?" Hunter asked.

"He was Filipino, about five feet six or five feet seven. He looked like one of us. Actually, he looked like one of the cabin stewards."

"Why do you say that?" Hunter asked.

"I don't know. He just didn't belong in the kitchen. He didn't seem comfortable in this area."

Scott and Hunter thanked Emilio and left. Hunter suggested that he and Scott mull over all of this in their minds while they socialize with their ladies, then briefly meet somewhere afterward and decide what they want to do about these new developments. Scott agreed, and the two of them headed for the Crooners Lounge not far away.

CHAPTER 18

The Crooners Lounge and Bar is one of a number of gathering places on the ship. By day, it is a favorite place for a number of people to sit and read. By night, it is, as the name implies, a crooners bar and lounge—that is, a place to drink and listen to sentimental songs. The Crooners is on the starboard side of the Promenade deck at midship, across from the three-story atrium, with the mid-ship or atrium glass windowed elevators and the curved atrium stairs that descend from the Promenade deck—deck seven—down to deck five where the International Café, among other features, sits.

The last cruise Hunter and Susan were on—the one they refer to as "the murder cruise"—was on the Ocean Princess, and the Crooners Lounge was on the port side. Many of the Princess ships have similar restaurants and lounges, just not on the same side of the ship or in the same location. But on Princess, if there is a Crooners Lounge, then there is the iconic baby grand piano in or near the center, manned by a master and often humorous crooner tickling the keyboard.

As Hunter and Scott approached the lounge, they could see that a large group of people had taken over almost the entire area of the lounge on the right side of the piano. It was close to eight o'clock, and Austin Parker wasn't due to start tickling the ivories until nine. This was a good thing as the group was talking up a storm, and Sue and Catalina were in the center of it. As Hunter and Scott worked their way into the center of the group and their saved seats, an attempt was made to introduce Hunter to everybody there. The loquacious group included all four winemaker couples: Tony and Maryanne Black from New Mexico, Jim and Linda Perdon from Arizona, Jay and Roxanne Patterson from Nebraska, and Ed and Joyce Cooling from California.

Also in the group were the "boys from Nebraska," brothers Mike and Larry Oncur and Hector and Paula Veracruz. Hector and Paula are friends with Scott and Catalina and also Grady and Silvia Flanigan (code name Jeep and Mrs. Jeep and leaders of the underground Protect California Wine group). Hector and Paula are the source of the information to Grady and Silvia regarding Scott and Catalina's plans for the blind wine taste testing on May 9th. Hector and Paula Veracruz are also friends with Ralph and Arleen Simpson (code names Schultz and Sandy and hosts of the secret offshoot of the Protect California Wine group) and owners of the Golden Hills Estate Winery in Napa Valley where the group holds their secret meetings.

The gathering was too large for the whole group to hear one person talk at a time, so the gaggle naturally divided into smaller conversation cells. By 8:45, all the seats in the Crooners Lounge were taken, and a few people were already standing outside the lounge's elegant silver metal and glass half-wall that separated the lounge from the Promenade deck thoroughfare.

"Boy," Scott said, "whoever the piano player is, he must have been a hit last night, judging from the crowd that has gathered. Do you guys know who the piano player is?"

Jim and Linda said they saw his name in the Princess Patter, the ship's daily newspaper, but didn't remember his name. Hunter and Sue said they didn't know either.

A few minutes later, the piano player appeared. He was wearing a black tuxedo with tails and a red bowtie. With a bit of fanfare, he pushed his tails out of the way and took his seat at the baby grand. As soon as he had taken his seat, Mimi, one of the two cocktail waitresses working the Crooners, brought a rum punch with two maraschino cherries perched on top and placed it on the small glass table just to the right of the piano. The piano player leaned forward and spoke into the microphone attached to the baby grand.

"Good evening, fellow cruisers. As some of you know from last night, my name is Austin Parker, and I am here to provide an evening of music and fun—or is it fun and frivolity? At any rate, I'm here. Are you?"

"That's the piano player from our last cruise," Hunter blurted out to Sue.

"It is," Sue said. She turned to Scott and Catalina and Jim and Linda and told them that she and Hunter have seen him before and they should really enjoy him.

Austin repeated, "I'm here. Are you? Let's just see if you are here." Austin shielded his eyes from the overhead lights and peered out into the audience to the right of the piano. After a few seconds, he said, "Boy, I don't see anyone I recognize from last night—or from any time. Oh, wait. I do see a couple that looks familiar, but not from last night." Austin looked square at Hunter and Sue and asked, "Have you been on any of the cruises I've performed on before?"

"Yes," Hunter said. "We were on the Ocean Princess trans-Atlantic cruise from Houston to England a couple of years ago."

"Oh yes, that's the one where…well, never mind. But refresh my memory. Tell me your names again."

"Hunter and Susan Kingsley."

"Oh yes. Hunter and Susan. Hunter hunts for Susan in the king's lair—Kingsley—king's lair. That was my mnemonic device for remembering your names."

"I guess it didn't work too well," Hunter said.

"Oh, Hunter. You have seen me before. You know it is all right to take potshots. I think I'd rather talk to your wife. She seems to be much nicer—a kinder, gentler person."

"Thank you," Susan said.

"And now I'm remembering," Austin said. "You and Mr. Potshot live in Sacramento, California."

"We did," Hunter said, "but we moved to Arizona late last year."

"What? California too cold for you?"

"No, no," Susan said. "We heard that you might be moving there."

"Boy, you're just as spirited as your husband. I think I want to talk to someone else. Maybe the couple on your right," Austin looked at Scott and Catalina.

"Are your friends always this direct?"

"Hunter was a fighter pilot," Scott said. "He learned to take quick aim and fire."

"Well, okay. So, what are your names, and where are you from?"

"Scott and Catalina from Albuquerque, New Mexico," Scott said.

"Scott and Catalina, do you have a lina? That might work as a mnemonic. Do you have javelinas in New Mexico—you know—those somewhat dangerous wild pigs?"

"Yes, we do," Scott said.

"So, Catalina, am I correct in perceiving that you and the people around you are part of some group—like a tour group?"

"Yes. The sixteen of us here are part of the wine lovers group that cruise together once a year with usually two winegrowers who bring their wines, and we, as a group, enjoy some special wine tastings and other events."

"Well, good for you guys. So the ship has thousands and thousands of bottles of wine on board, but that's not enough? You have to bring your own wine?" Austin paused for a moment, then continued. "Just kidding. Don't take a potshot at me. I totally understand. You have winegrowers on board who bring their own special wine for you to taste and enjoy. That's nice. I hope you all have fun and thoroughly enjoy the cruise. Your group can join me anytime."

"This is only a small part of our group," Catalina said. "There are one hundred and one of us on this cruise."

"Wow. That's a good group. I look forward to seeing you and your group throughout the cruise. Now, let me look over here on the other side of the ivories and quickly see if I recognize anyone. Ah, yes, Jeb and Belinda from Mississippi. Thanks for coming back again tonight."

Jeb smiled and said, "Our pleasure."

Let's see. James and Bernice. Hi again. And, yes, the four ladies from Tallahassee. The Tallahassee Lassies. Hi ladies." They waved. "Oh, and way in the back. The big guy in the black with a lovely lady, Duke. Good seeing you again, my friend."

Duke stretched his right arm straight out and pointed his index finger at Austin. "You too, Austin."

"I guess I'd better start playing some music before I get thrown overboard," Austin said. He then launched into a medley of tunes that showcased his versatility and humor.

"Hunter," Sue whispered, "is that the Duke that we followed around on the ship on our Atlantic cruise and who started dating the lady who murdered her husband?"

"That's him—Mr. Available."

"Mr. Available?"

"Yes. Duke Rawlings—Mr. Available. I found out after our murder cruise that he apparently has a business card that just says, 'Available' in bold letters with his contact information at the bottom."

"What does that mean—available?"

"I'm not sure. I learned that from the FBI agent who interviewed me on our murder cruise. Right now, Scott and I have to take care of something. We'll be back in a short while."

"Okay, honey."

Hunter then gave Scott a bump on the arm to get his attention, followed by a head nod to let him know they needed to leave. Scott whispered in Catalina's ear and then followed Hunter as the two of them quietly slipped out of the Crooners Lounge.

CHAPTER 19

"Where to, Hunter?" Scott asked.

"Either one of our cabins is the best bet. We know no one is going to overhear us there."

"Let's go to mine. We went to yours last time. Besides, I have an open bottle of excellent port that needs to be finished."

"Sounds good, Scott. Lead the way."

Upon arrival at Scott and Catalina's suite, Scott brought out the bottle of port, retrieved two stemmed wine glasses, and poured. The two gentlemen toasted each other, swirled, sniffed, swallowed, and savored.

"Yes, excellent, Scott," Hunter said as he picked up the bottle and read the label.

"It's a welcome aboard bottle to Catalina and me from Princess."

"Susan and I didn't get one."

"You didn't bring one hundred and one paying passengers with you either."

"No, we didn't. In light of that, they should have given you a case."

"They did upgrade us to this nice suite."

"That's right. They did. I'd say they adequately thanked you for the one hundred and one paying passengers."

"So," Scott said, "what do you think we should do about our escalating situation?"

"I think you should bow out. I think you should cancel the blind wine taste test on May 9th. It's getting too dicey. Someone is likely to get hurt. It's not cowardly to bow out. It's the prudent thing to do."

"Hunter…I can't believe you're saying that. That doesn't sound like you at all. Are you going soft on me?"

"Tactical withdraw. Live to fight another day—that type of thing."

"Well, I don't feel I can do that. I can't let people down. I can't chicken out at the first sign of trouble. I can't let people I don't even know intimidate me." Scott was standing now. "I'm not going to do it. I'm not going to bow out. I've got to go as planned. I don't expect you to put yourself or Susan in jeopardy, but Catalina and I have to see this through."

Scott realized he had become a little emotional, so he paused, sat back down on the couch catty-cornered from Hunter, and picked up his glass of wine. He peered into the glass as he gently swirled it, embarrassed to look at Hunter."You're sure?" Hunter asked.

Scott now looked at Hunter square-on. "Yes, I'm sure."

"Okay, then. Let's do this thing. I'm with you. I'm all in. I love you, man. I don't want anything to happen to you or Catalina, so I felt I had to make sure you weren't going to feign a strong stance if you really didn't have it in you—if you weren't fully committed."

Scott's eyes watered, and he swallowed hard.

Hunter noticed this and said, "That's right. You and Catalina are near and dear to Susan and me. We have to be careful, and we have to do this right."

Hunter's eyes moistened as he continued. "There's been two attempts—three, really, if you count the fake email—at commandeering your wine. You were abducted and told not to go through with your May 9th wine-tasting plan. And now, Susan and I just learned that Duke Rawlings is on board."

"Duke Rawlings?"

"Yes, he was the big guy in the back at the Crooners Lounge that Austin pointed out just before you and I left."

"Oh, yeah. So what's the deal with him?"

"The FBI, Scotland Yard, and I are fairly certain he is a gun for heir. He was on the last cruise Susan and I were on, and he married the woman who murdered her husband."

"Your murder cruise you told us about."

"He may very well be the guy who abducted you. You said he was a big, beefy guy. Duke is a big, beefy individual. I think he is six feet four to six feet five inches tall and weighs around two hundred and fifty to two hundred and seventy-five pounds."

"So what do you think we need to do, Hunter? Obviously, Catalina and I need to have our guard up and exercise caution in everything we do."

"Yes, absolutely. They've gone after your winemaker's wines, and they've gone after you. And they've used Catalina as a ruse to get to you. We need to protect your wine, and we need to protect you and Catalina."

"So we need to tell ship security."

"After thinking about it some more, I think not. They don't have the manpower to watch after you and Catalina and still perform their duties. Besides, if we tell them what has been going on, there's a good chance they will cancel your May 9th event, as that would be an easy solution to the threat. They might even cancel your whole program. And we think that's what your adversaries want anyway. So, no, we don't dare clue security in. We're on our own on this."

"Is there anything we can do then?" Scott asked.

"Here's what I'm thinking. You and Catalina don't go anywhere outside your cabin without at least one other person going with you."

"Secret Service stuff, eh? That's right up your alley."

"Yes. The concept is there. Maybe a very low-key, rudimentary facsimile of a Secret Service detail. If you and Catalina go somewhere together on the ship and stay together, that should be fine.

Otherwise, Susan or I or one of the boys from Nebraska, Mike or Larry, will accompany. I'll have to talk to them about it. I think they would enjoy it and be glad to help out.

"So, that will be our little pseudo-Secret Service detail. You and Catalina are the protectees, and Sue and I and Mike and Larry are the protection agents, to put it in Secret Service lingo. Also, I have some whistles and some little pepper sprays we can all carry."

"Pepper sprays? Did you have to sneak them on board?"

"I've been known to be a little sneaky at times."

"And what possessed you to bring whistles and pepper sprays? Do you always bring such things with you on trips?"

"They are compact and easy to bring, so why not? You never know, right?"

"Okay. Sure."

"Anyway, we'll talk more about this tomorrow morning sometime—all of us together—you and Catalina, me and Susan, and Mike and Larry. Right now, I think we can go back down and join Austin and our group."

CHAPTER 20

Hunter and Scott slipped back to their seats next to their wives in the Crooners Lounge. Austin was in the middle of the Elton John tune, Benny and the Jets, and had just about everyone in the lounge swinging and swaying with the music and even singing along. The song was so well received by the group that Austin turned it into a medley of Elton John songs. If there had been any room to dance, it's a safe bet that many in the group would have been stomping the floor.

In the middle of the Elton John medley, Hunter leaned over to Sue and whispered in her ear, "If Catalina gets up to go anywhere, go with her. Be on the lookout. Someone might try to harm her or abduct her."

Susan's eyes widened as she looked at Hunter after he said this. Hunter looked back at her and nodded. Susan nodded back.

Austin took a break at ten thirty. Several in the winemaker's group decided to call it a night. Susan accompanied Catalina to her cabin. Hunter and Scott grabbed the brothers from Nebraska, Mike and Larry, and the four of them walked over to the empty lobby area of the Princess Theater. They all sat down on one of the built-in couches. Hunter briefly filled Larry and Mike in on the threat to Scott and Catalina's safety and the need to have at least one other person with Scott—and with Catalina—whenever either of them left their cabin alone. Mike and Larry were eager to help. Hunter, Mike, and Larry walked with Scott to his cabin and then headed for theirs.

CHAPTER 21

Monday, May 1
Hearts and Minds Wedding Chapel

At 8:15 in the morning, Hunter and Susan meet Scott and Catalina at their cabin. The four of them walked to the Hearts and Minds wedding chapel across from the Wheelhouse Bar for the self-directed Bible study. The cruise line lists the event and the time and location in the ship's daily newspaper, the Princess Patter, but does not take charge of the Bible study. In fact, no one from the ship's staff is even there after the first day.

The passenger Bible study group selects someone from the group to lead them, and almost always, there is either a pastor or Bible study class leader in the group who is happy to lead. Hunter, being an at-large Christian Chaplain, had a study prepared just in case he was picked to lead. He wasn't picked, which was just as well, he figured, in case it conflicted with watching out for Scott and Catalina. Vacationing Ken Harmony, lead pastor of Calvary Chapel of Oklahoma City, was picked to lead the Bible Study.

Pastor Harmony told the group he could easily lead a study and discussion in the Book of Daniel, as that was the sermon series he and his congregation had just finished. Everyone agreed on a study of Daniel, and in the time left, Pastor Harmony passed out Bibles and began the study.

Vintners Jim and Linda Perdon from Leapfrog Vineyards were also at the Bible study. When the study ended, Jim and Linda went with Scott and Catalina to the Sabatini's specialty restaurant on the Promenade deck, aft of the Crooners Lounge and the Explorers Lounge, and across from the Photo Gallery. Scott and Catalina and Jim and Linda met with Sabatini's manager and the wine steward to start setting up for the eleven o'clock wine-tasting and lunch featuring Jim and Linda's wines.

CHAPTER 22

Hunter and Susan left the Bible study and walked around the corner to the Crooners Lounge. They sat down in the nearly deserted lounge among the smattering of people reading their books.

"I need to talk to Duke Rawlings—Mr. Available—and see if he is involved in any way with the harassment of Scott and Catalina," Hunter said.

"How are you going to contact him?" Susan asked.

"That's what we need to figure out. We need to think of a way to find out his cabin number so I can knock on his door or call him. We can't rely on a serendipitous encounter. I need to talk to him—feel him out—as soon as possible."

"Obviously, we can go to the passenger services desk and ask for his room number."

"True," Hunter said. "It's always worth a try, but it's unlikely they will give it to us. If we can think of some sort of ploy to entice them to give us the cabin number, that would be better. Otherwise, we'll have to think of something else."

After a minute or so, Susan spoke up. "Well, from the last cruise, we know he frequents the casino."

"And he went to the art auction. That's how we got his cabin number the last time—from the sign-in sheet at the art auction."

"And when we went by his cabin, we learned he was most likely from Denver, Colorado, because he had a sign on his door that said, 'Denver Duke.' He might have a sign like that on his cabin door this time, too. What if we walk by all the cabins and look for a 'Denver Duke' sign?"

"Good idea," Hunter said, "and we get some exercise in to boot. He had a mini-suite last time, so I say we start on the mini-suite deck—the Dolphin deck—deck nine."

Hunter and Susan decided to cruise the Dolphin deck together rather than split up. When they reached cabin D 320, on the port side, bingo, there it was. Or was it? The sign on the door read, "Arizona Duke," and had a picture of a cowboy sitting on a horse. Sue took a photo of the sign and the cabin number with her cell phone, and then she and Hunter returned to the same seats in the Crooner's Lounge.

"You think that's him?" Susan asked. "Do you think Denver Duke is now Arizona Duke?"

"I don't know. We know he lived in an apartment in a suburb of Denver. Then, he married Vivian Swenson, the lady who murdered her husband. But later, she was in a terrible accident and died."

"So, he became single again and is back to his single ways—advertising himself on his cabin door."

"Unless the lady he was with here at the Crooners Lounge last night is a new wife."

"But if he remarried, I don't think he'd put a sign on his door advertising himself."

"Enough of this speculation," Hunter said. "I think we can now go to the front desk and get them to confirm or deny that Duke Rawlings is in cabin D 320."

After a short wait in the queue at the passenger services desk on deck six, Hunter and Susan stood in front of a petite dark-haired lady with a name tag that read "Sue Lynn Wang."

"Sue Lynn," Susan said as she smiled, "we have a friend by the name of Duke Rawlings. We were walking by cabin D 320 and saw a sign on the door that read 'Arizona Duke.' We're pretty sure that has to be our friend, Duke Rawlings, but we want to be sure before we bother someone we don't know. Is cabin D 320 his cabin?"

Sue Lynn thought for a moment, smiled, then looked up something on the computer. "Yes, Mr. Duke Rawlings is in cabin D 320."

"Thank you, Sue Lynn," Susan said.

"Yes, thank you, Sue Lynn," Hunter echoed.

Hunter and Susan stepped around the corner and into the entrance to the Grand Casino. "Well done, Suzie Q," Hunter said. "That was smooth. People are a little more reluctant to give out information than they were a few years ago."

"Yes, but maybe unnecessary."

"How so?" Hunter asked.

"See the two big guys over at the craps table..."

"There he is. Mr. Duke Rawlings. Let me see if I can talk to him—one on one."

"I know...man to man, without me present. But I do agree with that. I think he's a man-to-man kind of guy. I think he'll be a lot more open that way. I'm going to go see if I can help Scott and Catalina with the setup for the wine tasting and luncheon. Don't forget, Hunter, eleven o'clock at Sabatine's. Good luck with talking with Duke."

"Okay. Thanks. See you at lunch. Love you."

"Love you."

CHAPTER 23

Hunter walked over to the craps table and stood near Duke Rawlings. Besides the gentleman who was similar in height and build to Big Duke, there were several other people at the craps table. Hunter stood and watched for a while.

Hunter pulled the business card of Passenger Services representative Sue Lynn Wang he had grabbed from the counter a few minutes ago. On the back of the card, Hunter printed the word "Available," followed by a question mark. He handed the card to Duke. Duke looked at the card, looked at Hunter, thought for a second, then said yes. Hunter turned and motioned for Duke to follow him out of the casino and a short distance to the Churchill Lounge.

The Churchill Lounge is a cigar-smoking lounge with a bar and is obviously named after Sir Winston Churchill, who liked to drink and smoke cigars. The décor is, of course, English with dark wood and brass and plush leather chairs. Churchill memorabilia and photos of Sir Winston at different historical events adorn the walls and counters.

Fortunately for Hunter and Duke, who do not smoke—anything—no one else was in the lounge. Hunter, at six feet two inches, and Duke, at six feet four to five inches—both muscular and solid—sat down in a little alcove area with a couch and two stuffed leather chairs. Duke sat down in one of the chairs at the end of the coffee table, and Hunter sat down on the end of the couch with Duke ninety degrees to his right.

Duke studied Hunter for a few seconds, then said, "You do look somewhat familiar, but I sure can't place you. Do we know each other?"

"No, not directly. I was involved in the investigation and arrest of your wife."

"Oh, Vivian. I still don't remember seeing you."

"My wife and I were on the cruise you were on when you met Vivian Swenson—just after she murdered her husband."

"Oh... Okay. I still don't remember you specifically."

"Not surprising. I tried to stay out of your sight—and Vivian's, as she tried to accuse me of having something to do with her husband's death."

"What is your name?"

"I'm sorry. I guess I neglected to introduce myself. My name is Hunter—Hunter Kingsley," Hunter said as he stood up and held out his hand.

Duke stood up and hesitantly shook Hunter's hand. The two men sat back down, and Duke said, "I remember your name. Yes, Vivian tried to blame you for her husband's death. She thought you had stressed him out—stressed his weak heart—and that it had at least contributed to his death. I went along with some of her conjectures and genuinely believed her husband had died of a heart attack. It took me a long time before I realized that she had actually outright murdered her husband.

"But that's all water under the bridge. Vivian met an untimely death—a vehicle accident. I remarried. Married Vivian's best friend, Yvonne Davies. Yvonne tried to do me in—tried to poison me. I was going to reverse it—do her in—but I thought better of it and divorced her instead. We had to sell the house in Golden to split the proceeds, so I had to move. I like warmer weather and golf, so I moved to Arizona."

"Really. My wife and I moved to Arizona from California not too long ago. Where in Arizona did you move to?"

"Scottsdale. I'm renting a very nice house there. I may buy

something later, but right now, I'm really enjoying my rental. What about you? Where did you move to?"

"Carefree," Hunter said.

"Carefree. That's not that far from Scottsdale. At least it's in the same neck of the woods."

"Yes, it is. We're practically neighbors."

"Okay, neighbor, you asked me if I was available. I suspect you got that from my business card, and you know that I am available to do various odd jobs. If so, how can I be of service to you, Hunter, neighbor of mine?"

"Well, yes, good question. From what I know of you, I take you to be a straight shooter. Therefore, I won't beat around the bush but come right out with it. My wife and I are with good friends of ours, Scott and Catalina Poncetran."

"Don't know them."

"Scott and Catalina are heading up what they call a wine lovers cruise, and they have one hundred and one fellow wine enthusiasts with them on board this ship. One of the things they do is host various wine-tasting events. They are planning a big wine-tasting event on May 9th—the day before everyone disembarks in Vancouver. Certain things have taken place to discourage them from having this event. The question is, are you in any way involved in doing things to try to discourage them? Has someone hired you to keep Scott and Catalina from carrying on with their wine-tasting event?"

"Boy, you certainly are direct. But the answer is no, and no," Duke said as he looked Hunter straight in the eyes.

"Good. I appreciate your straightforwardness. Let me ask you this. If someone did hire you to keep my friends from doing their big wine-tasting event, would you be honest and tell me?"

"No."

"So, I don't know if someone hired you to do this or not."

"Correct."

"Did someone hire you to do any kind of job while you're on the cruise?"

"No."

"This is purely a pleasure cruise for you?"

"Of course."

"Well, Duke, I enjoyed our little chat. I actually feel you're being honest with me to the extent you can be honest."

"I am. And I wouldn't mind chatting with you some more. I sense you may have a somewhat similar background to myself... And we're neighbors. We should get to know each other better."

"We should." The two stood up and shook hands. Hunter left, and Duke sat back down. Both thought about the strange meeting that had just ensued.

CHAPTER 24

It was close to eleven o'clock, so Hunter headed for Sabatini's restaurant for the wine tasting and luncheon. People were sauntering in, and Hunter spotted Susan at a table with Jim and Linda Perdon, the wine-tasting presenters for the gathering. Hunter kissed his wife on the cheek, greeted Jim and Linda, and sat down.

"I'm looking forward to your presentation and tasting your wines," Hunter said. "Susan may have told you, but we've had your Meritage before, which was excellent. Our local wine store carries your wines, but at the time, the Meritage was the only one they had in stock."

"You and Susan will have to come and visit our winery," Linda said. "Let us know when and we'll be sure to give you a personal tour."

"That would be fantastic," Hunter said.

"Hunter," Susan said as she put her hand on top of his, "Jim and Linda told me a curious thing about one of the bottles of wine they were going to use for the tasting today."

"Yes," Jim said. "As we were loading the cart with the wines we were going to use today, we noticed that one of the bottles had a small hole in the foil at the top, and apparently through the cork—maybe made with a syringe. It was a Chardanay, and it appeared to be slightly darker in color than the other bottles of Chardanay."

"Strange," Hunter said.

"Yes," Linda said, "so we carefully checked all the other bottles and discarded the one with the hole in the cap."

"That's good," Hunter said. "If it happens again, save the compromised bottle or bottles and give them to me. And continue to thoroughly check any wine on this trip before you use it."

Just then, Scott Poncetran stood up, walked over to the front of Jim and Linda's wine display, and started clanging his glass to quiet the crowd. "Welcome everyone to our second of four wine presentations and tastings from our four winemakers with us on this cruise. Today, Jim and Linda Perdon from their Leapfrog Vineyards in Camp Verde, Arizona, are our featured winemakers. Since I don't feel I have to remind you again that drinking wine is better than drinking poopy water, I'll ask Jim and Linda to come on up and tell you a little about their vineyard and their wines."

As Jim and Linda stood up and started walking forward, Sue leaned over and asked Hunter in a low voice how it went with Duke. Hunter told her that Duke denied having anything to do with harassing Scott and Catalina. He also told her that Duke admitted that if he were working for anybody to do such a thing, he would also deny it. Sue whispered, "Well, then we don't know any more than we did before."

Hunter said, "True, but it was worth a shot. And, he does now know that if he is involved, we may be on to him."

Jim and Linda gave the group of enthusiastic wine imbibers a smattering of information about the history and operation of their winery in Camp Verde, near Cottonwood, Arizona. Jim told everyone that the rocky limestone soil and sunny climate of the Verde Valley are very similar to the wine-making regions of France and Italy. In fact, he said, the Verde Valley and its twenty-plus wineries could easily become the next Paso Robles, Temecula, or Napa Valley.

Joyce, of Los Amigos Cellars of Napa Valley, leaned over to Ed and whispered, "They're after us."

Ed whispered back, "I guess that's a good thing. They want to be like us."

Linda gave the audience a quick overview of their Leapfrog winery and stated that since its beginning in 2004, the winery has been growing by leaps and bounds, which is partly where the name came from. She said that she and Jim started out calling it Perdon Winery, but they quickly changed the name to Leapfrog Vineyards because of the growth and because of their visit to Stag's Leap Wine Cellars in Napa Valley in 2005. They liked the winery, and they liked the name Stag's Leap. And she added that she and Jim hope that someday their winery will be as famous in Arizona as Stag's Leap is in California.

She said their winery is in an ideal location to make it a travel destination with the different outdoor activities available in the immediate area. Linda said the winery is surrounded on three sides by the Verde River, at the confluence of the Verde River and Oak Creek, and one of the things people like to do is take the two-hour water to wine kayak trip from Cottonwood to their winery, or to one of the other wineries along the Verde River. Besides all the local activities the area has to offer, she said, it is an easy and picturesque drive to Prescott, Jerome, and Sedona, and all the activities they have to offer.

Jim took over again and started the wine tasting. As before, all five wines had been pre-poured and sat before each participant—a white, a rose, and three reds. The white was a Pinot Grigio. The Rose they called Lovely. The three reds were a Sangiovese, a Merlot, and a Cabernet Sauvignon. The tasting was followed by an excellent lunch of either seafood linguine, beef pappardelle, or linguine carbonara. Dessert was a choice of tiramisu, vanilla panna cotta, or chocolate journeys rocher.

At around 1:15, Scott walked up to the front of the group and asked everyone to give a hearty round of applause to Jim and Linda, once again, and also to the manager, the servers, and the kitchen crew at Sabatini's for such excellent service. Scott then reminded everyone that the ship would be cruising Hubbard Glacier tomorrow, and there would be no wine lovers event. But the day after, Wednesday, May 3rd, there would be a wine-tasting luncheon at the Savoy dining room on the ship even though they will be in port at Icy Strait Point. Scott said Icy Strait Point is a fishing village of about seven hundred inhabitants, and unless they had booked one of the few shore excursions available, they would have plenty of time to see the village either before or after lunch.

With that, the wine lovers started getting up and making their way out of the restaurant. Many lingered, no doubt because it was such a delightful event people were sorry it had to end.

Hunter and Susan told Jim and Linda and Scott and Catalina that they would stay and help tear down the wine display and cart things off. After everyone else had cleared the restaurant, the six gathered by Jim and Linda's wine display, and Hunter asked Jim and Linda if they had told Scott and Catalina about the tainted bottle of wine. They had. Scott said he would let the other winemakers know to be on the lookout for tampered wine bottles.

After taking care of the wine display, Catalina, Sue, and Linda said they were meeting Maryanne, Roxanne, and Joyce, and they were all going to the afternoon movie in the Princess Theater. Scott asked, "Well, what about us guys?"

Catalina said, "It's a chick flick. We knew you men wouldn't be interested."

CHAPTER 25

Scott, Hunter, and Jim looked at each other. Jim said, "There must be something for us guys to do."

"Yes, there must be," Hunter said as he pulled the folded copy of the Princess Patter from his back pocket. "Let's see. There is an ice carving demonstration going on right now. It just started. And, in less than half an hour, there is a golf putting contest on the Club Fusion dance floor."

"How does that work," Scott asked, "putting on a dance floor?"

"Pretty good, I think," Jim said. "A guy told me about it yesterday. He said he was on a Princess cruise last year, and they have a big putting green carpet they roll out on the dance floor and put down one of those raised mental golf holes. He said it works fine, and it was a lot of fun."

"I'm game," Scott said, "if you guys are."

"I'm in," Hunter said.

"Me too," Jim said.

"I'll call the other guys—Tony, Jay, and Ed," Scott said. "Since their wives are going to the chick flick, they also may be looking for something to do. I'll tell them to meet us just inside Club Fusion in fifteen minutes."

"Club Fusion is not too far away," Hunter said, "and there's a restroom and a house phone just outside."

"Good," Jim said. "I need to use the head."

The three gentlemen left Sabatini's and turned aft toward Club

Fusion. Jim went to the restroom, and Scott and Hunter went around the corner, by the aft elevators, to the house phone on the wall. Hunter leaned his backside against the wall as Scott called the cabins of Tony, Jay, and Ed. Surprisingly, all three were in their cabins, and all three agreed to meet for the putting contest.

Jim finished his business, and as he turned around and walked over to the sink area, he saw a letter-sized envelope with his name on it propped up against the mirror. Jim washed his hands, grabbed the envelope, then walked out of the restroom and around the corner and found Scott and Hunter by the house phone.

"What do you have there?" Hunter asked.

"An envelope with my name on it," Jim said. "It was by the sink, in the restroom, when I turned around to wash my hands. I'm sure it wasn't there when I walked in."

"Did anybody go in the restroom after you entered?" Hunter asked. "Somebody must have, right?"

"Yeah, but I didn't see who it was. My back was to the door and the sinks. All I know is that the door opened and closed while I was relieving myself."

"Did you open it yet?" Scott asked.

"No," Jim said as he placed his finger under the flap and opened the envelope. He pulled out a tri-fold eight-and-a-half by-eleven sheet of paper. Jim unfolded the letter and read it out loud to Hunter and Scott:

Back off Buckaroo. Refuse to participate in the May 9th wine taste test. Tell your other winemakers not to participate either and everything will be fine.

"We're being watched," Hunter said, "more so than I thought."

"Why?" Jim asked. "And why would someone write me a note telling me not to participate in the blind wine taste test you have coming up, Scott?"

"We're going to have to let Jim in on the things that have been going on," Scott said.

"Yes," Hunter said. "I think we should forgo the putting contest and clue all four winemakers in on what has happened."

"You're right," Scott said. "Catalina is at the movie, so we can meet in my cabin if you want."

"Excellent," Hunter said. "Let's walk over to the Club Fusion entrance and wait for the other guys to show up. Then we'll all go up to your cabin."

A few minutes later, Tony, Jay, and Ed showed up in rapid succession at the entrance to Club Fusion. The six of them then rode one of the aft elevators to deck ten and Scott and Catalina's Glacier Bay suite, C 755.

After the four winemakers complimented Scott on his spacious suite with his view of the propeller-churning water trail, the six men gathered around the coffee table in the living room. After offering bottled water to everyone, Scott started the discussion.

"Thank you, guys, for agreeing to forgo the putting contest to come up here and discuss a matter that is of concern to Catalina and me and to you, four vintners, and your wines. There have been several incidents now that make Hunter and me certain that someone doesn't want us to have the blind taste test Catalina and I have planned for May 9th. We've talked to you and your wives about the event at different times before the cruise, and you all seemed to be on board with it, despite maybe a little reluctance by you and your wife, Ed, at first."

"That's right," Ed said. "Joyce and I do feel that maybe our California wineries are being targeted by you Arizona, New Mexico, and Nebraska boys, but we have decided we're cool with it. We're not afraid of a little friendly competition. We're not afraid to taste-test our wines against any others."

"Good," Scott said. "Glad you're still on board with it, but it has become clear over the last few days that there is someone who doesn't want our May 9th tasting event to take place. And we realize now that whoever it is, they seem to be serious about putting a stop to it."

"Yes," Hunter said. "Yesterday, Scott was grabbed from behind and chloroformed by a very big man and told to cancel May 9th. Then today, while we were getting ready to meet you guys for the putting contest at Club Fusion, about a half hour ago, someone slipped Jim here a note in an envelope with his name on it telling him not to participate in the May 9th event."

"So," Scott said, "I hate to do it because I think it would be a great event that would benefit us all—and Catalina and I have put so much into it, including sommelier judges and so forth, but I think, for the safety of everyone, we should cancel the event. I don't want anyone to get hurt."

"No, don't do it," Ed said. "Don't cancel. At least, don't do it on our account—Joyce and me. It would be a shame to cancel the main wine lovers event of the whole cruise. Everything has been leading up to this event. All the wine lovers would be very disappointed."

"Yeah, I agree," Jim said. "That really galls me—someone I don't even know giving me a letter ordering me around—trying to tell me what I can and cannot do."

"Right," Jay of Silver Leaf Vineyards said. "Back in Nebraska, we don't take kindly to people trying to boss us around. We have ways of taking care of people like that. You have to press on with your itinerary, Scott. You and Catalina have put too much into it to now kowtow to someone you don't know trying to ruin your plans and hard work."

"You were grabbed from behind and chloroformed, Scott?" Tony asked. "I'm with everybody on this, but that's a pretty aggressive act—grabbing someone and chloroforming them. I'm concerned but agree. We winemakers work hard and don't like anybody to try to push us around. I say full steam ahead on May 9th. We just need to be a little careful, I guess."

"Yes," Hunter said, "careful, watchful, and suspicious are the watchwords. Be aware of your surroundings—who's around you and what they're doing and what they have in their hands, and so forth. And be leery of anything out of the ordinary—like what they did with Scott. Someone called his cabin and said Catalina needed him at the medical center right away. Scott rushed to the medical facility, and as soon as he got off the elevator on deck four, he was grabbed.

"So, watch out for ploys like that, and try not to go anywhere by yourself. When we are in port, definitely stay vigilant and definitely don't walk around by yourself.

"Anyone else want to comment?" Hunter asked.

"Yes," Jim said. "Thinking about it, it seems that whoever is trying to stop the taste test would have their best chance by going after Scott and Catalina."

"Yes," Hunter said, "that's what Scott and I think. These people have been only going after Scott and Catalina and the wines you vintners brought aboard. But now we don't let Scott or Catalina go anywhere alone. It's a lot harder to get to them now. So, the next logical thing for the bad guys to do is to go after you vintners to see if they can convince one or more of you to drop out.

"Any other comments or thoughts?" Hunter asked.

No one said anything for a beat or two, then Jay said, "We're with you, Scott. Right, everyone?" The others nodded. "What can we do to help?"

"Like we said," Hunter reiterated, "watch your back. Let Scott or me know of anything that happens pertaining to this. We are obviously being watched. Give us a description of anyone you feel is following you or watching you—and tell your wives all of this."

"Thank you, guys," Scott said. "Thank you so much. Your understanding and support means a lot to Catalina and me."

"You and Catalina are the greatest," Tony said. "We're going to stick with you on this." The others affirmed what Tony said with a hardy "yes" and a slap on Scott's back.

A few seconds later, Ed said, "That didn't take long. "Does anyone want to go back down and see if we can still get in on the putting contest?" They all did.

CHAPTER 26

Tuesday, May 2
Hubbard Glacier Scenic Cruising

Late morning on May 2nd, the Alaskan Princess left the Gulf of Alaska and entered Yakutat Bay. The ship continued on to where Yakutat Bay narrowed considerably to become Disenchantment Bay. Captain Horatio Bustamante approached magnificent Hubbard Glacier head-on, and by the time he came as close as he dared to go, he had slowed the Alaskan Princess to a crawl. The Captain then used the side thrusters to present the ship's port side to the glacier.

Hubbard Glacier is famous for being North America's largest tidewater glacier. It is over seventy-five miles long and seven miles wide and flows directly into Disenchantment Bay. The glacier is six hundred feet high at its terminal face—three hundred and fifty feet of it above the waterline and two hundred and fifty feet below the waterline.

Because of the part of the glacier that is underwater and because of the waves and icebergs created when the glacier calves (chunks break off from the face), cruise ship captains maintain a safe distance from the glaciers.

After thirty minutes with the port side of the Alaskan Princess opposite the glacier, Captain Bustamante used the side thrusters to slowly turn the ship one hundred and eighty degrees. Now, the starboard passengers with balconies could see and hear the mighty glacier calve and creek and groan as it slowly inched its way further into Disenchantment Bay. It is a curious thing that where most glaciers are receding, Hubbard Glacier is still expanding.

By mid-afternoon, the Alaskan Princess had started slowly moving forward, out of Disenchantment and Yakutat Bays and on toward Icy Strait Point for an eight o'clock arrival the next morning.

During the Hubbard Glacier cruising, Scott and Catalina had lunch with and spent time with the four passenger sommeliers and the two free-lance wine reporters and their spouses at Sabatini's. The four restaurant sommeliers: Amy Christine from Anasazi in Santa Fe, New Mexico; Brian Downey from Lon's at the Hermosa Inn in Paradise Valley, Arizona; Reggie Narito from the Grange in downtown Sacramento, California; and Nickolas Paris from Au Courant in Omaha, Nebraska, had all meet Scott and Catalina at various times before the cruise. The same with the two free-lance reporters, John Carr and Alex Bullon, and their wives. Scott and Catalina had met them previously during their travels. In fact, Alex had done a feature article on Scott for New Mexico's Wine Enthusiast magazine.

The sommeliers and reporters were not part of Scott and Catalina's one hundred and one wine lovers group and did not participate in any winemakers functions. Scott and Catalina thought it was best to keep these judges and reporters at a distance from the winemakers functions so they would not be unduly influenced when it came time for them to judge and report at the May 9th event. They paid their own way for the cruise, as did the four featured winemakers, Tony and Maryanne Black, Jim and Linda Perdon, Jay and Roxanne Patterson, and Ed and Joyce Cooling.

During the gathering, Scott and Catalina told the group that someone was trying to undermine the May 9th blind wine tasting with demands to cancel the event. Scott and Catalina told them that they had no intention of canceling this premier event, but everyone connected with the event, including them, should use caution and stay vigilant.

CHAPTER 27

Hunter and Susan watched and took photos of Hubbard Glacier from their cabin balcony while the port side of the ship was directly across from the ice and snow mass. Once the Alaskan Princess had started its slow one-hundred-and-eighty-degree turn to position the starboard side opposite the glacier, Hunter and Susan took the stairs to deck fifteen to continue watching for the calving of the glacier. Along with others who braved the cold, Hunter and his wife periodically changed locations on the topside deck for the best observation position as the ship made its turn, even climbing up to the crow's nest platform once.

When the Alaskan Princess started to ease out of Disenchantment Bay, the Kingsleys went to their cabin and dropped off their parkas and hats and scarves and went down to deck five and the International Café. Sue ordered a hot Double Chocolate Mocha Madness coffee. Hunter, not being a fan of the coffee bean, ordered a hot Silk Road Chai tea along with a yogurt parfait. Sue grabbed the only table left while Hunter waited for the order.

The couple chatted about the glacier and how they were enjoying the cruise thus far while they thoroughly enjoyed warming up their insides with their hot drinks. As they were finishing up and getting ready to leave, Susan said, "That looks like Duke Rawlings over there next to the windows. I think he's with that same lady we saw him with last night at the Crooners Lounge."

"I think I'll go over and say hello," Hunter said as he and Susan were scooting their chairs out from under the table in order to leave.

"I'm going to go get my book and find a cozy place to read," Susan said. "I'll see you a little later."

"Okay, love ya."

"Love you too."

CHAPTER 28

Hunter bussed his table and then headed over to say hello to Duke. Duke and his lady friend were standing, and she turned to leave as Hunter approached.

"I didn't mean to scare anyone off," Hunter said.

"You didn't scare me off," the lady said. "I have an appointment at the spa."

"Hello again, Hunter," Duke said. "Kimberly, this is, I think, a friend of mine, Hunter Kingsley. It is Kingsley, isn't it?"

"Yes, you got it right," Hunter said.

"And Hunter, this is also a new friend of mine, Kimberly Howe."

Hunter extended his hand, and Kimberly lightly shook it. "Nice to meet you, Mr. Hunter Kingsley. Good chatting with you, Duke. Now, off to the spa I go."

Hunter and Duke both watched as Kimberly walked away. Duke then turned to Hunter and said, "Have a seat."

"Oh no, that's all right. I didn't mean to interrupt. I saw you—actually, my wife spotted you over here. She left, so I thought I'd come over and say hi."

"That's good of you. Unless you have another glacier you need to see, let's go someplace where we can get a real drink, like the Explorers Lounge or the Wheelhouse Bar. They're both just an easy elevator ride two decks up from here."

"The Wheelhouse Bar is the safer bet. It's about time for trivia or one of those other games in the Explorers."

"The Wheelhouse works just fine."

The two gentlemen took one of the midship panoramic elevators up to deck seven and the Wheelhouse Bar. They found a suitable table at the very back next to the windows that look out past the outdoor Promenade deck to the sea beyond.

Riviera, the cocktail waitress, came over to the two large men, one large and one extra-large, and asked what they would like to drink.

Duke spoke up with a smirk on his face. "A manly drink for manly men."

"We have several manly drinks. Do you have an idea on which one you would like?"

"A hearty Cabernet for me," Hunter said.

"That's not a manly drink," Duke said.

"Well, it's manlier than a Chardonnay or a Pinot noir," Hunter said.

"Wine has its place," Duke said, "but I'm talking about a drink—a drink drink. Cancel my friend's Cabernet. We'll each have a Four Horsemen."

"I can't think of a more manly drink," Riviera said. "I'll be right back with your Horsemen, gentlemen."

Duke and Hunter both handed Riviera their cruise card with the unlimited drink package endorsement.

"Four Horsemen," Hunter said. "I don't know about the drink, but the Four Horsemen is biblical—the Four Horsemen of the Apocalypse—from the Book of Revelation."

"Are you one of those Bible thumpers, Hunter?"

"It depends on what you mean by that. I am an evangelical, born-again Christian who wholeheartedly believes the Bible is the inspired word of God. I have accepted Jesus Christ as my Lord and Savior and believe everyone is going to live forever in either heaven or hell."

"Okay, Hunter. Wow. I'd say you're not wishy-washy about it."

"Yes. It's not good to be lukewarm about it. The Bible makes that clear. I take it you're not a believer—not a Christian."

"Well, I'm not. I'm not against Christianity, but I just don't know much about it. It's interesting, though, the lady I introduced you to—Kimberly Howe—is a Christian. I just met her yesterday."

"Very nice looking."

"Yes. She said there's a Bible class that meets every day here on the ship, and she's trying to get me to go to it."

"Are you going to go?"

"Probably not."

"Why not?"

Just then, Riviera showed up with the Four Horsemen manly drinks. "Sorry for the slight delay, gentlemen, but we had to go to one of the other bars for one of the ingredients."

"What's in the Four Horsemen?" Hunter asked.

"Equal portions of Jim Beam bourbon, Jack Daniels whiskey, Johnnie Walker scotch, and Jose Cuervo gold tequila."

"What mix do you put in it?" Hunter asked

"No mix, just Jim, Jack, Johnnie, and Jose."

"Yikes," Hunter exclaimed.

Riviera smiled and left.

"Here's to ya," Duke said as he raised his glass to Hunter. Hunter did likewise.

Duke took a swig, set his glass down, and let out a satisfied "ah."

Hunter took a swig and exclaimed, "Whoa, that's some potent brew."

"It's good for whatever ails ya," Duke said.

"I think it's also good as a paint remover."

"Probably."

"So," Hunter asked again, "why don't you go to the Bible class with Kimberly? Susan, my wife, and I go. You'd learn more about God and what He has for us. You'd learn about the Four Horsemen other than just a drink."

"Yeah, I know. I think I would be uncomfortable. I'd be surrounded by Christians like you who know the Bible pretty well—and I don't."

"That's why you go: to learn. Someone gives a lesson from part of the Bible, and then there is a discussion. But you don't have to say anything if you don't want to. Besides, you'd be with Kimberly, and she seems like a nice person to be with."

"True, not that I would ever want to, but I don't think I could ever become a Christian. I've done some pretty horrendous things in my life."

"Well, that's the point of Christianity. If you confess your wrongdoings to God and are truly sorry for them and don't want to do them anymore, God will forgive you, and He will help you live a more righteous life, not a perfect life by any means, but a more pleasing life to Him and to you. And when you die, you will go immediately to paradise—to heaven—and then you will be perfect and whole and will be continually filled with joy."

"Well, okay, Hunter, I'll think about it."

"Good for you, Duke. Once you open up your heart, even a little bit, God will start talking to you, working with you."

"We'll see. But let me ask you this. Why do you even care if I become a Christian? Why do Christians seem so concerned about people who aren't Christians? Why can't Christians just worry about themselves and let other people believe whatever they want to believe?"

"A good question. I don't think I've ever really thought about it much. I think it has to do with the truth. What is true and what is not. What is reality and what is not. If you're not living in the truth—not being guided by what's true—then you're living a lie. And that's not going to work—not in the long term. If you're on an airplane heading for Los Angeles, but you believe you're heading for New York, well, that's not going to work out very well for you."

"So you believe Christianity has the truth—exclusively. There is no other truth out there."

"People can arrive at something in different ways, but the original source of truth is from God. Scientists could perform all kinds of different experiments and conclude that heavenly bodies—planets and stars and so forth—have gravity; they attract other objects, but the original source of that truth is God. God made the planets and the stars. God made everything, so He is the source of all truth. Jesus said He is the way, the truth, and the life."

"And that's another thing. You said Jesus said He is the truth. God didn't say that."

"Jesus is God. Jesus said He and the Father—Father God—are one. But I know what you're getting at—the trinity—Father, Son, and Holy Spirit. Three distinct entities, yet the same—all three God. How does that work? We don't really know. But it's not a concept totally out of left field. A man can be a father and a son at the same time. Ice, water, and steam contain the same substance but in three distinct forms. Not the best example, but there is no exact comparison. Father, Son, and Holy Spirit is unique—the only one of its kind.

"Okay. That helps a little."

"Oh, another reason that just popped into my head on why we Christians like to get everyone to become fellow believers is that fraternal feeling—the fellowship of congenial spirits."

"The fellowship of congenial spirits? That sounds familiar. That sounds like a saying from my old college fraternity, Kappa Sigma."

"Kappa Sigma. You're a Kappa Sig? I can't believe it. So am I."

"No kidding. What chapter?"

"Beta Theta, Indiana University. What about you?"

"Pi Xi, Colorado State University."

"Well, I'll be," Hunter said as he stood up and extended his hand.

Duke stood up and shook Hunter's hand.

"Do you remember the secret handshake, Duke?"

"I think so. Let's do it."

The two fraternity brothers exchanged the secret handshake as Hunter said, "A. E. K. D. B., my brother."

Duke returned with, "A. E. K. D. B., my brother."

The two fraternity brothers sat back down with elation and amazement still on their faces.

"Well," Hunter said, "not to belabor the point, but being a Christian is something like being a member of a fraternity or sorority. You are part of a group of like-minded individuals who enjoy the fellowship of congenial spirts. It's a lot more than that, but great fellowship is a part of it."

"Okay, Hunter, my brother, I'll give it a shot. I'll call Kimberly and see if I can go to the Bible study tomorrow with her."

"Really! Good for you. And if Kimberly is not going to be there for some reason, Susan and I will be there—so, either way, you will know someone in the class."

"Okay. That's good."

"Anyway, I'm going to go look for my wife. We need to start getting ready for our early dinner with our wine lovers group. See you tomorrow at the Bible study." Hunter started to get up.

"Right. I actually think I'm looking forward to it."

"Excellent."

"You're not going to finish your drink, Hunter?"

"No. I'm pretty much a wine-only kind of guy."

"Okay. See you tomorrow, brother."

"Tomorrow."

CHAPTER 29

Wednesday, May 3, 10:00 a.m.
Icy Strait Point

"Hello, this is Jeep."

"Yeah, Available here. I'm calling from Icy Strait Point."

"Okay. How's it going? Should I start smiling yet?"

"I'm not smiling. What should be a simple job is not working out that way. This Poncetran couple is not getting the message. Indications are they are still planning on having the blind taste test against your California representative. I found out they have four reputable sommeliers on board, in addition to the ship's sommelier, and they plan to use them as judges for the tasting. And they have two free-lance wine reporters who are going to write articles about the event. The Poncetrans have invested a good amount of effort and time into this thing, and we have not been able to dissuade them."

"This is not good news."

"No. And now we can't seem to catch either of the Poncentrans alone, so we can give them a much stronger message about forgetting to do this big May 9th event. We do, fortunately, have some other options, but we're going to require more money."

"Listen, you came highly recommended to us. We were told you were a 'can do' type operation. Now you're waffling."

"Like I said, complications have arisen. I told you and your cohort that operations like this are not always cut-and-dried. A good amount of ad-libbing is often required. And that turns out to be the case here. Now, we can just call it a day, or we can employ more persuasive tactics. Your choice. It depends on just how important stopping this May 9th event is to you and your friends."

"We want the job done. We need to have it done. It's important."

"Okay then. It's going to cost you more money."

"How much more?"

"Twenty thousand."

"Twenty thousand! That's a lot extra to pay for a job that should have been done already."

"It comes with a guarantee. A guarantee that you will get your desired results."

"I thought we already had that guarantee."

"You put restrictions on us. You said you didn't want anybody to get hurt. We tried it that way, and it didn't work. Remove those restrictions, and we're free to do whatever it takes to get the job done."

"Well, okay. Just don't hurt anybody too bad."

"That's a restriction."

"Okay. No restrictions."

"Good. Now, I'll make it easy for you since you've given us free rein. You can pay half the additional money now and the other half when the job is done. The ship will be in Juneau tomorrow, and you can wire the ten thousand to me there. Let me know later today when and where it will be. We are there from 8:00 a.m. to 10:00 p.m., so you have all day."

"Okay. I'll call you later today with the particulars."

"Good."

CHAPTER 30

Wednesday, May 3, 11:00 a.m.
Savoy Dining Room

The Savoy is a mid-sized dining room on deck five just aft of the panoramic lifts, which are just aft of the Plaza where the International Café is located. It has a subdued royal blue carpet with a British Coat of Arms design, dark brown wood and upholstered chairs, square and round table-clothed tables for four, and built-in seating along the sides and rear with tables for four. The brass railings throughout add to the British Pub feel. The restaurant is one of the five main dining rooms at night and is open on certain days for a traditional British pub-style lunch. Classics such as steak and kidney pie and bangers and mash with bread and butter pudding for dessert are included in the menu choices. Available drinks include Bass and Guinness and Strongbow cider, among others.

Today, the Savoy is the location for the third of the four winemakers tastings and luncheons—all leading up to the May 9th grand finale blind wine tasting competition of wines from all four of the winemakers—with reputations and awards at stake.

Following the same format as before, sitting before each patron were five pre-poured wines sitting in a semi-circle on a James Suckling's Great Wines of the World paper matt. The matt had a circle for each of the wine glasses to sit on, along with a synopsis of the basics of wine evaluation.

Without much ado, Scott Poncetran introduced Jay and Roxanne Patterson of Silver Leaf Vineyards of Lincoln, Nebraska.

Jay did the presentation. "Thank you, Scott, for that lackluster introduction." People laughed but almost immediately curtailed their laughter. Scott's introduction certainly seemed lackluster, and maybe Jay was serious with his jab. "No offense, Scott, but ever since Roxanne and I opened our winery just outside of Lincoln, we've had to put up with sneers and jokes about making wine in Nebraska. That's okay, Scott. Come on out to our winery sometime, and maybe I'll let you drive the tractor. Better yet, let me drive the tractor while you stand in front of it. Just kidding, Scott. Seriously, though, come visit our winery, and you can see that our grapes really aren't plastic. I'll let you touch one and even squeeze it, and you can see that it really does have juice."

Scott, who had been sitting on the sidelines and who was a little red-faced now, stood up, shaking his head from side to side, and walked over to Jay. He put his right arm across Jay's back and placed his hand on Jay's right shoulder. He rocked Jay back and forth as best he could, as they were both about the same size and weight. Scott looked out and said to everyone, "I know it's hard to tell, but Jay and I are actually very good friends—right, Jay?"

"Of course, Scott, whatever you say. But seriously, you and Catalina come out to our winery for a visit. I know you said you tried to once, but you couldn't find Nebraska."

"We're coming. Catalina and I are coming for a visit soon. And I do want to drive the tractor and squeeze the grapes." Scott walked back to his sidelines chair, still a little red in the face, shaking his head back and forth once again.

By now, most in the group were in full-blown laughter, although several were still not sure if Jay's sort of put-down humor was normal for him, and they were not sure if Scott was genuinely caught off guard or if he was just playing along with Jay.

"Well, folks, Roxanne and I understand why most people don't associate Nebraska with winemaking. Nebraska has come on the scene as a winemaker only recently. Nebraska's oldest existing winery was established in 1994, and there are currently just over thirty operating wineries in the state. Nebraska's long, hot summers and cold winters perfectly suit the commonly grown French-American hybrid grapes, such as Edelweiss, La Crosse, Frontenac, St. Croix, and Vignoles. It's safe to say that Nebraska winemakers produce the best Edelweiss wines in the world. Several Nebraska winemakers have won Best of Show and Double Gold with their dry Edelweiss wines. A Nebraska Brianna wine won the U.S. National Competition in Sonoma, California, in 2012, beating all comers, including California wines.

"So, bottom line, don't sell Nebraska winemakers short. Now, enough about Nebraska wines deserving at least some respect. Let's see what you all think of our Silver Leaf Vineyards wines. Starting with the wine on your left, we have our Edelweiss. Over the years, this has been our most popular and most awarded wine. It is a semi-sweet white made from one hundred percent Edelweiss grapes. It is a well-balanced wine that creates quite a sensation of sweetness in the front of the palate with a burst of tartness as it dances..." As soon as Jay said the word "dances," he lifted up his arms with his wine glass in hand and started dancing forward with a few dance steps. He continued his comment, "...as it dances across the tongue and heads for the finish, creating a sweet yet complex taste experience. Full of green apple flavors, this is a wine that won't be forgotten."

Jay continued presenting the wines and, at times, visually demonstrated his words. In the end, Jay received a standing ovation from the smiling crowd. Scott reminded everyone that the next day, May 4th, they would be in Juneau all day, and they would have their final wine-tasting luncheon. He said it would be at the usual time, eleven o'clock, in the Vivaldi dining room on board the ship with Ed and Joyce Cooling from Los Amigos Cellars of Napa

Valley presenting. Catalina walked up and stood next to Scott, and they both thanked everyone for coming.

CHAPTER 31

Wednesday, May 3, 1:00 p.m.
Icy Strait Point

"It's about time you called, Schultz," Jeep said over his burner phone.

"Yeah, well, this is the first day I could. We were at sea the first two days. Besides, I had nothing to report. And I still don't. I don't think our fantastic 'Mr. Available' has done anything yet. In fact, I haven't even seen him."

"He called me this morning," Jeep said. "He said he made several attempts to just get rid of the wine, but all attempts failed. He said he then tried to give Mr. Poncetran a message more directly, but that didn't work either. Now, he wants more money—twenty thousand—and free rein to do whatever he deems necessary. But he guarantees the job will get done."

"This taste test looks like it's going to be a big deal, with a good amount of publicity," Schultz said. "We definitely don't want this thing to take place. I think we have to stick with our guy and give him the extra money. Twenty thousand dollars is nothing compared to the possible damage to the California wine industry that could come out of this May 9th thing."

"Agreed. I already figured to pay the extra if you didn't call. And remember, we still have an ace up our sleeve: you. If Mr. Available and company doesn't come through, say by May 8th at the latest, then you've got to do something to stop this thing."

"We'd better make sure Mr. Available comes through. I don't know what I could do. Remember, we agreed my wife and I are not supposed to get involved. We are supposed to enjoy the cruise and, at most, confirm that Mr. Available got the job done. If we get involved and are found out, it could come back to ruin our whole wine group operation."

"Yeah, yeah."

"That's why Sandy and I did not sign up to be part of the wine lovers group with the Poncetrans. We need to monitor and observe from a distance. Plus, we want to keep a safe distance from Ed and Joyce Cooling. If they see us, they would probably recognize us—which is all right—but it's better if they don't and we keep our distance from them."

"That's right. There's bad blood between you and them—that water rights debacle."

"Exactly. Plus, I just really don't like them."

"Well, you're not alone. Not everyone in the valley does."

"That's for sure."

"Okay. So, I'll wire Mr. Available half of the twenty thousand tomorrow, like he asked. Then we pay the other ten thousand when the job is complete."

"How you going to wire him money? We don't know his real name."

"He gave me a name to send it to. He apparently has an account and I. D. under that name. Heck, maybe that is his real name."

"What's the name he gave you? Just out of curiosity."

"Antone Gillespie."

"I guess that could be his real name. Hard to tell. If he had said, 'Dizzy Gillespie,' I would say no, that's not his real name."

"We don't care what his real name is," Jeep said. "All we care about is that he comes through and gets the job done. By the way, have you run into Hector and Paula Veracruz? You met them at our last party a little while back. They were in Napa visiting. They used to live there but moved to Albuquerque a few years ago. They are good friends of ours and also of Scott and Catalina Poncetran."

"Okay. I know who you're talking about. No, I haven't run into them, but I'll keep a watch out for them."

"Yeah, they are part of the wine lovers group with the Poncetrans. When the May 9th event gets canceled, they will know."

"Good. I'll look for them. I do have a source for the events on the ship and if they get changed or canceled. But it never hurts to have a backup."

"For sure. Listen, Schultz, keep on top of this. Call me as soon as something happens."

"Will do. Talk to you later."

CHAPTER 32

May 4, 7:30 a.m.
Juneau, Alaska
Cabin C 232

As Hunter and Susan Kingsley were getting ready for the eight-thirty Bible class, Captain Bustamante made the announcement over the public address system of the ships arrival in Juneau. He confirmed something they already knew—it was a bit chilly outside.

"Let's get there a little early in case Duke shows up by himself before Kimberly shows up."

"Sure. Okay," Susan said. "One more minute, and I'll be ready. So do you really think Duke is sincere about wanting to learn more about God?"

"He seemed pretty attentive yesterday in class, so, I think so. But he does seem a little hesitant at times. I think something is holding him back."

"One step at a time," Susan said.

"I know. Baby steps."

"What about his possible involvement in what's been going on with the wine and the harassment of Scott and Catalina and all that? Do you think he's sincere in saying he's not involved?"

"Good question. I think he's sincere, but I am also hesitant to fully believe him. He's the kind of guy who can look you in the eyes and tell you a bold-faced lie and never flinch."

"Okay, I'm ready."

"Good, let's go grab some breakfast before class."

CHAPTER 33

May 4, 11:00 a.m.
Vivaldi dining room
Deck Five

The Vivaldi dining room is almost the mirror image of the Savoy dining room right next to it. Instead of the British pub look and feel, the Vivaldi has a Venetian ambiance with warm colors, glittering accents, and rich wood furniture. The room was named after the Venetian composer, virtuoso violinist, and impresario of Baroque music, Antonio Lucio Vivaldi.

At eleven o'clock, Scott Poncetran stepped up in front of the group of wine enthusiasts and started clinking an empty wine glass in order to quiet the group. Not all of the one hundred and one were present, as a few of them had morning excursions in and around Juneau.

"Good morning—getting close to lunchtime—everyone. Welcome to our fourth wine tasting featuring wines from the four winemakers we have on board. We've enjoyed wines from New Mexico, Arizona, and Nebraska thus far. And now, last but not least by any means, we will enjoy wines from California—more specifically, Napa Valley—and, more specifically still, Northern Napa Valley. I say that because wine growers get even more specific than that and talk in terms of microclimates, and Northern Napa Valley has the better microclimate for grapes.

"Our friends, Ed and Joyce Cooling, own and operate Los

Amigos Cellars in Northern Napa Valley. Their winery offers a pleasant alternative to the corporate-run vineyards and wineries that are all over Napa Valley and California in general. California has room for both. But if you are looking for the level of hospitality the smaller, family-run operations offer, you certainly can't go wrong with a visit to Los Amigos. Ed and Joyce often host the tastings themselves.

"So, please give a warm round of applause as Ed comes up front to tell you more and to lead you in the tasting of their fine wines.

"Thank you, Scott," Ed said. "Joyce and I are so glad that we were finally able to join you and Catalina on one of your wine lovers cruises. Thanks again for inviting us. If any of you here have a chance to visit our winery, let us know in advance, and we will arrange a special tour for you and your friends. Our wine-tasting fee is fifty dollars a person, but if you tell us you were on Scott and Catalina's Alaskan cruise, we'll discount it to twenty-five dollars each. That's the best we can do. In case you haven't heard, things in California are expensive. Wine-tasting prices in Napa Valley are anywhere from fifty to one hundred and twenty-five for basic wine-tasting. Special wine tastings can be up to five hundred dollars and more. I guess that's the price of fame.

"But before we get started with the wine tasting, a few facts about California wineries. There are over 450 wineries in Napa Valley. That is, wineries with tasting rooms that you can go and visit. There are over 6.000 wineries in California. Compare that with Washington State at number two with about 1,400 wineries, and, believe it or not, Texas at number three with about 950 wineries. Arizona has about 160 wineries, New Mexico 120, and Nebraska 45.

"While some California vintners may be worried about competition from up-and-coming wineries in other states, we are not. California wines will reign supreme, production-wise, well into the future. However, taste-wise, that can be a different story. Joyce and I have to admit we have tasted some very good non-California wines these last few days. So, if Scott and Catalina want to have a few sommeliers taste test our wines along with wines from New Mexico, Arizona, and Nebraska—and give out a few awards in the process—Joyce and I say, have at it." At that, an enthusiastic round of applause erupted from the audience.

"Unless anyone has a comment or a question, we will start our wine tasting. Oh, I see a hand. There is a question or comment. Yes, ma'am."

"What about the recent fires in California and in the wine country?"

"Yes, we do have our problems in California. Fires have always been a concern. Also, we've had some recent state legislation regarding water rights that have not been helpful to our wineries. But we forge ahead and do the best we can. Anyone else have a question or comment?

"No. Good. Let's start with the wine on your left. It, obviously, is a white wine…"

Ed continued with the wine tasting and, when finished, received a healthy round of applause. Lunch was served, and at the end, Scott reminded everyone that Skagway was tomorrow, and the day after that was scenic cruising in Glacier Bay National Park. He told everyone that no formal wine lovers events were planned for the next two days but encouraged people to have their own little wine gatherings.

As people started to file out of the restaurant, Scott and Catalina went around to their close friends and invited them to their "cruise out of Glacier Bay" party in their rear balcony suite on Glacier Bay afternoon, starting as the ship begins to motor back out of Glacier Bay, after the scenic cruising.

CHAPTER 34

May 4, 2:00 p.m.
Juneau, Alaska
Bank of America

"You ran out of money, Mr. Gillespie?"

"Yes, that's right. Stayed in the casino too long."

"That can happen. Good thing you have friends who can send you money."

"It is."

"And you want seven of the ten thousand in cash?"

"Yes, in hundreds."

A few minutes later, Gillespie, aka Mr. Available, headed out the door and back to the ship to put the money in his cabin safe.

CHAPTER 35

May 4, 4:00 p.m.
Juneau, Alaska

"Hey, Jeep, it's Schultz."

"Yeah. You still in Juneau? I thought you'd be leaving by now."

"No, we're here until ten tonight. Anyway, Ed and Joyce Cooling of Los Amigos Cellars did their wine-tasting lunch today. I caught Hector and Paula Veracruz as they were coming out of the luncheon. I asked them if anything was said about the big wine tasting on May 9th—like if it was still going to take place. They seemed surprised I had asked and said that it was still planned. In fact, they said Ed and Joyce are apparently looking forward to it, even though they may not come out number one in everything. And my other ears and eyes in the wine lovers group confirmed it. It's full speed ahead for the May 9th taste test.

"I was afraid of that. I don't know them very well, but I've never quite figured out Ed and Joyce. I don't think they have a clue as to what's going on. I don't think they realize they are being set up for a fall. They don't understand what a laughing stock the whole California wine industry could become if an Arizona or a New Mexico wine, let alone a Nebraska wine wins a superior taste test over their California wines. Ed and Joyce make some good wines, but I would feel a lot better if we had someone like Stags Leap Vineyards representing California."

"I hear you, Jeep, but we had no control over that. Besides, this whole wine taste-testing thing is not as cut and dried as a lot of people think. Even though Stags Leap 1973 Cabernet won the 1976 Judgement of Paris and put Napa Valley on the map, subsequent judgments have found that the Stags Leap Cabernet does not come out on top most of the time."

"I know. That's what I'm afraid of—what we're afraid of—that the mystique surrounding the superiority of California wines will be dismantled, shattered. One or two bottles of—oh, I can't even say it. One or two bottles of—egad—Nebraska wine could shatter the mystique of our California wines irreparable. That's why we have to stop this. We have to do whatever it takes to stop this crazy contest against our California wines."

"Yes. I wholeheartedly agree. I know what Mr. Available looks like, but I haven't seen him since boarding the ship. I'm sure he's laying low, but I'll keep my eye out for him, and if I see him, I'll emphasize to him that this thing has to be done, no matter what it takes."

"Yes, and I'll call him as well and make sure he understands. I'm sure he'll go to town tomorrow, to Skagway, so you might check all the watering holes for him. We can't fail at this. People are depending on us."

"No, we can't fail. We'll keep in touch."

CHAPTER 36

May 5
Skagway, Alaska

The Alaskan Princess was fast alongside the dock at Skagway at 7:00 a.m. on May 5th. One other ship was in port. It had docked a half an hour earlier. Two other cruise ships were on their way. Four ships at Skagway at the same time was typical. The weather forecast showed a high of 45 degrees and a low of 32 degrees Fahrenheit, relative humidity of 80 percent, and rain likely. Again, typical.

Hunter and Susan, Scott and Catalina, Tony and Maryanne Black, and Hector and Paula Veracruz were all booked on the White Pass and Yukon Railroad excursion at nine o'clock. In the afternoon, they all planned to explore downtown Skagway.

Mike and Larry Oncur—the boys from Nebraska—were originally going to hike the 33-mile Chilkoot trail but decided to instead do the more reasonable bike, hike, and float trip down the glacially-fed Taiya River.

Jim and Linda Perdon, Jay and Roxanne Patterson, and Ed and Joyce Cooling were all going together on the Skagway dog sledding and glacier helicopter tour. A little pricy but a once-in-a-lifetime experience.

Ralph and Arleen Simpson (code-named Schultz and Sandy) planned to go to the famous Red Onion Saloon for lunch and then explore the town afterward.

Antone Gillespie (aka Mr. Available) and his accomplice, Wit Kraske, decided they would go into town and have a beer or two or three.

At approximately 1:30 p.m., as Ralph and Arleen Simpson were finishing their lunch at the Red Onion, Ralph saw Mr. Available and another man walk into the saloon. "Can you take care of the check, Arleen? There is a guy I have to go say hello to. I won't be long."

"Well, if you are, I'll be in the jewelry store down the street."

"Okay." Ralph walked over to the entrance area where Mr. Available and Wit were standing and waiting for a table. "Mr. A, I know you talked to Jeep on the phone a time or two and…"

"Ah, Schultz. Listen, we really shouldn't be seen together. What is it?"

"I want to emphasize even more than Jeep probably did that the job absolutely has to be done. So, if I can help, if you could use my help—and you'll still get your money—I'm handy, I'm here, I'm available."

"I'll think about it. Meet me tomorrow at 6:00 a.m. by the ice cream counter at the Horizon Court on deck fourteen, and we'll discuss it."

"The ice cream shop is not going to be open at that time."

"That's right. If anybody's around, then we'll go someplace else. Now, you'd better get lost."

CHAPTER 37

Friday, May 5
Charthouse Dining Room
Deck Six

At 5:30 dinner, the wine lovers' tables were lively with discussions of the different adventures everyone had enjoyed in and around Skagway earlier in the day. The three couples, who had gone on the Skagway dog sledding and glacier helicopter tour, were excited to relive their experience with their table mates. They actually rode in a dog sled pulled by Alaskan huskies on a glacier.

Scott and Catalina and company thoroughly enjoyed their train trip into the Yukon on the 1898 railroad built during the Klondike Gold Rush. The scenery was spectacular, and so many photos were taken by the group.

The brothers from Nebraska, Mike and Larry, witnessed some great scenery as well on their combination bike, hike, and float trip. They passed their many phone photos around the tables.

After dinner, a few in the group went to the Crooners Lounge to hear Austin Parker. Others went to the Princess Theater to see the production show "New York, New York." Others went to Club Fusion or the Explores Club to dance. One couple went to the Wheelhouse Bar for a nightcap. The rest called it a night and went back to their cabins. All hoped for good weather tomorrow for the scenic cruise into Glacier Bay.

CHAPTER 38

Saturday, May 6, 6:00 a.m.
Ice Cream Shop
Deck Fourteen

"Right on time, Schultz," Mr. Available said.

"Yeah, a little early for me. But, what the hey. I made it. I'm surprised at the number of people up at this hour."

Wit Kraske smiled.

"Probably more than usual," Mr. A said. We are just entering Glacier Bay. Won't be at the glaciers for a little while yet, but there are some people who don't want to miss anything."

"So, you got a plan?" Schultz asked. "Do you want my help? No charge. I just want to make sure the job gets done."

"Yeah, yeah. Let's go over to that table in the corner, out of the way of any foot traffic that might come through here. We'll talk."

The three men sat down at the out-of-the-way table and talked. Fifteen minutes later, the three men stood up. Schultz went his way, and Mr. Available and Wit went their way.

Captain Bustamante announced over the public address system that the ship had entered Glacier Bay National Park and would be parked alongside the main glacier, the Margerie Glacier, in approximately two and a half hours. He said the ship would spend about thirty minutes with the port side facing the glacier, then would slowly turn one hundred and eighty degrees, and the starboard side would face the glacier for another thirty minutes. Then the Alaskan Princess would slowly cruise back out of Glacier Bay and on into Icy Strait, then the Gulf of Alaska, and head south for their next port of call, Sitka.

CHAPTER 39

Glacier Bay, Alaska

It was an exciting day aboard the Alaskan Princess. For not a small number of people, an Alaskan cruise means Glacier Bay. The other glaciers cruise ships can get to are worth seeing, but Glacier Bay has received the most publicity and has become the "must-see" wonder of a cruise trip to Alaska.

Glacier Bay National Park features nine giant tidewater glaciers. Cruise ships normally cruise up the inlet sixty-five miles to the Johns Hopkins, the Grand Pacific, and the Margerie glaciers and spend a little over an hour in front of the Margerie Glacier. Margerie Glacier is the most famous glacier in the park, with one of the most active glacial faces. That is, Margerie normally does the most calving, where huge chunks of ice break off the face and fall into the sea.

At Gustavus, at the entrance to the Glacier Bay Inlet, a boat comes alongside the ship, and two Park Rangers board the ship for the day and offer commentary over the loudspeakers. Often, a Huna Tlingit cultural guide will also board and offer commentary regarding the local Tlingit people. Sightings of wildlife such as puffins, harbor seals, humpback whales, brown bears, bald eagles, and ravens are usually pointed out by the Park Rangers. Glacier Bay is a UNESCO World Heritage Site, and only two cruise ships per day are allowed in.

Many people who have balcony cabins spent the day on their

balcony during the cruise in and out of Glacier Bay. The advantage is you can slip into your toasty warm cabin anytime you want and get a drink, go to the bathroom, and so forth. The disadvantage is that if a wildlife sighting or waterfall is pointed out by the Park Ranger and it's on the other side of the ship, you miss out. So, the best place for viewing the scenery, as long as you dress warm enough, is on the upper decks, where it's easy to go from one side of the ship to the other.

Scott and Catalina, Hunter and Susan, Hector and Paula Veracruz, brothers Mike and Larry, all the winemakers, along with a few others from the wine lovers group, all braved the cold and gathered as a loose group out on deck fifteen as the Alaskan Princess cruised toward the glaciers of Glacier Bay. The winemakers and wine lovers were among many other hearty passengers out on deck fifteen, and periodically, individuals and couples went inside to warm up, maybe get a hot drink from the Horizon Court one deck below, and maybe go to the restroom. At one point, Ed and Joyce Cooling, owners and operators of Los Amigos Cellars in Upper Napa Valley, took a turn inside. No one took note, but they never came back out.

CHAPTER 40

Glacier Bay, Alaska

A little while later, the Alaskan Princess was positioned opposite the Margerie Glacier, with the port side of the ship facing the two-hundred-and-fifty-foot-tall monster. The ship's engines were at idle, and the weather now was almost perfect. Just then, with a roar and a spectacular crash into the water, a giant chunk of the face of the glacier broke off and plummeted into the sea. Now, everyone's appetite was wetted, so to speak, and they wanted to see more. Many had missed getting a photo or video of the event as it had happened so fast. People were now staring at the glacier with their cameras ready.

And suddenly, there they were—two people with orange life jackets, a male and a female—with their heads bobbing up and down in the frigid water floating in between small chunks of ice. It was hard to tell what they were at first, especially for people on the top decks. Finally, a woman on deck fifteen yelled, "Those are people—those are people swimming in the water." They weren't swimming. They were bobbing up and down in the choppy water with their lifeless arms sloshing back and forth.

Hunter ran inside to a house phone and called security. The person who answered said one of the crewmen had also just spotted the two people in the water, and a crew was already preparing to launch an emergency raft to retrieve them. Hunter went back outside and yelled to everyone that help was on the way.

People watched as a yellow rubber raft with three crewmen retrieved the two bobbers and returned to the ship. People started wondering and asking each other why someone would think they could go swimming in such freezing water. Hunter knew they hadn't gone swimming. He was afraid it might be someone connected with the wine lovers group. Hunter realized that he and Scott had to now talk to security and tell them about the harassment attempts. Hunter knew they might have some explaining to do. Hunter knew that he and Scott might be in trouble for not alerting security to the shenanigans that had been going on regarding the wine lovers group.

Hunter located Susan and Scott and Catalina in the deck fifteen crowd. He grabbed Scott by the upper arm and said, "We have to talk to security, Scott. The couple in the water is probably somebody you know."

"I didn't think of that. You may be right."

"Yes. If it is someone in the wine lovers group, you may speed up the identification of the couple, and you probably have information about them that will help security."

"Ladies," Hunter said, "Scott and I are going to go down to security just in case the swimmers are somebody in the wine lovers group."

"Do you want us to go with you?" Sue asked.

"Better not," Hunter said. "They might not even talk to us, but two of us have a better chance than four of us."

"Okay," Sue said.

"I sure hope it's not someone from our group," Catalina said.

"Yeah, I hope not," Scott said.

"We'll see you guys back here in a little while," Hunter said. "Get some good photos while we're gone."

***

On the way down to deck four in the mid-ship elevators, Hunter asked Scott if he was aware of anyone who was missing from their group. He said no, and Hunter said he wasn't either.

Hunter and Scott got off the elevator on deck four and walked the short distance from the medical center lobby into the crew-only area and over to security. The door was closed and locked. Hunter knocked several times, but there was no answer. Hunter and Scott then walked further down the corridor and turned right at a short corridor that led to an open area and a port side hatch that was open. Just inside the hatch, laid out on the floor, were the two people who had just been retrieved from the icy water.

The orange life vests had been removed, and two crewmembers were administering CPR. The ship's doctor, Doctor Hazlett, knelt down and started checking vital signs. After a couple of minutes, Doctor Hazlett looked at the two CPR crewmembers and said, "It's too late." Doctor Hazlett then looked at his nurse, Nurse Palma, and said, "Both pronounced dead at 12:35 p.m." He then looked at the Chief of Security, Carter Watts.

Chief Watts nodded and said, "Got it, 12:35 p.m." Watts turned and looked around and noticed Hunter and Scott, who were standing back and to the side, out of the way, but able to see everything. Watts exploded. "Who are you, and what are you doing here? You are not supposed to be here. This is a crew-only area."

"Yes, sir," Hunter said, "we may be able to help. We may be able to identify the couple and possibly shed some light on what may have happened."

"Well, go wait in the foyer in front of the medical facility, or go in the medical facility and have a seat in the waiting area. I can't talk to you now. Officer Yates, escort these gentlemen out of here."

Security Officer Yates made a move toward Hunter and Scott. Hunter said, "We'll be in the medical clinic waiting area. We know the way." Hunter and Scott turned and walked away.

CHAPTER 41

"May I help you?" medical clinic nurse and receptionist Lily Wu asked Hunter and Scott.

"We were told we could wait here," Hunter said. "Security might want to talk to us. It's about the two people who were pulled out of the water. Do you happen to know anything about that?"

"No. I know Doctor Hazlett and Nurse Palma were called to attend to them. I hope they're all right. It's crazy what some people will do for a thrill."

"How's that?" Hunter asked.

"Going for a swim in Glacier Bay. It seems to be a 'thing.' It seems to be the 'thing to do.' Three people tried it last cruise. They didn't make it, though."

"They drowned?" Scott asked.

"No. They didn't make it into the water. One of the crew caught them trying to open the hatch. Security gave them a good talking to. Crazy people."

"Yeah, crazy," Scott said.

Scott and Hunter sat silent for a moment, then Scott said in a low voice, "I didn't get much of a look at them. Did you?"

"No. We'll just have to wait and see."

"I guess security is going to let us see if we can identify them."

"I think so."

"This is all my fault, Hunter. We should have told security right from the start what was going on—the attempts at getting the wine, the threats, me being abducted. But I wanted to keep things under wraps. I wanted a little mystery surrounding the event."

"I don't agree. If this couple is from the wine lovers group, it's not your fault. You should have the right to do above-board, legitimate things without being told by someone or some group that you can't do that. People who do harm are responsible for that harm."

Just then, Chief Security Officer Carter Watts opened the door to the medical clinic and poked his head inside. "You two come with me."

Hunter and Scott stood up and followed Watts out the door and to the security office. Watts motioned for Hunter and Scott to take the two chairs in front of his desk as he took his chair behind it.

"I am Chief of Security Carter Watts. Your names and cabin numbers, please."

Scott and Hunter gave Watts the information.

"So, what information do you have for me regarding this couple who decided to take a swim?"

Scott spoke up. "My wife and I are hosting the wine lovers group on board, and if the couple that went swimming is one of our group, I can help identify them. That is, I take it that they are no longer alive."

"They are not. And we know who they are. Their cruise cards were on their person."

"Who are they?" Scott asked.

"I can't tell you that. Not at this time."

"Then I don't know if I know them. I don't know if I can confirm their identification. Don't you need that?"

"Their names are Ed and Joyce Cooling from Napa Valley, California."

Scott let out a sigh. "Oh boy. I was afraid of that. Hunter and I know them. They are—they were part of our wine lovers group."

"Sorry. But why do you think they would try to take a swim in Glacier Bay? Was that some sort of dare—some sort of prank your group conjured up?"

"No," Scott said, "absolutely not! We're pretty sure they were chloroformed and abducted."

"Really. And why is that?"

"We are certain someone is trying to stop my wife and me from doing our wine-tasting event on May 9th in Sabatini's restaurant."

"Why? Why would someone want to prevent your wine-tasting event? And why would chloroforming Ed and Joyce Cooling and tossing them in the bay stop that event?"

"They were two of the winemakers whose wines were going to be taste tested. So, if they are not there for the event, I guess someone might think that would stop the taste testing."

"Would it?"

"I don't know. I haven't thought about it."

"Well, I'll keep your concerns in mind, but this looks like a simple case of two people wanting to go for a swim in Glacier Bay—for the notoriety. It looks like it's becoming a minor fad. Once something like this gets around on social media, then everybody wants to do it. Anyway, Doctor Hazlett will examine them as best he can to see if there is any evidence of foul play, but I think we have another case of 'swim Glacier Bayitis.' Except, unlike some of the others, they didn't live to tell about it."

"It's so hard to believe," Scott said. "They are good friends of me and my wife. We were just with them a little bit ago. They didn't give any indication they might do something like this. I still think they were forced into the water against their will. I know they don't have any relatives on board. Do you want me to give a positive identification?"

"Okay. It's not all that necessary, but it won't hurt. But just you, Mr. Poncetran."

"Mr. Kingsley knows them too."

"Okay then, both of you. They're in the morgue now. I'll call over and make sure it's all right."

Watts made the call, and the three of them walked over to the medical center. Doctor Hazlett met Chief Watts and company, and Scott and Hunter confirmed that the couple in the morgue was, in fact, Ed and Joyce Cooling. Hunter noticed evidence of bruising on Ed and Joyce's upper arms and said that that could be evidence that they were grabbed and forced into the water. Watts said that the bruising could just as well have taken place when the crewmen pulled them up out of the water and into the raft. Doctor Hazlett said it was hard to tell. The bruising could have happened either way.

Chief Watts told Scott and Hunter he was sorry for the loss of their friends, but it was just an unfortunate accident. He said the ship's personnel would take care of the necessary paperwork and inform the "in case of an emergency" contact persons they had listed for the couple.

Scott and Hunter walked out of the medical clinic and over to the mid-ship elevators across the way. "Well, I guess we go back up to deck fifteen and let Catalina and Susan and our friends know the sad news."

"Yep, got to do it," Hunter said.

CHAPTER 42

While Scott and Hunter were gone, the Alaskan Princess had done its half hour with the port side facing the glacier, its slow turn using the side thrusters, and its half hour with the starboard side parallel with the glacier. The ship was now creeping back out of Glacier Bay.

Some of the deck fifteen crowd were staying on for the cruise out while others were heading for warmth and other parts of the ship. Scott and Hunter spotted their wives among the lingering deck fifteen group.

"There you are," Catalina said to Scott as he walked up to her. "You're just in time. Remember, we invited some of our friends to our cabin for hors d'oeuvres and warm-up wine for a little cruise out of the bay party."

"Oh yes, I almost forgot."

"So, what did you find out about that couple—the swimmers? Everybody is affectionately calling them the 'Glacier Bay show-offs.'"

"It's not good news," Scott told Catalina in a low voice. "It was our friends, Ed and Joyce. The cold got to them. They didn't make it. They died."

"Oh no," Catalina managed to mouth as she started to faint and collapse.

Scott caught her and kept her from going down. She quickly regained consciousness and looked at Scott.

"Let's let everyone still come to our cabin, and we'll tell everyone at that time," Scott said.

"Okay. That is probably a good way to break the news to everyone—together in a private setting."

Scott and Catalina headed for their cabin and told Hunter and Susan to remind anyone in the group they see to come to suite C 755—the Glacier Bay suite, on deck ten at the rear of the ship for a cruise out of the bay party.

A few minutes after Scott and Catalina had arrived at their stateroom, people started showing up. Catalina quickly set out the hors d'oeuvres she had previously prepared, and Scott started pouring the wine. When it seemed like everyone who was coming was there, Scott clanged his glass to get everyone's attention. He then started to relay the sad news.

"Thanks for coming, everyone. I wish this were more the happy occasion it was intended to be, but I'm afraid I have some sad news to pass on." With that, even the little bit of murmuring that was still going on abruptly ceased. "Our friends—your friends—Ed and Joyce Cooling of Los Amigos Cellars in Napa Valley are the Glacier Bay swimmers you may have seen or heard about today. They did not survive the ordeal. They died." Scott waited for the gasps and other reaction expressions to subside before he continued. "Catalina and I are so sorry this happened. We don't know how they came to wind up in Glacier Bay or exactly what caused their death. Hopefully, we'll learn more at some point. The security team on board seems to think they got caught up in what is apparently a minor fad on these cruises—going for a swim in Glacier Bay.

"Well, anyway, out of respect for Ed and Joyce, Catalina and I are thinking of canceling our May 9th blind wine taste test event. It doesn't seem appropriate or proper in light of the loss of our friends."

Without hesitation, Tony Black stood up and spoke. "Listen, I think it's very appropriate. Maryanne and I didn't know Ed and

Joyce as well as you and Catalina, but we met them that time they came to visit you, and you brought them to our winery. We also got to spend some time with them on this trip. We know them as a fun-loving couple who love wine and the wine business. I sincerely believe they would want you to go ahead and have the wine-tasting event you and Catalina have planned. I think it would honor them.

"Their wine that was going to be used in the taste test is still on board. Going ahead with the event using their wine to represent them, I think, would be very fitting. I think they would wholeheartedly approve."

Tony abruptly sat back down and sheepishly looked around, feeling he had said too much. But a few people started clapping. Then, most everybody joined in.

Scott looked around at everyone clapping, waited for it to subside, and said, "Okay." Tony, who doesn't always say a lot, said a mouthful, "I take it that most everyone of you agrees with Tony's sentiment, so the taste test on May 9th is still on." Scott looked up at the ceiling and raised his glass of wine. "I hope we're doing right by you, Ed and Joyce."

The sail out of the bay party continued in a strange, upbeat, but somber mood. There were not enough places for everyone to sit, and some people anyway preferred to stand out on Scott and Catalina's elongated balcony and watch the ship's propeller churning trail and the scenery disappear. Somehow, to many, it felt like Ed and Joyce were still among them.

CHAPTER 43

Sunday, May 7, 7:00 a.m.
Charthouse Restaurant

Scott and Catalina, Hunter and Susan, and brothers Mike and Larry meet for a sit-down and be served breakfast at the Charthouse—the ship's main dining room.

"I can't get over what happened to Ed and Joyce," Catalina said. "I can't believe they were this spontaneous couple who all of a sudden decided to go swimming in Glacier Bay, even if it is some sort of up-and-coming, latest thing to do in Alaska fad."

"Yeah, that's not like them," Scott said. "I think they were chloroformed, like what happened to me. They were grabbed, made unconscious, had life jackets put on them, and were thrown into the water, still unconscious."

"I agree," Hunter said. "I've come to the same conclusion. They were with our group and a whole gang of other people on deck fifteen, watching the glacier, looking for pieces to break off. Nobody was paying much attention to anybody else at that point. But somebody was watching—but not the glacier. They were watching you, Scott, and you, Catalina. And they were watching Ed and Joyce. Primarily, you four people. You four are the key people as to whether there is a wine test comparing California wines against those from the other three states. And, secondarily, they were watching the other three winemaker couples, Tony and Maryanne, Jim and Linda, and Jay and Roxanne.

"So, at some point, Ed and Joyce slipped away and didn't tell anyone because everyone was preoccupied with watching the glacier. They went to the restroom—went to get coffee—went to warm up—something—and they were grabbed and were chloroformed, just like you were, Scott, and taken all the way down to deck four. They—the big guy who grabbed you, Scott, and the lookout, and very possibly a third person—took Ed and Joyce down the crew corridor to a deck four hatch. They put life jackets on them as they wanted people to see them as they were sending a message to you, Scott and Catalina, primarily, and to the other winemakers. Then, they tossed Ed and Joyce into the water, closed the hatch, and disappeared back through the empty crew corridor—empty because everybody's working—and back into the passenger population.

"Whoever the one or two lookout guys are who watch, we may have seen any number of times in amongst the rest of the passengers. But we see lots of passengers we don't know lots of times because the passenger group is a finite number of people—about two thousand. I'm sure the big guy, however, the guy who grabbed you, Scott, stays in the shadows because he would stand out. People would take note and remember him. In fact, he could have been the other big guy I saw in the casino the other day when I saw my friend Duke.

"So, a long dissertation to say, again, I agree with you, Scott. Ed and Joyce didn't go swimming by choice. The trouble is, we have no evidence to back up what we're sure about—the way Ed and Joyce came to be floating in Glacier Bay. And security doesn't seem to want to look into it because they believe Ed and Joyce pulled a prank, and they apparently haven't uncovered any evidence to the contrary. Since no evidence of foul play, they won't call the FBI."

"But you're convinced it was murder?" Mike asked.

"Yes," Scott said.

"Murder or manslaughter," Hunter said.

"So what do we do?" Larry asked. "We've been trying to help make sure Scott and Catalina don't go anywhere alone."

"That has obviously been working," Hunter said. "In fact, I'm afraid that has been working so well that they momentarily gave up on Scott and Catalina and went after the secondary target of Ed and Joyce."

"That makes sense," Mike said.

"I say we turn the tables and go after them," Hunter said. "I say we go on the offense."

"But we don't know who they are," Susan said. "How do we go on the offense if we don't know who we're dealing with?"

"Yeah, how does that work?" Catalina asked.

"Point well taken," Hunter said. "You're right. We have to identify them first. So...we set them up. We bait them. We make them follow one or two of us so we can have a go at identifying them.

"In a moving vehicle surveillance, when the bad guy leaves the scene of the crime in his vehicle, he usually cleans himself up. That is, he makes sure no one is tailing him by making some abrupt moves, like suddenly turning right or left or making a U-turn. If the good guy tailing him sticks with him and makes the same sudden move—bingo—he's been made—he's been identified by the bad guy as a probable tail. One or two more sudden moves will tell for sure."

"So we get them to follow us, and we make some sudden moves?" Catalina asked.

"Yes," Hunter said. "We probably do this on foot, in town. We entice them to follow one of us, and that person makes some different moves. If the bad guys are following our guy and his moves, our other team members—our counter-surveillance people, who are even further back—will see and identify the individuals who continue to follow our guy. Thus, we have identified the bad guys."

"Then what?" Catalina asked.

"Then we either take note of what the bad guys look like so that now we know to watch out for them, or, better yet, we deal with them right then and there."

"You mean we beat them to a pulp?" Mike asked.

"No. You never know how that's going to turn out. I had more in mind that we confront them. Let them know we're on to them. Tell them we're going to go to the police with what we know."

"You mean, just talk to them?" Catalina asked.

"Yes, in a persuasive manner. We might have to initially twist their arms or apply some pressure points on them or simply pepper spray them to get their attention. But, once they know they've been exposed, they will have to really watch themselves. And, after the wine tasting on May 9th is over, it's too late for them. They failed in their mission to stop the event. They have to lick their wounds and go home. They're done."

"It's too bad we can't get them for causing the deaths of Ed and Joyce," Susan said.

"We'll continue to be on the lookout for evidence to that effect, but, so far, nothing. Scott and I snuck back to the hatch area after talking to security in the hopes of finding something, like a chloroformed rag, a torn piece of clothing, a blunt instrument with blood on it, any kind of evidence of a struggle, but nothing."

"When do we do this reverse surveillance, or whatever you want to call it?" Larry asked.

"Maybe this afternoon in Sitka. Maybe tomorrow in Ketchikan. We first have to let their inadvertent source of wine lovers cruise information have time to work."

"Who's that?" Catalina asked.

"I'm almost certain I know, but I don't want to say yet, in case I'm wrong. I think that with Ed and Joyce Cooling out of the picture, our bad guys figure mission accomplishment. They'll figure that you two, Scott and Catalina, will either cancel the May 9th wine event altogether or, if you do have it, you will have it without a California wine representation. Either way, they've accomplished their mission. But once they talk to their inside source, who was at your sail out of the bay party yesterday, if I'm right about who it is, they will definitely know that the wine-tasting event is on, and with Ed and Joyce's California wines still a part of it.

"They will be very upset and desperate, and I think they will make an all-out effort to get to you, Scott and Catalina, and not just tell you to cancel the event but cancel you, put you two out of commission so you can't have the event."

Scott and Catalina shuttered, raised their eyebrows, and turned and looked at each other. Hunter looked straight at them and said, "So now these guys are going to go after you with a vengeance, and having a couple of other people with you will not deter them this time. I think we go to town this afternoon, after lunch, and we use you two as bait to flush them out. Are you two up for it?"

Scott and Catalina turned and looked at each other again. "Sure," Scott said, "we're up for a little adventure, aren't we, my lovely?" Catalina displayed a tentative smile.

"Good," Hunter said. "We know they have a big guy. Scott knows only too well that there is a big guy on their team. I'm going to see if we can also have a big guy on our team."

CHAPTER 44

Sunday, May 7, 8:00 a.m.
Sitka, Alaska

"Mr. A, I hope you're phoning with good news."

"Yes, Jeep, you can relax now. This Scott character may still have a wine taste test, but Ed and Joyce Cooling won't be part of it. They, unfortunately, went for a swim in some ice-cold water and died."

"What? Murder was not supposed to have any part in this. We agreed on that. You assured us that no one would get hurt too badly."

"It wasn't murder. Yes, they inadvertently died, but the intent was to send a message—to scare the you-know-what out of everybody involved in the wine taste test. So, we sent a little stronger message than originally intended. Like I said in the beginning, persuasion is not an exact science. And you gave me the go-ahead to do whatever it takes."

"Yes, but...well, okay, good job. And you're sure the blind taste test on May 9th has been canceled?"

"I don't know if the event has been canceled, but Ed and Joyce Cooling of Napa Valley are not going to be a part of it. Scott and Catalina Poncetran may taste-test Arizona, New Mexico, and Nebraska wines against each other, but so what? Who cares? They don't have much of a reputation to uphold—not like California. California is not going to be put to the test now, and its wine reputation will remain intact. Mission accomplished. That's what you wanted. So, I completed the job, and you can pay me the rest of the money. Oh, and by the way, your boy Schultz helped a bit, but that doesn't give you any discount."

"I know. I'll pay but after May 9th."

"Understood."

CHAPTER 45

Sunday, May 7, 8:30 a.m.
Hearts and Minds Wedding Chapel

At the start of the self-directed Bible class, leader Ken Harmony opened in prayer, including prayer for the relatives and friends that Ed and Joyce Cooling left behind. Ken knew Ed and Joyce had died because Hunter and Susan had told him. However, the general passenger population did not know, at least officially, of the fate of the two Glacier Bay swimmers. It is not customary for cruise ship personnel to make public announcements regarding passengers who die during the cruise. There are exceptions, as on Hunter and Susan's previous cruise across the Atlantic two years before.

This morning, Ken finished the lesson on Daniel chapter 4 and concluded by saying that Daniel teaches us to take political changes in stride. Rulers come and go, kings rise and fall, but, as Daniel 4:26 says, "Heaven rules." Ken said that this doesn't mean we ignore politics. Daniel didn't. He was right in the middle of the Babylonian and Persian governments and what was going on at the time. But he kept his balance because he knew God was sovereign—controlling events, guiding history, and moving the times toward their ultimate consummation.

Pastor Ken went on to say that we are living in days like those of Daniel, where politics are turbulent, the leaders are egocentric, and the times are reaching their fulfillment. He then said, "Let's pray. We pray, God, that You give us a solid spiritual foundation, a determined heart for You, Lord, a hunger for Your word and for Your promises about tomorrow, a habit of daily prayer, and a grasp of Your absolute sovereign power. Amen."

"Well, we still have a few minutes," Ken said. "Does anyone have any questions or comments before we adjourn?"

"Yes," Duke Rawlings said. "Everyone here knows I don't know a lot about God or the Bible, but something I've always wondered—and it is kind of touched on in our lesson—is, well, which way is it? Does God really control events? Because it sure doesn't seem like He does most of the time. And if He does control events, then where is our free will? I thought God was supposed to be pretty much hands-off to let us humans do things and decide things without His interference, or, I guess, a better word is, without His intervention. So, the way I see it, if God controls events and guides history, then humans don't have free will."

"Does anyone want to take a stab at offering insight to Duke's question in our remaining three minutes?" Pastor Ken asked. Most everyone chuckled or laughed. "Duke, I trust you realize that no one is laughing at you. They are laughing because we could have thirty hours and still not fully resolve the question. You have brought up a mystery that has perplexed mankind since Adam and Eve. But let's make that something to ponder, and in a couple of days, we'll start off with a discussion of this dilemma. Thanks for bringing this conundrum up, Duke. Until tomorrow, enjoy your day in Sitka, everyone, and may the Lord be with you."

As everyone was getting up to leave, Hunter and Susan walked over to Duke and Duke's friend, Kimberly Howe. "Great question you brought up, Duke," Hunter said. "How about if we buy you two a cup of coffee at the International Café?"

"I'm game," Duke said. "What about you, Kimberly?"

"Sure."

***

A few minutes later, Hunter, Susan, Duke, and Kimberly were sitting at a table by the window with their specialty coffees, and a non-coffee drinker Hunter with his specialty tea. "So, what's up, brother Hunter?"

"Did Duke tell you, Kimberly, that he and I are fraternity brothers—Kappa Sigs?"

"Yes, he did. You and Duke and Robert Redford. And I'm a Sigma Kappa, your sorority counterpart."

"No kidding," Hunter said, "our sister sorority. Fantastic. And to add a few more Greek letters to the mix, Susan is a Pi Beta Phi."

"A Pi Phi," Kimberly said. "Where did you go to school?"

"Arizona State, in Tempe, not that far from where Hunter and I live now. What about you, Kimberly? Where did you go to school?"

"I went to Clemson University in South Carolina."

"You do have a bit of a southern accent," Susan said. "Did you grow up in South Carolina?"

"I did. I grew up in Columbia, the capital."

"Interesting," Hunter said, "we all went to college, but none of us asked what anybody's major was or what degree, or degrees, any of us graduated with."

"Yes, interesting," Kimberly said. "I guess for a lot of careers, the specific degree wasn't as important as the fact that you did go to college and graduated."

"Now people are starting to realize that college degrees don't have that much importance for a lot of jobs," Susan said. "Try calling a political science or humanities major over to fix your plumbing."

"People are waking up to the fact that being skilled in a trade is much more important than many of the degree programs colleges offer," Duke said.

"Exactly," Hunter said. "For example, what is your degree in, Duke?"

"Political assassination."

"And has that helped you in your chosen field of work?"

"Immensely."

Sue and Kimberly were now staring at Duke and Hunter with wide eyes and half-open mouths. Hunter noticed this and said, "Duke's kidding, aren't you, Duke?"

Duke smiled but didn't say anything. After a short period of silence, Kimberly said, "Duke and I were thinking about going into town early this afternoon. What are you guys doing?"

"Funny you should ask," Hunter said, "there's a little project that just might be up Duke's alley, so to speak. And maybe you would be interested in it too, Kimberly. And it involves going into town. However, there might be an element of danger involved."

"Oh, yeah?" Duke said. "What have you got going?"

"Basically, we want to flush out some bad guys."

"Snuff out some bad guys? I'm in," Duke said.

"No, flush some bad guys out."

"Okay, I'm still in."

CHAPTER 46

Sunday, May 7, 11:00 a.m.
Sitka, Alaska

"Yes, Mr. Available. You're calling back to chat some more?"

"Yeah, Jeep. This time, it's not good news. Not good news at all. The wine taste test is still on for May 9th, and they are going to use the Los Amigos Cellars Napa Valley wines in the comparisons even though Ed and Joyce obviously won't be there. I just found out from my source that there was a meeting last night, and this Scott and Catalina couple decided it would be a fitting tribute to Ed and Joyce to include their wines in the contest."

"Well, Mr. A, I think you should have anticipated this might happen. If you were going to eliminate anybody, you should have eliminated Scott and Catalina Poncetran. If you had disposed of them, there definitely would be no big May 9th wine event."

"Yeah, no kidding. They were the primary target all along, but after I put the scare into him with the knock-out chemical on the rag, his friends decided to act like bodyguards, and I could never get close to him or to his wife after that. But don't you worry, Jeep, I'm going to take care of this—and at no extra charge. This is personal now. This Poncetran couple has really ticked me off.

"I'll call you back when things are really taken care of. It may be today; it may be tomorrow, but I'll be calling you back with the news you want to hear."

"Okay, then. I'll look forward to your call."

CHAPTER 47

After lunch, Hunter's counter-surveillance team met in Scott and Catalina's suite. Upon opening the cabin door for Kimberly, Duke happened to glance down and noticed a very small black metallic device attached to the outside of the door at the very bottom left edge. He let Kimberly go on in the cabin, after which he squatted down and took a closer look at the curious device. A few seconds later, Duke stood up and went into the cabin.

Duke went over to Hunter. "I see how the bad guys know when Scott and Catalina leave their suite. They don't have to have somebody watching their cabin door. They have a tiny little device attached to the bottom of the door that is sensitive to movement. Every time the door is opened or closed, it sends a signal to a receiver that the bad guys apparently have."

"Well, I'll be. I wondered why I never saw anyone hanging around Scott and Catalina's door, yet they seemed to know when Scott and Catalina left their cabin."

"Yes, and if they have a gizmo like that, which is state of the art, they probably have other surveillance aids as well."

"Like what, do you think?"

"Hard telling. They may have used some ruse to gain access to the cabin, like maintenance men, and planted some very small tracking devices on their clothing or on their shoes."

"We should check."

"Since you said you were going to use your friends as bait to flush these guys out, it's probably best to leave any devices they may have planted intact. I left the device on the door in place. If we remove any of these devices, then they will know that we're on to them. Besides, you want them to track Scott and Catalina, so we don't want to make it too hard for them."

"Right. It is, however, going to make it a little harder for us to identify them since they don't have to follow our friends so close. In fact, if they did plant some tracking devices on their apparel somehow, then they don't even have to have an eyeball on them most of the time."

"However, when the bad guys don't have the eyeball on your friends, then they will have to be periodically looking at their monitoring devices, which could be in the form of a watch or a cell phone, or something like that. So, if we notice anyone who is following the general direction your friends are going, and they are periodically looking at their cell phone or watch, good possibility that's one of the bad guys."

"Right."

Just then, there was a knock on Scott and Catalina's cabin door. Catalina opened it for Tony and Maryanne Black.

"Okay, we're all here," Hunter announced to everyone. Scott and Catalina, our guinea pigs, Duke Rawlings, Kimberly Howe, brothers Mike and Larry Oncur, Jim and Linda Perdon, and Tony and Maryanne Black. Jay and Roxanne Patterson would have joined us, but they are on an all-day tour.

"So, as most, or all of you know, there are some people—we think two or three people, most likely male, one of which is a very big gentleman—probably about the size of Duke here..."

"Maybe it is Duke," someone said.

"Well, for a while, I thought it might be, but never mind that. Anyway, these people have tried different ways to get Scott and Catalina to call off the May 9th wine taste test the day after tomorrow. We're not totally sure why, but we think that someone—some group of people—is concerned that the taste test will somehow harm the California wine industry. That's not really a possibility, but nonetheless, someone doesn't want the event to take place.

"But more importantly, we think these people are responsible for the deaths of Ed and Joyce Cooling. Murder may not have been their intent—we don't know—regardless, Ed and Joyce are dead, and we think that they are going to go after Scott and Catalina now. So, our mission is two-fold. First, we want to stop these people from trying to get to Scott and Catalina and doing them harm. Second, we want to identify these guys so we can alert the authorities.

"Duke here happens to have a good friend in the Ketchikan Police Force, where we will be tomorrow. If we can discover who these guys are and get a description—and better yet, photos—then we can turn them over to the Ketchikan police. Duke's friend, Detective Bob Blackhorn, has agreed to look into the matter. If we can get good enough photos of these yahoos, Blackhorn can use his resources to try to see exactly who these guys are. He can also take them to our ship's security people, who can probably match them up with the passenger photos. If ship security doesn't cooperate, since the police department doesn't have jurisdiction on the ship, he can contact the FBI, which does.

"So, our mission is to discover and identify who the bad guys are and to turn our information and photos over to law enforcement. We plan to do this by conducting a little counter-surveillance on these people who we think will try to follow and get to Scott and Catalina as they wander the streets of Sitka this afternoon.

"Now, there is some danger in doing this as these guys are going to be looking for an opportunity to abduct or do harm to Scott and, or Catalina. They may try to come up to the Poncetrans from behind with a rag or cloth with a knock-out chemical on it and hold it against their nose and mouth. So be looking for anyone with a cloth or rag and a bottle of liquid. Also, be looking for anyone with a device or phone or watch that they look at fairly often, as they may be monitoring electronic devices that may have been planted on Scott and Catalina.

"Scott and Catalina are going to wander through town as tourists and casual shoppers and will be stopping and window shopping fairly often. If the bad guys are going to try to get to Scott and Catalina, even though they may be using tracking devices, they will have to try to stay close enough to grab them if they think they see an opportunity.

"Mike and Larry will keep a little distance from Scott and Catalina but will keep them in sight and be close enough for a quick reaction if there's trouble. Also, Mike and Larry and Scott and Catalina will have pepper spray. Additionally, Scott and Catalina will have whistles." Hunter blew one of the whistles. "If you hear that sound, everybody come running to Scott and Catalina.

"Any questions?"

"Yes," Maryanne Black said. "Scott and Catalina, are you okay with this?"

"Yes, we are," Catalina said. "These people killed our friends. We really want to get these guys."

"Anyone else have a question?" Hunter asked. "No. So, everyone, stay loose, have fun, be yourselves, and try to get good photos of anyone you suspect is tailing the Poncetrans. Good face shots are the priority. Use the zoom on your cameras and phones if necessary. Remember, you're tourists, so taking photos is part of the gig. And don't worry about blowing your cover, so to speak, with the bad guys. I doubt if they are going to suspect a counter-surveillance.

CHAPTER 48

By two-thirty in the afternoon, Hunter's counter-surveillance team had arrived by various means and was in place in Sitka in the area of St Michael's Cathedral, a Russian Orthodox church in the middle of Lincoln Street. The street actually splits and goes around the church on both sides. There are a few shops, watering holes, and restaurants in the area, and this is where Scott and Catalina did their stroll with starts and stops and browsing while Hunter's team looked for the bad guys. Photos were taken, and descriptions written down of possible candidates.

By five o'clock, Hunter's team was back on the ship, and all reconvened in Scott and Catalina's suite on deck ten. The likely bad guy candidate photos were all loaded on Duke's cell phone as he had an appointment to see his detective friend, Bob Blackhorn, tomorrow at the Ketchikan Police Department. The surveillance team had narrowed the bad guy candidates down to four men and one woman.

Hunter complimented the team of amateur counter-surveillance operatives and said that Scott and Catalina did such a good job of moving around and starting and stopping that the bad guys apparently didn't have a chance to get close enough for an abduction attempt. However, Hunter said, tomorrow would be a different story. "Tomorrow, we actually want the bad guys to attempt to abduct Scott and Catalina. If we get it set up right, Detective Blackhorn and the Ketchikan P D will be there to arrest the ne'er-do-wells in the very act of committing a crime."

CHAPTER 49

Monday, May 8, 8:00 a.m.
Ketchikan, Alaska

At 8:00 a.m., the Alaskan Princess was fast alongside Berth 2 in Ketchikan, Alaska. Hunter Kingsley and Duke Rawlings were among the first few people off the ship. They immediately headed for the Ketchikan Police Department at 361 Main Street, which was a short walking distance from the ship—two to three blocks, depending on how you measure blocks. They had an appointment with Duke's longtime friend, Lieutenant of Investigations Bob Blackhorn.

Upon arrival, Duke and Hunter were shown to Lieutenant Blackhorn's office, where they also met Detective Sergeant Nick Purcell. Duke and Bob gave each other longtime friend manly hugs. Hunter shook hands with Bob and Nick. Duke shook hands with Nick, and Nick, at five feet ten inches, seemed almost dwarfed next to Duke at six feet four and a half inches. Bob, at six feet three inches, and Hunter, at six feet two inches, both solidly built, were a pretty even match. Coffee was offered and accepted—tea, of course, for Hunter. Duke gave Bob his cell phone with the suspect bad guy photos. Bob loaded them into his computer and made copies.

"Now, the next step is to drive over to your ship and see if security will I. D. your suspect passengers. The police department doesn't have any official jurisdiction over cruise ships that come into port, but they are generally very cooperative. Do either of you have a contact number?"

Hunter handed a business card to Lieutenant Blackhorn with Alaskan Princess Chief of Security Carter Watts' phone contact information. Blackhorn then punched up one of the phone numbers. "Chief of Security Carter Watts, please."

"This is Chief Carter Watts."

"Yes, this is Lieutenant Bob Blackhorn over at the Ketchikan Police Department Investigations. How's your morning going so far?"

"Not bad. How about yours?"

"Good. Listen, I've got a couple of your passenger guests over here in my office, and they have some photos of a few of your passengers that I would like to see if you can identify."

"Is there a problem with any of them?"

"There could be. If it's convenient for you, we can be over in fifteen minutes."

"Sure, Lieutenant, come right over. I'll have someone waiting at the top of the gangway to escort you."

"Good. See you in a bit, Chief."

"Smooth," Hunter said.

"Bob is a smoothie," Duke said.

"You want to come with us, Sergeant, and see what a cruise ship security office looks like?" Blackhorn asked. "I guarantee it will make you appreciate your office that much more."

"Sure, I'll go. I wouldn't think it should take too long."

The four of them rode the short distance to the ship in Lieutenant Blackhorn's unmarked vehicle. When Chief of Security Watts saw Hunter, he smiled and said, "Somehow, I knew it was you."

The photo matching didn't take all that long, and three men and one woman were confirmed as ship passengers. They were identified as Ralph and Arleen Simpson of Napa Valley, California (Schultz and Sandy), Antone Gillespie (Mr. Available) of Las Vegas,

Nevada, and Wit Kraske, also of Las Vegas. The four thanked Chief Watts and rode back to the police station. While Sergeant Purcell ran the names through the crime databases, Lieutenant Blackhorn and Hunter and Duke finalized their plans for the setup—for giving the now-identified bad guys the opportunity to try to abduct Scott and Catalina Poncetran.

They decided that Scott and Catalina would have lunch at Annabelle's Famous Keg and Chowder House at 326 Front Street, basically located about halfway between the police station and the ship. Tony and Maryanne Black and Jim and Linda Perdon will walk with Scott and Catalina from their cabin to the restaurant to make sure there is no abduction attempt en route to the restaurant. As Scott and Catalina approach the entrance to the restaurant, Tony, Maryanne, Jim, and Linda will peel off and go elsewhere. Scott and Catalina will enter the restaurant and sit at a prearranged table for two. Lieutenant Blackhorn, Sergeant Purcell, and Duke Rawlings will already be sitting at a table very near Scott and Catalina's table. Hunter Kingsley and Detective James Garver, with the police department, will be stationed on the street near the entrance to Annabelle's. There is no easy back way out from the restaurant, so it was decided not to try to cover that... That was the plan.

Sergeant Purcell was able to pull up a hit on the two gentlemen from Las Vegas, Antone Gillespie and Wit Kraske. Gillespie had a few aliases. No arrests, but he was a person of interest with the FBI. Kraske had arrests for breaking and entering and burglary with the Las Vegas P D. Ralph and Arleen Simpson were clean.

Hunter and Duke walked the two blocks or so back to the ship and went to Scott and Catalina's cabin. The Poncetrans were given the plan, and they were okay with it. Catalina telephoned Tony and Maryanne and Jim and Linda and asked them to meet Scott and her at their cabin at 11:30 for the walk over to Annabelle's.

Things were now set. Scott and Catalina and Hunter and Duke prayed for mission success and no injuries.

CHAPTER 50

At 11:30, Maryanne Black knocked on Scott and Catalina's cabin door. Scott and Catalina emerged, paused, smiled, took a deep breath, and said, "Thanks, you guys. Let's do this thing." The six of them, Scott and Catalina, Tony and Maryanne Black, and Jim and Linda Perdon, walked together along the starboard deck ten corridor to the midship elevators. They took an elevator down to deck four and walked over to the security checkpoint, where they showed their cruise cards. They walked down the gangplank, across the concrete open area, and over to Front Street and to Annabelle's restaurant. Scott and Catalina told their friends to have a good time on their sightseeing adventure and waved goodbye. The Poncetrans then entered the restaurant and walked over to the maître d' stand.

Sally, the maître d', looked over at Hunter, who was seated in the small waiting area. Hunter gave a slight nod. Sally then escorted Scott and Catalina to a table for two not far from the entrance. After they were seated, she handed them a couple of menus. She smiled and said the waitress would be with them shortly.

Seated at a table a little further into the restaurant but close to Scott and Catalina were three gentlemen looking a little kicked back, seemingly enjoying their beers while looking at their lunch menus.

On the walk over, both Maryanne Black and Jim Perdon whispered to Scott and Catalina that they were pretty sure two of the men they had seen yesterday during the counter-surveillance exercise had followed them. While perusing the menu, it slipped out of Scott's hands and fell on the floor. Scott quickly picked it up and resumed looking it over. It was an agreed-on signal to the nearby beer drinkers that Scott and Catalina were fairly certain they had been followed.

Shortly after the Poncetrans had been seated, Hunter stood up from his waiting area seat by the entrance and walked out. He walked down the street a few paces to where Detective James Garver was hanging out in front of the Totem Pole Saloon adjacent to Annabelle's. As Hunter approached Garver, the two of them started up a good old boy conversation, which fit right in with the kind of lunchtime crowd that was wandering into the Totem Pole. During the conversation with Garver, Hunter told him, "It looks like it's going to go down." The lunchtime foot traffic going up and down the sidewalk also helped good old boys Hunter Kingsley and James Garver blend into the scene even more.

Nothing happened until about 12:15 when a mud-caked white SUV slowly drove by Hunter and Garver and the Totem Pole, past the entrance to Annabelle's, and parallel parked in front of the building on the other side of Annabelle's, the Ketchikan City Hall. Hunter and Garver couldn't see the woman driver very well, but the man who got out of the passenger side of the vehicle Hunter was sure was Ralph Simpson, one of the suspects. He figured the woman driver was probably his wife, Arleen.

Arleen Simpson stayed behind the wheel of the dirty SUV. Ralph Simpson looked around, closed the passenger door, walked over to the entrance to Annabelle's, and went in. He walked past the maître d stand, looked around, saw the restroom sign pointing to the rear, and went into the men's restroom. A minute or so later, he came out and casually walked out of Annabelle's, turned right, and parked himself in front of the City Hall building directly opposite the dirty SUV. As he watched the entrance to the restaurant, he pulled out his cell phone and made a call.

"They're in there. They are in the left-hand section of the restaurant where the bar is and are toward the front and are the first table behind the check-in stand. The restaurant's pretty full, mostly all couples and groups of two and four. There is one table of three guys near your target, but they are drinking beer and yucking it up. Nobody seemed to pay any attention to me, so I think we're good to go. You'll be in and out of there with the package before anyone has a clue as to what just happened."

"Okay, good job, Simpson," Antone Gillespie said. "We'll be there in a few. Stay near the SUV. We'll key on you as we come out. Remember, as soon as we go in, open the sidewalk side rear door of the SUV and keep it open. We're going to dump them in there."

"Right. Got it."

A few minutes later, big guy Antone Gillespie, aka Mr. Available, and Wit Kraske came from across the street and walked up to the entrance to Annabelle's. They stopped, looked around, nodded at Ralph Simpson just up the street, and went in.

Hunter couldn't believe it! Suddenly, his wife appeared across the street exactly where Gillespie and Kraske had been just a few seconds before. Susan had her cell phone camera out and aimed at the entrance to Annabelle's, and she appeared to be taking a video.

About twenty seconds later, big guy Gillespie came out of the restaurant with his arms wrapped around Scott and holding a rag over Scott's nose and mouth. Scott's feet were barely touching the ground as Gillespie was basically carrying Scott out the door.

In a similar fashion, Kraske had a bear hug from behind on Catalina, with a rag over her nose and mouth, and was helping her out the door with the weight of his body.

Two big guys and a medium-sized guy were right behind, spilling out the door. It was quite the spectacle: seven bodies, one right behind the other, in mass, pushing and stumbling out the single entrance door to Annabelle's. It looked like a human centipede trying to scurry away.

Lieutenant Blackhorn was immediately behind Kraske and was actually toughing his back and helping him out the door. Sergeant Purcell was behind Lieutenant Blackhorn with his hand on Blackhorn's back. Duke was behind Purcell with his hand on Purcell's back and was halfway turned around, protecting the rear from a possible intrusion from behind.

This whole gaggle of bodies spilled out onto the sidewalk, headed for the mud-caked SUV with the rear curbside door open.

Hunter Kingsley and Detective Garver ran out into the street past the gaggle of bodies. Hunter ran up to the SUV, pulled open the driver-side door, pulled Arleen Simpson by her arm and shoulder out of the SUV, and put her up against the side of the vehicle. He then pulled out a set of cuffs and handcuffed Arleen's wrists behind her back.

While Hunter was busy with Arleen Simpson, Detective Garver ran past Hunter, went around the front of the SUV, and over to Ralph Simpson, where he promptly arrested and handcuffed him.

At the same time Hunter and Detective Garver were doing their tasks, as soon as he had cleared the entrance to Annabelle's, Lieutenant Blackhorn ran around Kraske and Catalina and grabbed Gillespie. Blackhorn hooked his right arm over Gillespie's right arm, pulled it back away from Scott's face, and continued it on around Gillespie's back into a come-along hold and on into a reverse wrist control hold. Blackhorn applied the pressure to Gillespie's wrist to the point where Gillespie yipped in pain and let go of Scott. Maintaining the reverse wrist pressure, Blackhorn marched Gillespie over to the face of the Ketchikan City Hall building and handcuffed him. Blackhorn had to interlock two sets of cuffs to cuff Gillespie since he was so beefy and non-agile.

While the Lieutenant was taking care of Gillespie, Sergeant Purcell performed a similar maneuver on Kraske.

In less than thirty seconds after the gaggle of bad guys and good guys came out of Annabelle's, four bad guys were up against the wall and handcuffed—Antone Gillespie and Wit Kreske from Las Vegas, and Ralph and Arleen Simpson from Napa Valley. Sergeant Purcell then had the four suspects sit down on the sidewalk with their backs to the wall. It was harder to run that way if any of them were thinking about doing such a thing. Duke Rawlings was right there, ready to grab anyone that did try to run.

Lieutenant Blackhorn called for the two squad cars that were standing by with engines running at the police department a block away. Sergeant Purcell and Detective Garver rode back to the police station with the suspects while Lieutenant Blackhorn walked back with Duke, Hunter, Scott, Catalina, and spur of the moment videographer Susan Kingsley.

CHAPTER 51

At the Ketchikan Police Station, Lieutenant Blackhorn held a quick debriefing while police officers processed the four arrestees. All involved in the setup and arrest were in attendance: Lieutenant Blackhorn, Sergeant Purcell, Detective Garver, Scott and Catalina, Hunter, Duke, and surprise videographer Susan Kingsley. Lieutenant Blackhorn, of course, wanted a copy of Susan's video for training purposes.

Lieutenant Blackhorn complimented everyone on a job well done and then opened it up for an informal debriefing. Everyone thought, overall, the operation went very well. One possible improvement area that Duke and Sergeant Purcell brought up was the gaggle of people trying to pile out of the entrance to the restaurant. That was kicked around a bit.

Hunter and Sergeant Purcell both commented that the non-use of radios—for fear of spooking the bad guys—they thought went well. Susan commented that she thought it was amazing how fast the whole thing went down. She said that from the time that the two bad guys entered the restaurant until the time all four suspects were handcuffed and against the building, was forty-five seconds, give or take a second. Blackhorn said he wasn't surprised. He said most crimes are a done deal in a matter of seconds, and the forty-five seconds for this one included the pursuit and handcuffing of the suspects.

Blackhorn told everyone that all four of the suspects would be charged with abduction under Alaska state law, but more importantly, the FBI would probably get involved. He said he had already alerted the FBI office in Juneau, and if any arrests were made, two FBI agents were prepared to come down tomorrow morning by boat and interview the arrestees. He said there are apparently federal statutes relating to assaults within maritime jurisdictions that include attempted suffocation of a person by covering the nose or mouth of that person, regardless of whether that conduct resulted in any injury to the person or whether there was any intent to kill or injure the person.

"In other words," Blackhorn said, "what these guys did is serious stuff. And Antone Gillespie, we know, was already a person of interest by the FBI for possible involvement in other schemes.

"Anyway, thank you guys for your help, and thank you, Susan Kingsley, for your training video. It will be put to good use. My detectives and I have work to do, so Sergeant Purcell is going to take you all to another room with a big table. We need to get statements from all of you. And Scott and Catalina, be sure to describe in detail the part about having the rag or cloth put over your face and how that affected your breathing ability and so forth. Enjoy the rest of your cruise, everyone."

When they all had finished their statements, Scott and Catalina, Hunter and Susan, and Duke walked back to the ship together. None of them had eaten lunch, but it was getting close to the early dinner time for the wine lovers group. Hunter asked Scott and Catalina if it was all right if Duke and his friend Kimberly could join them for dinner in the wine lovers area of the Charthouse dining room. Catalina said that would be great as Jim and Linda Perdon wouldn't be there as they were doing a specialty dinner at Sabatini's tonight. Hunter then asked Duke if he was interested.

"Eat with a bunch of wine imbibers? Sure. What time?"

"Five thirty," Hunter said. "Just tell the desk at the front of the Charthouse that you'll be dining with the wine lovers group and you'll be led to the back by the big windows."

"Okay. I'll see if I can interest Kimberly. If not, I'll come alone."

"Right, O," Hunter said. "See you in a bit."

CHAPTER 52

Hunter and Susan Kingsley showed up a few minutes early for dinner, and Hunter snagged one of the few tables for four set aside for the wine lovers group. Hunter hadn't said anything to Susan, but Susan could tell Hunter was dying to discuss something. Hunter pulled out a chair for Susan, but he remained standing by his chair with an eye out for Duke and Kimberly. When he saw them approaching, he waved them over.

As was the custom, Scott and Catalina usually walked around amongst the dinner tables and personally greeted everyone. Scott usually had a white and red wine recommendation, such as: "If you order entrée such and such, I would recommend the so and so wine." Often, Sommelier Alex Lapierre would also make an appearance with the wine lovers group and would offer his pairing recommendations. Sometimes, Scott's and Alex's recommendations matched, and sometimes they didn't.

Scott came over to Hunter and Susan's table, and Hunter said, "It looks like you recovered all right from being chloroformed today."

"I did. As soon as I got back to the cabin, I had a glass of Tempranillo. That helped. Speaking of wine, if you order the New Zealand ling cod, I recommend the Cloudy Bay Sauvignon Blanc. If you order the chateaubriand, I recommend the Salentein Argentinian Malbec."

"Scott," Susan said, "you've met Duke Rawlings, but I don't think you have met his friend, Kimberly Howe."

"Pleased to formally meet you, Kimberly. I have seen you in Bible study but was never formally introduced."

"Oh, that's right," Susan said.

"Anyway," Scott said, "I'd better move on. If Alex comes by with a different wine recommendation, go with his. Or, better yet, just drink what you like. You know your pallet better than we do. Catch you all later."

After Hunter, Susan, Duke, and Kimberly had received their wine, and after dinner orders had been taken, Hunter raised his glass. "I propose a toast."

The other three raised their glasses and held them up along with Hunter's. "A toast to what?" Duke asked.

"A toast to an opportunity," Hunter said.

"Well, okay," Duke said. "I can drink to that."

"What's the opportunity?" Susan asked. And she knew Hunter was bursting at the seams about something.

"I think I want to become a PI."

"A private investigator?" Duke asked.

"Yes, a private investigator. Not necessarily full-time. Part-time. Because I do want to play golf whenever I want, but it will be something to keep me interested. Something to keep me in the mix."

"Wow," Kimberly said as she looked at Susan. "You don't seem all that surprised, Susan. Did you already know about this?"

"Not formally, but Hunter's been dancing around with the idea ever since he retired from the Secret Service. And after the little escapade this afternoon, Hunter's had the biggest grin on his face that I've seen in a long time. I knew he was probably going to say something tonight, so I brought my big purse to dinner."

Susan leaned down and opened her purse that was on the floor. She pulled out a Sherlock Holmes black and white hound's-tooth cap, a calabash curved fake ivory pipe, and a large magnifying glass and presented them to Hunter.

Hunter couldn't believe it. He laughed a laugh of endearment, then gave Susan a big hug. Duke and Kimberly roared with laughter. Hunter put on the hat and stuck the simulated curved ivory pipe in his mouth and brought the magnifying glass up to his eye. People in the immediate surrounding tables saw this and also started laughing. People at tables a little further away started looking around to see what was so funny.

Scott was the master, but Hunter had a little showmanship in him also. Hunter stood up so everyone could see and did some gesturing with his Sherlock Holmes ivory pipe and magnifying glass. More and more people started laughing until almost the whole dining room, well beyond the wine lovers group, was now laughing. As the laughter started to subside, Hunter sat down, then abruptly stood up again. He took the pipe out of his mouth, held it in a Sherlock Holmes-type pose, and said, "Elementary, my dear Watson, red wine goes with red meat, and white wine goes with white meat." The room erupted in laughter again, and Hunter sat down.

Susan and Kimberly were laughing so hard they had tears in their eyes and couldn't talk. Duke had a giant smile on his face and gave Hunter a big high five. Several people came up to the table to take Hunter's picture. After a few minutes, Hunter took off his hat and put the pipe down. Several people yelled, "No, put the hat back on." Hunter wore the hat the rest of the evening.

Dinner was served, and periodically, people continued to come up to the table and take Hunter's picture. Hunter always accommodated by putting the pipe in his mouth and peering through the magnifying glass.

As dessert was served, Hunter said, "Duke, I'd like you to consider partnering with me on occasion when the job calls for more than one person. I know I could use your expertise and help from time to time. We live close enough to each other that I think it would work out."

"Well," Duke said, "you know I'm available."

Hunter smiled, stood up, and reached out to shake Duke's hand. Duke smiled, stood up, and shook Hunter's hand. There's something about men not shaking hands while sitting down. Maybe it's part of the code of the West. Whatever it is, Hunter and Duke understood this. As Hunter and Duke sat back down, Susan and Kimberly gave Hunter and Duke big, approving smiles.

After most everyone in the wine lovers group was done with dessert, Scott stood up and started clinking his wine glass. When the group had quieted, Scott looked over at Hunter, still sporting his Sherlock Holmes chapeau, and said, "Boy, I'm going to have to take a few showmanship lessons from Hunter." Hunter smiled. "Now, before you go, don't forget: tomorrow is a sea day, and we have a big event, our grand finale, at Sabatini's at eleven o'clock. Now, it won't be a wine tasting for you guys. You all have tasted all the wines our vintners brought already at our four previous wine tastings. It will be a taste test for a panel of five sommeliers that are here on the ship. You, of course, know the ship's sommelier, Alex Lapierre.

"The other four sommeliers are here on the ship with their families and have purposely not been included in any of our wine gatherings, particularly the four wine tastings we had, so as not to sway or influence them in any way. But tomorrow, they are going to taste-test all the wines from our four vintners that you all have tasted, and they are going to rank them based on the accepted criteria that most sommeliers go by. There are strict criteria that sommeliers use to judge wine. We'll talk about that more tomorrow.

"This will be what is known as a blind taste test. That is, all the bottles of wine will be covered up so no one can tell which wine they are tasting. At the end of the whole process, after the wines have been ranked and scored—now that's two different things, and I'll explain that a little more tomorrow—after the wines have been ranked and scored, then the covers on the wine bottles will be taken off, and everyone will see which wines had the best scores. And probably, some will have scored high enough to win medals. More about that tomorrow also.

"Anyway, you don't want to miss tomorrow. After the sommeliers have finished—you will watch them go through their ritual of judging, with the swishing and the spit bucket and all that—we will have a fantastic lunch and use up all the remaining wine. So, you don't want to miss our never-been-done-before on a wine lovers cruise newsworthy grand finale. See you all tomorrow."

CHAPTER 53

Tuesday, May 9, 8:30 a.m.
Hearts and Minds Chapel

The Bible study began in prayer, and then leader Ken Harmony said, "The other day, our friend Duke brought up a perplexing question. Is God sovereign? That is, does He rule in the affairs of men and women, or has He granted men and women free will? In other words, can men and women do whatever they want without interference from God? The two concepts seem to be an either-or situation—meaning, if one is true, then the other can't be true. We didn't have time to discuss it the other day, so I asked everyone to ponder the question for a couple of days.

"There are a number of verses in scripture that support both positions or concepts. I'll give you three that support the sovereignty of God." Ken turned to the Book of Job in his Bible. "Job 42:2 says, 'I know that you can do all things; no plan of yours can be thwarted.'" Ken turned to Isaiah 14. "Isaiah chapter 14, verse 24 says, 'The Lord Almighty has sworn, Surely, as I have planned, so it will be, and as I have purposed, so it will stand.' And Proverbs 19:21 reads, 'Many are the plans in a man's heart, but it is the Lord's purpose that prevails.'

"So, according to these three short passages, it's pretty clear that God is in control, and whatever he wants is going to happen. But, on the other hand, I'll read you two verses that definitely indicate that God allows man to make choices—to exercise free will. The first one is Galatians 5:13—one second, while I find it—Galatians 5, verse 13 reads, 'You, my brothers, were called to be free. But do not use your freedom to indulge the sinful nature; rather, serve one another in love.' Then, Deuteronomy 30:19 reads, 'This day I call heaven and earth as witnesses against you that I have set before you life and death, blessings and curses. Now choose life, so that you and your children may live.'

"So, what do we think? Let me ask Duke to start off. What do you think, Duke?"

"I don't know the Bible very well, so I can't quote any scripture off the top of my head to support what I think, but it seems to me that God allows me to do whatever I want. If He does intervene in people's lives, maybe He only does it with Christians. I'm not a Christian, but I'm looking into it."

Bob Bickford spoke up. "I go along with Duke. I am a believer—and Duke, I hope you eventually become one too—but I feel God allows me to make my own choices on things. Sometimes, I make some dumb choices. Usually, in those cases, I wish God had intervened. Then, sometimes I pray about a situation or choice I need to make, and it seems that if I give Him time, He helps me make my choice, and it usually turns out good."

"So," Ken said, "you believe God honors your free will, but if you pray for help, He sometimes helps you make a good choice?"

"Yes, so I obviously should pray for His help anytime I have to make a decision. I think He still lets me make the choice, but He seems to make it clear to me which is the best choice."

"You know what I think," Denise Chapman said. "I think Bob had a good observation. Maybe God lets us run with our free will and doesn't interfere unless we ask Him to in prayer. I say this because our prayers are often asking God to change something—maybe to heal someone of cancer or to change someone's heart or way of thinking."

"When we pray for the salvation of someone," Susan Kingsley

said, "I think that is exactly what we are asking God to do: to violate that person's free will, to intervene and change that person's mindset."

"Using Susan's example," Janine Brooks said, "if a person comes to salvation because of our prayers, maybe God didn't go against that person's will to reject God, but God provided more opportunities for that person to come to God on their own. So that person freely chose God, not because God changed his or her mind, but because God provided more opportunities for that person to see the light."

"So, God gets his way," Pastor Ken said, "not by violating the person's free will, but by other ways without directly intervening."

"Yeah," Janine said.

"I think we're coming to a conclusion, or realization," Hunter Kingsley said, "that both are true. God is sovereign and rules over everything, including the affairs of men and women. And, at the same time, God allows men and women to exercise the free will He has given them. We may not understand how both of these could be true and operate at the same time, but scripture clearly indicates that they are. Just like when you put it all together, scripture clearly indicates that Jesus was fully man and fully God at the same time. And scripture clearly indicates that there is only one true God, but He exists in three persons: God the Father, God the Son, and God the Holy Spirit."

"What do you think, guys?" pastor Ken asked. "Is this another one of those paradoxes or mysteries in the Bible that, in our limited way of thinking, we cannot fully understand now, but someday might?"

"Yes," Jim and Linda Perdon said, "we think so."

"Yes," Jan White said, "Dwayne and I have also come to that conclusion. God lets us exercise our free will, and if something one of us chooses or does would somehow stand in the way of His purpose, He will just work around it."

"Well, interesting discussion," pastor Ken said. "I wish we had more time. There is a lot more we could bring up and discuss on this topic. But let me leave you with this quote I pulled off the internet from the Topical Bible Studies website: 'God, in his sovereignty, has granted a certain amount of autonomy to humanity. This free will allows humanity to act in ways that are contrary to how God might wish for them to act. It is not that God is powerless to stop them, rather, he has granted us permission to act as we do. Yet, even though we might act contrary to God's will, his purpose in creation will be accomplished. There is nothing we can do that will thwart his purpose.'"

Someone said, "Amen." Others followed.

"This obviously is our last meeting," Ken said, "as tomorrow we dock in Vancouver and our little trip is over. Thank you all for allowing me to help facilitate our daily gatherings, and thank you all for your participation. May God bless you and watch over you on your continued travels or on your journey home. Stay in touch with some of the people you met in our group if you can, and hopefully, some of us will see each other again."

Everyone stood up, mingled, and slowly started filing out of the Hearts and Minds Chapel. Some people hugged, and some people shook hands. Most everyone felt a little sadness that their daily gathering was over so quickly, but also joy in the meeting and gathering together of a new group of fellow believers and seekers. Duke also experienced a tinge of the two emotions.

CHAPTER 54

Tuesday, May 9, 11:00 a.m.
Sabatini's Specialty Restaurant

Today is the day that Scott and Catalina had been anticipating and looking forward to ever since the idea for a blind wine tasting, with wines from different states, had been conceived in discussion with their friends, Hector and Paula Veracruz, several months ago. The long, narrow table at the far end of the restaurant had five chairs behind it arranged so that the five sommeliers would be facing the audience. On the white linen-covered table in front of each of the chairs was a line of four wine glasses with a silver discard bucket to the right of each of the sets of glasses.

On a separate table to the right of the audience was an arrangement of five groups of wine bottles, with four in each group. Each of the wine bottles was completely covered with white taped-on paper so that the wine labels were not visible. On the white paper of each bottle of wine was a letter and a number. The letters A, B, C, D, and E designated which group the bottle was in. The numbers 1, 2, 3, and 4 designated which bottle was in that grouping. Each grouping contained a similar type of wine from each of the four represented vineyards from each of the four states: California, Arizona, New Mexico, and Nebraska.

Most of the one hundred and one wine lovers on the cruise had already tasted all of these wines during the earlier four wine-tasting events. The difference between then and now is that at the four previous wine-tasting gatherings, only wines from one state were being compared to each other. In this event, similar wines from each state would be compared with each other. And it would not be a comparison only, as the recognized hundred-point scale for judging wine, very familiar to the five sommeliers, would be used.

Scott explained all of this to the wine lovers group and went on to say that he and Catalina had medals to award any wines that scored high enough on the hundred-point scale to win one. Scott held up each of the four types of medals for everyone to see: a double gold, a gold, a silver, and a bronze.

"And now," Scott said, "I'm going to introduce the five sommelier judges. First of all, a man now very familiar to us, the Alaskan Princess sommelier, Alex Lapierre." Scott started clapping, and everyone else followed suit as Alex came in from the entrance to the restaurant, walked to the far end of Sabatini's, and took his seat at the head table.

"Next, we have Amy Christine from the Anasazi restaurant in Santa Fe, New Mexico." Amy entered the restaurant, walked the aisle between the tables, and took her seat at the head table.

"And Brian Downey from Lon's at the Hermosa Inn in Paradise Valley, Arizona." Brian walked the friendly gauntlet of clapping people and took his seat at the judge's table next to Amy.

"Reggie Narito of the Grange restaurant in downtown Sacramento, California." Reggie had a big smile as he walked past the tables of wine lovers and took his seat.

"And, last but not least, Nickolas Paris from the Au Courant restaurant in Omaha, Nebraska." Nickolas took the remaining seat on the audience's right side of the table.

Scott gestured for the five sommeliers to stand again. "Let's hear it again for our five sommelier judges." After another round of applause, the sommeliers once again took their seats.

Scott now introduced Emilio Suarez, one of the wine stewards on board the Alaskan Princess. He and his two assistants were set to do the wine pours for the judges and to set up clean glasses for the judges after each of the five rounds of taste testing. Scott then introduced John Carr and Stephen Bullon, the two freelance wine reporters.

"Each of you has a glass of wine in front of you. It is one of the twenty different wines from our four vintners almost everyone has already tasted during our four different wine luncheons. Your job is to ascertain which of the twenty it is. We will also be starting the lunch service in a few minutes, all of this while our sommeliers are busy up here, working, doing their version of look, smell, taste, and conclude. Feel free to converse during all this. As long as it does not get too loud, and Hunter does not put on his sleuthing hat, it will not bother our sommeliers.

"Finally, before we begin, a little background. In 1976, Steven Spurrier, an Englishman who had a wine shop in Paris, arranged and hosted a blind taste test of certain premium California wines against certain premium French wines. To everyone's surprise, the California wines won over the French wines in two of the flights or groups of wine taste tested. This became known as the Judgement of Paris and put Napa Valley and California on the map as a recognized source of good wines. As a result of that, we know, and the world knows, that California has good wines. What about New Mexico, Arizona, and Nebraska? Stay tuned, and we'll see. Okay, Emilio, begin the pours!"

CHAPTER 55

Emilio took bottle number 1 from flight A from the side table and opened it. He poured a sampling of the wine into the first glass, sitting in front of each of the five sommeliers. Each of the sommeliers then went through their ritual of evaluating and scoring the wine. They each wrote down their score on the score sheet provided, and Lilly Carver, one of the wine lovers from the group, sitting at her own table near the head table, got up and collected the five score sheets. She then added the five scores and divided the answer by five to get the average score for that wine. Afterward, she wrote the consensus score for that wine on the master score sheet.

Each time Lilly collected the score sheets, Emilio would pour the next wine. This process ran smoothly through the entire twenty bottles of wine. Before dessert could be served to everyone, the five sommeliers and Lilly had completed their tasks. All twenty bottles in the five different flights were evaluated and scored, and the scores were averaged and entered onto the master score sheet. Emilio had also done his job well. After each pour, Emilio placed the bottle back in its place in the group. And, just as an extra but probably unnecessary precaution, in case there was any question of impropriety, William Strollmyer, an appellate court judge from California from the wine lovers group, stood behind the tables and watched the whole process.

Scott stood up before the group in front of the head table and made the announcement after the group had quieted. "Ladies and gentlemen, all of the wines have been scored, and the scores have been tabulated. Please give a round of applause to our five sommeliers as they leave and trot off to another room, where they will now get to eat lunch. In the meantime, Emilio and I will take the master score sheet and rearrange the bottles in each flight in the order in which they scored. That is, the bottle that received the highest score of the four wines in that flight will be put in front. The bottle with the next highest score will be placed right behind the front bottle, and so forth. After dessert, I will have my lovely wife Catalina help me unmask the wine bottles so we can see which wines won the taste test in each flight and also which wines scored high enough for a medal. So, until then, enjoy your dessert and another glass of wine if you so desire."

After dessert, Scott and Catalina stood up from their table, walked over to the side table with the covered-up twenty bottles of wine, and stood. Scott didn't have to quiet the room as everyone stopped talking in anticipation of the great unveiling. This moment had been subtly promoted and hinted at throughout the cruise by Scott and Catalina. And now, the excitement in the room was not unlike that of the Academy Awards or the Grammys. The two reporters, John Carr and Stephen Bullon, took up their positions with cameras and recorders ready.

To add a little frivolity to the unveiling, Scott asked for a drum roll like the one in the movie "National Lampoon's Christmas Vacation" just before Clark Griswold plugged in the thousands of Christmas lights on the house. As everyone did their best at imitating a drum roll, Scott picked up the front bottle, the one that had received the highest score on the hundred-point system, from flight A, and held it in front of him as Catalina peeled off the cover.

With the cover now off, Scott looked at the label and announced, "And the winner of flight A, which consisted of white wine from each of our four winemakers, is the Los Amigos Cellars of Napa Valley, California, Barrel Select Chardonnay, with seventy-nine points. Seventy-nine points—that's a bronze medal. One more point, and it would have been a silver medal." Scott raised the glass of wine he had brought with him, looked up to the ceiling, and said, "Well done, Ed and Joyce. We're sorry you're not with us to enjoy the moment." Those who still had wine also raised their glasses.

Scott continued. "Next, the winner of flight B, which were all roses, is..." Catalina peeled off the cover, and Scott looked at the label and then at the score sheet for flight B, "...again, Los Amigos Cellars of Napa Valley, California, with their Amigos Rose and a point total of eighty-five. It wins a silver medal. Congratulations again, Ed and Joyce Cooling.

"And now to group or flight C. These last three groups are all reds, paired together with comparable varietals. Catalina picked up the front bottle, pulled the cover off, and handed it to Scott. Scott looked at the label, then looked at the score sheet for flight C, and said, "The winner is Black's Smuggler Winery of Bosque, New Mexico, with their Smuggler's Tempranillo. And they won with a score of ninety-three points. That's a gold medal. Congratulations, Tony and Maryanne Black." Scott and others lifted their glasses to where Tony and Maryanne were sitting while others applauded.

"The winning bottle for flight D, please, my dear," Scott said. Catalina peeled the cover off and handed the bottle to Scott. "The winner of flight D, which were all medium-bodied reds, is a Merlot called Leaping Merlot from Leapfrog Vineyards in Camp Verde, Arizona. And, with ninety-two points, it also wins a gold medal." Scott raised and pointed his glass toward Jim and Linda Perdon as others did the same or applauded.

"And for our last group, wine lady, unveil the bottle, please." Catalina handed the bottle to Scott, and Scott looked at the E flight score sheet. "The wines in this last group were all that we could call hearty reds. And, also with ninety-two points, the winner is, again, Los Amigos Cellars with their Three Amigos Cabernet. It is actually a blend of 90 percent Cabernet, 5 percent Merlot, and 5 percent Tempranillo. Congratulations for the third time, Ed and Joyce," Scott said as he looked up.

"Well," Scott continued, "there we have the winners of each of the five flights. And each one was also a medal winner. And there may be more medal winners because we are dealing with some very good premium wines here. To speed things up, because I know you've been here a while, I'm going to skip the wine bottle unmasking and merely look at the score sheets for all the second, third, and fourth-place wines. If any of these other wines received a score of seventy or better, which is the lowest score to get a bronze, then they also are a medal winner. To refresh your memory, seventy to seventy-nine points wins a bronze, eighty to eighty-nine points wins a silver, ninety to ninety-five points wins a gold, and ninety-six to a perfect score of a hundred wins a double gold. Obviously, none of our wines today won a double gold.

"Okay, looking at the score sheets, quickly—looking for a score of seventy or above, ah, here we go. In flight A, with seventy-five points, Leapfrog Vineyards of Arizona also received a bronze for their Pinot Grigio. In flight B, with eighty-three points and a silver medal is Silver Leaf Vineyards in Lincoln, Nebraska, with their Eden's Blush. In flight C, with a ninety-point gold—just made it—is Silver Leaf Vineyards again with their Nebraska Red, a blend of St Croix, St Vincent, and Frontenac varietals. Also, in flight C, it looks like Leapfrog Vineyards and Los Amigos both won a bronze with scores of seventy-three and seventy-two, respectively.

"Flight D, Los Amigos won a silver, and Black's Smuggler won a bronze. And flight E—the hearty reds flight—Leapfrog won a silver with their Cabernet, and Black's Smuggler won a silver with their Rattle Snake Red. That looks like it. That's quite a few medals. No wonder we enjoyed the wines so much. I think everyone here deserves a round of applause—our vintners, our judges, our reporters, the staff and servers here at Sabatini's, and you all—for sitting for an extended time. I want to thank everyone for attending. You all are a part of wine history now. In the coming weeks and months, check your favorite wine periodicals, like Wine Spectator and Wine Enthusiast, for articles about what you have just witnessed. Good day and God bless all of you." A standing ovation followed, which Scott and Catalina later admitted choked them up.

CHAPTER 56

Scott and Catalina, Hunter and Susan, and the three winemaker couples, Tony and Maryanne Black, Jim and Linda Perdon, and Jay and Roxanne Patterson, gathered by the wine table after everyone but the clean-up crew had left Sabatini's. The three winemaker couples congratulated Scott and Catalina on a fantastic event and a fantastic job of hosting it, as did Hunter and Susan. Comments were also made to the effect that they believed Ed and Joyce would have also been pleased with the event and how it turned out. Scott said that all the medal winnings would really help with the recognition and sales of not only the medal-winning wines but also the wineries they came from.

Emilio came with a cart to get the twenty partially filled bottles of wine from the wine table and said that this wine would be made available to the wine lovers group at dinner tonight. Roxanne asked about the people who tried to stop Scott and Catalina from having this wine taste test in the first place. Hunter said that his friend, Duke Rawlings, was going to check on the status of the bad guys later in the day through ship security.

Scott and Catalina looked tired—tired but relieved. After helping Emilio load the wine on the cart, they went to their cabin to take a nap. The rest of the group also broke up and went their way.

Hunter and Susan headed for their cabin. Sue wanted to start packing for tomorrow's debarkation in Vancouver. The larger suitcases of all the passengers were supposed to be tagged and in the hallways by midnight tonight. Hunter wanted to make sure his

Sherlock Holmes hounds-tooth cap and calabash pipe and magnifying glass did not get packed in the big suitcases as he wanted to use them tomorrow. Susan gave him a look that he couldn't quite figure out.

CHAPTER 57

Shortly after Hunter and Susan had started packing, their cabin phone rang. Hunter answered, "Yes?"

"Hunter, it's Duke. I just talked to my buddy Bob Blackhiorn at the Ketchikan PD. He gave me an update on our big arrests yesterday. If you've got a few minutes, I'll meet you somewhere and fill you in."

"Good. How about the Wheelhouse in five?"

"You got it."

***

Hunter walked into the Wheelhouse Bar and found Duke all the way back and to the right at a table over by the windows.

"You beat me," Hunter said, "and I thought I was pretty quick."

"I called you from a house phone by the casino, so I was close by."

"So, you heard from Bob Blackhorn. I didn't think we got cell phone reception this far from shore."

"Probably not, but he called ship security, Chief Carter Watts, on the ship to shore set up. Watts called me, and I went down to security and talked to Blackhorn directly."

"Good. What did you find out? I've been wondering about it all day."

"Well, at first, none of the guys would talk. But when it came down to the woman, Arleen Simpson, she sang like a bird. The trouble is, she didn't really know a whole lot. She said her husband, Ralph, got her to drive the SUV by telling her there was a couple trying to ruin their business.

"Then the Simpson woman started talking about some super-secret meetings her husband would have at their winery every once in a while—their winery back in California—in Napa Valley. She said she would help set out wine and snacks for the meetings—and she would see some of the people as they started showing up—all guys—no women, but before the meeting would start, she had to leave and walk back to the house.

"She said she didn't recognize all of the men who came to the meetings but was sure they were all owners and, or, operators of other vineyards in the valley. All her husband ever told her about the meetings was that they had to do with protecting their livelihood—their wine businesses."

"Did she know anything about the murders of Ed and Joyce Cooling?"

"She said she knew Ed and Joyce as they had a winery not all that far from her and her husband's winery. She said she and Ralph didn't know Ed and Joyce too well and had only heard that they had drowned, not that they had been murdered."

"Have any of the guys talked yet?"

"Not yet. Antone Gillespie and Wit Kraske lawyered up right away. Arleen's husband, Ralph, may turn, but he hasn't yet. Gillespie and Kraske have an FBI hold on them, so we'll see what happens there."

"Good. Keep me updated if you would."

"Of course. We're partners," Duke said.

"You really are serious, then. You really want to go through with this—this enterprise."

"Yes. What about you? Are you serious?"

"I have to be. I've got my investigator's cap and pipe and magnifying glass. There's no turning back now."

"So," Duke said, "we'll talk when we get back?"

"Yes. Let's meet and talk. Are you staying over in Vancouver or going back right away?"

"I'm going back right away. I'll be home tomorrow early evening. What about you?"

"Susan and I are spending an extra day in Vancouver with Scott and Catalina. I don't know what we'll do, but we'll do something. We'll be home Thursday, the day after you. We could meet Saturday, somewhere, if you want. I need Friday as a day to unwind."

"I can't. I'm playing golf. Hey, why don't you join me for golf, then we'll talk afterward? You said you play, right?"

"Yes, but don't you have a foursome already?"

"No, only a twosome, so now it can be a threesome."

"What's the course?"

"TPC Scottsdale."

"TPC Scottsdale? That's a private club, isn't it, and a little expensive."

"You'll be my guest. I'm single again. I have to spend my money somewhere. Besides, it might be good for us. A good source of leads—of people with money who can afford to pay for private investigators."

"Okay. What time?"

"I think it's around eight o'clock. I'll call you Friday with the exact tee time."

"Great. I'm looking forward to it. I've never played TPC Scottsdale. That's got to be a nice course."

"It is."

"I see it's getting close to the wine lovers early dinner time. Do you or you and Kimberly want to join the wine lovers group again for dinner? I think there will be space."

"Thanks, but no. Kimberly and I are going to eat at that specialty restaurant, the Sterling Steak House."

"Do tell. Are you and Kimberly an item, as my wife would say?"

"I'm not saying anything. I'm just taking it slow. Very slow.

And we'll see what happens, if anything. I've taken things a little too fast in the past. Kimberly is a nice lady. I'm not saying anything more."

"She happens to live in the Phoenix area, doesn't she?"

"She does. Again, I'm not saying any more."

"I got ya. I better get going. So, if not before, I'll see you at the golf course on Saturday."

"Right. Looking forward to it, brother."

The two stood up and used the secret fraternity handshake. Hunter headed for the Charthouse restaurant for the 5:30 dining. Duke sat back down for a second. A minute or so later, cocktail waitress Riviera came over to Duke's table.

"Hi. I didn't know anybody was back here. I saw a gentleman just walk by the bar from back here, so I thought I'd check. Have you been here long?"

"Ten minutes? Twenty minutes? I don't know. Not that long."

"Can I get you anything from the bar? Better late than never, right?"

"Better late than never?"

"Yeah, you know, in a lot of things. If you get in on it late, and it's a good thing, well, too bad you didn't get in on it earlier, but better late than never."

"You're right. Better late than never. So, I'm looking into this Christianity thing, and it looks like it's a good thing. So, if I go for it and get in, well, better late than never."

"Sure."

"Are you a Christian, Riviera?"

"Yes, well, I think I am."

"Do you go to church?"

"No."

"Well. I'm dating a Christian lady. I've never dated a Christian lady before—at least one that goes to church every Sunday. And she's nice. She's very nice, but we are different. She goes to church, and I don't. But I've been going to the Bible study on the ship. It's not bad. Well, anyway. I don't think I want a drink. I think I'd like to sit here for a little bit. Is that all right?"

"Yes, it is."

"You know, you should go to church. I should go to church."

"You're right, I should. I should go to church. Let me know if you need anything."

"Thanks. I do need something, but it's not from the bar. Thanks again for checking on me."

"You're welcome."

CHAPTER 58

It was 5:26 in the afternoon as Hunter walked into the Charthouse restaurant. He told the maître d' standing near the kiosk that he was with the wine lovers group in the back, and he knew the way. The maître d' nodded and smiled. Hunter double-timed it to the back as he was late, and he didn't like being late, although it seemed that he was always cutting it close. He wasn't late by civilian standards, but he was way late by military standards. In the Air Force, for a big assembly, the wing commander wanted you there five minutes before the scheduled time. The squadron commander wanted you there five minutes before that, and your flight leader wanted you there five minutes earlier than that. So, by military standards, Hunter was eleven minutes late.

He found Sue and sat down next to her in the seat she had saved for him. Sue looked up from the menu and smiled. "It's the last night on the cruise, and lobster is available at no extra charge."

As Hunter glanced at the menu, he said, "I'm going to have the shrimp cocktail appetizer and two lobsters for the main course. What about you, Susan?"

"I'm going to have the French onion soup, romaine and kale Caesar salad, and one lobster."

"Yeah, salad is a good idea. I also need a little roughage, so I'll have the Caesar salad along with you."

Scott Poncetran stood up and quickly reminded the group that the leftover wine from this afternoon's wine-tasting event was available. He said, to make it simple, Alex and Emilio were going to place one or two of the bottles on each table. If you wanted any of that particular wine, then have at it. Otherwise, you could order off the wine menu.

The conversations among the group were light, with most everyone talking about the wonderful time they had on the cruise and whether or not they were going straight home tomorrow or spending time in Vancouver before heading home. One couple was getting off the ship tomorrow and going directly to another ship sailing to the Hawaiian Islands. From cold and rainy to warm and sunny—somewhat of a packing challenge.

At the end of the dinner, Scott announced that next year's wine lovers cruise was from Miami, Florida, to Los Angeles, California, through the Panama Canal. He told everyone that if they had never sailed through the Panama Canal, they should, as the Panama Canal is one of the man-made wonders of the world. And, Scott said, if you're ever going to sail through the Panama Canal, their cruise next year is the one to go on as they will wine and wind their way through the canal.

Catalina then walked up, stood next to Scott, and they both thanked everyone for being on the cruise. Catalina then reminded everyone, "Remember, there are small ships, and there are big ships, but the best ships are friendships. Have a safe trip home, and hopefully, we will see everyone next year in Miami. God bless you all."

With that, people started getting up from the tables, wishing others goodbye, shaking hands, hugging, and slowly making their way out of the dining room. Some were heading toward the Princess Theater for the production show, some were heading to the Crooners Lounge to hear Austin Parker tickle the ivories one last time, and some were heading to their cabins to finish packing.

Meanwhile, another couple was having dinner at the Sterling Steakhouse, where the lights were low, soft music was playing, and the food and drink were extra special.

CHAPTER 59

The Sterling Steakhouse
Deck Fourteen

"You know, I'm going to miss you, Duke."

"Not unless you don't plan on seeing me back in Phoenix."

"Are you going to call on me?"

"You mean, ask you out on a date?"

"Yes."

"I plan to. If I do, will you accept?"

"That depends. Are you married?"

"No. I told you already that I'm not."

"I know. Just giving you one more chance to come clean if you are."

"Well, I'm not."

"Have you ever been married?"

"Yes."

"Once?'

"More than once."

"How many times?"

"Four."

"You don't give up easily, do you?"

"No."

"That's not a very good matrimonial record. Do you think you're doing something wrong?"

"I think so, but I have no idea what it is. Are you married?"

"No."

"Have you ever been married?"

"No."

"Ever been engaged?"

"Yes."

"But you didn't follow through?"

"I'm careful."

"How careful do you think you have to be with me?"

"Very."

"If I'm going to ask you out, I should know your schedule."

"As I mentioned before, I work for myself, so I'm flexible."

"That's good because I can be spontaneous at times."

"That sounds exciting. I think I might like spontaneous. What kind of work do you do? You never said much at all about your work."

Duke showed her one of his business cards that had the word "Available" in bold letters on the face.

Kimberly looked at it and said, "That sounds like what I do—freelance work. What kind of freelance work do you do?"

"It's odd jobs, mostly. Not so much handyman-type stuff, although I can do some of that. It's more like helping resolve things in more personal type situations. And, as you know, I may be working with Hunter Kingsley if he really goes through with becoming a PI. We're going to have a meeting about it on Saturday. We'll see how that goes."

"That's a plus. We both have flexible jobs."

"Do I have any minuses?"

"A few."

"Really. What would you say is the main one?"

"We're not equally yoked."

"Equally yoked? I've never heard of that. What does that mean?"

"In Bible times, oxen were often used to plow the fields. It was important that the oxen be of similar size and temperament and mindset and so forth so that when they were harnessed or yoked together with these heaven wooden yokes over their necks and shoulders, they would work in concert with each other. In the same way, it's important in a relationship, and in particular, a marriage, that the man and woman be equally yoked—that is, on the same page in regard to the important things in life, in particular, their relationship with God. Second Corinthians 6:14 puts it this way: 'Do not be yoked together with unbelievers. For what do righteousness and wickedness have in common? Or what fellowship can light have with darkness?'"

"That's pretty straightforward," Duke said. "I know I'm the darkness with my checkered past."

"How checkered?"

"You know what a checkerboard looks like?"

"Yes."

"That checkered."

"I have hope for you. I think you're coming around. To use an old cliché, 'you're beginning to see the light.'"

"Maybe, but I have to do it at my own pace. I don't want to be rushed or pushed."

"I know. I don't think I'm pushing. Do you think I'm pushing?"

"No, not at all."

"Well, if I don't stop eating, I may have to push myself away from the table a bit to make room for the food."

"Does that mean no dessert?"

"I didn't say that," Kimberly said with a smile.

The two did have dessert: Kimberly had a strawberry Sunday, and Duke a crème brulee. Duke then walked Kimberly to her cabin as she wanted to turn in early. They both had the same early flight back to Phoenix the next day.

CHAPTER 60

Wednesday, May 10
Vancouver, British Columbia, Canada

Duke Rawlings and Kimberly Howe were in the first group to disembark from the Alaskan Princess as they had a late morning flight back to Phoenix, Arizona. They shared a cab, and when they checked in at the airport, Duke asked if they could change their seats so they could sit together. The flight wasn't quite full due to a few last-minute cancellations. Two of the cancellations were for two business-class seats together. Duke paid the extra to upgrade both of them.

"Duke, my gosh, I'm glad we're going to be able to sit together, but that's a lot of money to spend just to sit in bigger seats for three hours."

"Not to be concerned. I have the money. There have been times when I didn't have the money, and I wouldn't have done it. But I have the money, so I'm happy to do it. Every once in a while, I think it's good to splurge for an unexpected pleasure. And, just so you know, I'm not expecting any favors in return."

"I appreciate that. But, just so you know, money wouldn't buy you any favors anyway. Also, just so you know, I think you're an honorable and forthright man, and I have a lot of respect for you for that."

The boarding of the Air Canada flight took place without incident, and Kimberly and Duke settled into their roomy business class seats for taxi and take off. When the Boeing 737 Max 8 reached altitude, the flight attendant offered them drinks. Kimberly asked for coffee, and Duke asked for a Bloody Mary. Kimberly looked at Duke, and Duke said, "No, I don't normally have a drink this early, but it's complimentary."

After Kimberly was served her coffee and Duke his Bloody Mary, Duke said, "I feel like you're judging me at times."

"I'm sorry I'm coming across that way. I'm really just observing you. I'm not used to a down-to-earth, plain-spoken, accept-me-as-I-am type of person. I am somewhat in awe of you, and that may be why you're interpreting it as judgmental. Please just keep being you, and I'll try not to come across as judgmental."

"That is just fine and dandy with me. And, you know, I may be a little in awe of you."

"Really. I'm flattered. How so?"

"I'm not sure. Let me think a second and see if I can come up with anything." After a short pause, "Okay, I think I have something."

"You're not going to make something up, are you?"

"Me? No. But it is hard for a guy like me to figure stuff like this out, and then even harder to put it into words."

"Give it a shot."

"Give it a shot? Who are you—Annie Oakley?"

"No, but I am sort of a cowgirl. I like horses. In fact, I have a horse—two horses. I like wide open spaces. And I like to wear blue jeans."

"That's it. I think that's why I am in awe of you. You're not prissy, not catty. You're kind of a down-home girl."

"Sort of a plain Jane?"

"No. No, not at all. You're beautiful, but it's a natural beauty. You don't appear to wear a lot of make-up or jewelry. You're just plain and simply beautiful. I bet you don't even color your hair."

"No, not yet, anyway."

"What color would you call that—your hair? It's kind of reddish-brown."

"I just simply call it auburn. That's what I put on my driver's license, anyway."

"You see, that's what I mean. You're simple, in a good way. You're not pretentious. Let me see something here." Duke started tugging at and then unclipped Kimberly's hair barrette. He helped her hair out of the bun she had it in and let it fall down over her shoulders. "There. That's nice."

"You don't like my hair up?"

"Oh, I do, but it also looks very nice down, spilling over your shoulders. A little sexier."

"I'm not trying to look sexy. I'm trying to look business-like."

"Oh, I know. I wanted to see the more relaxed, less business-like look. I like both looks, but if I had to choose one over the other, I'd choose the sexier, more relaxed look."

"So, Duke, tell me more about your move to Arizona. You said you moved recently from Colorado?"

"Yes, I did. And the abrupt subject change is all right. I'm not surprised. I sensed you were getting a little uncomfortable."

"Maybe, but I would like to hear more about your divorce and sudden move to Arizona."

"Well, I could make it a long, drawn-out story, but the bottom line is, she tried to murder me. So, I thought, under the circumstances, it would be a good time to get a divorce, sell the house, and get out of Colorado."

"Do you think she's going to come after you—hunt you down? Is that why you felt you had to leave the state? Why did she want to murder you in the first place?"

"I don't know why other than she thought I was in the way of her trying to destroy herself. She became addicted to gambling and couldn't walk away from it. It consumed her. It became more important to her than anything else, including our marriage.

"She went to therapy to try to break its hold on her. It worked for a while, but then it came back with a vengeance. She wasn't that way when I married her. She changed almost overnight. If I had stayed in town, I wouldn't put it past her to come after me and try something. I don't think she'll try to hunt me down in Arizona."

"For your sake, I sure hope not."

"See what you missed by not getting married."

"Well, things can happen."

"Yes, they can. But one thing that didn't happen is you didn't get married."

"No, I didn't—yet. I'm not an old maid. It can still happen. But I'm not desperately looking around for someone. I'm content. I have my work, I have my horses, and I have the Lord."

"Your work—you said it was some kind of computer work?"

"Yes. It's nothing too complicated. I work out of my house, and I design websites for people and companies. I work a lot with a gal who lives in Prescott—Prescott, Arizona, north of Phoenix. She also has a horse. Prescott is a big rodeo town. During Prescott Frontier Days, I usually go up there, and we go to the rodeo together. It goes on for days."

"So, your work, your horses, and God. What do you do with God?"

"In a way, I do everything with God. He is always with me. So, anything I do, anywhere I go, He is right there. I can't physically see Him, of course, but I always am aware of His presence. I am never alone because He is always right there."

"Okay."

"And thank you again, by the way, for coming to the Bible class with me on the ship. It was special having you there. It's always great to see someone new to the faith checking it out—testing it out—cautiously sticking their big toe in the waters of Christianity, so to speak."

"It was Hunter Kingsley who challenged me to come to the Bible class. His challenge made me decide to give it a try."

"I'm glad he challenged you to come, and I'm glad you accepted his challenge."

"You know, before we land, I think I need a little power nap. Fifteen minutes. Maybe half an hour."

"Me too. I'm going to shut my eyes, too."

Duke closed his eyes and thought, Kimberly here really seems to have it going on. I wonder if it really is because God is so real to her. It could be her job. It could be her horses. But I bet her contentment comes mostly from God. Probably all of it comes from God.

CHAPTER 61

Wednesday, May 10
Vancouver, British Columbia

At around 10:00 a.m., Hunter and Susan Kingsley and Scott and Catalina Poncetran walked off the Alaskan Princess, retrieved their bags, and jumped in the Uber Scott had arranged. They rode to the Chateau Granville Hotel at 1100 Granville Street. It was too early to check in, so they arranged for the front desk to hold their bags while they checked out Vancouver.

They walked across the lobby to the concierge desk and asked the friendly-looking lady what would be a fun and interesting thing to do for an afternoon in Vancouver. Victoria mentioned several things: Stanley Park, Queen Elizabeth Park, Van Dusen Botanical Garden, and the Capilano Suspension Bridge. None of these seemed to perk the interest of any of the four tourists, so Victoria suggested a few more possibilities: half-day whale watching, harbor cruise, Fraser Valley wine tour, and the Vancouver aquarium.

The four travelers looked at each other and shook their heads. Scott told Victoria that they had just come from a ten-day Alaskan wine lovers cruise, so a wine tour, harbor cruise, and whale watching didn't appeal to them.

Catalina asked Victoria if there was something enjoyable that they could do in the afternoon that was nearby—even within walking distance—like sightseeing with a little shopping. Victoria then said she thought the perfect thing for them to do would be to explore the Gastown area of the city. She said it was full of restaurants and pubs and shops and cute boutiques. And it was an easy walk from the hotel. She said that Yaletown and Chinatown were adjacent to Gastown and were also worth exploring if they had time.

Scott told Victoria that they couldn't check into their rooms yet, so maybe they could go have lunch at a nearby place, come back and check in, then explore Gastown. Victoria said there were plenty of pizza parlors and fast food places, along with other restaurants. Scott said they would prefer a fun place that had some local flavor. He said a pub-type restaurant would be great.

Victoria said the Pawn Shop, which is a very good Mexican restaurant, is right across the street, but if they didn't mind walking a block and a half and they want an experience besides good food, she recommended the Moose on Nelson Street.

The four adventurers agreed on the Moose. They walked out of the front of the hotel, turned right and walked up Granville Street, turned left on Nelson, walked half a block, and walked into the Moose's Down Under Bar and Grill. As soon as they checked in with the hostess at the front, they realized that only Aussie and Canadian were spoken at the Down Under.

They were shown to a table in the corner and given menus. The menu was simple—not a lot of choices, and the drink menu was the same. Susan ordered the barbeque back ribs, and Catalina ordered the jambalaya. Hunter asked for the drunken chicken ciabatta, and Scott decided to try the moose burger. The wine choices were extremely simple—red or white. The beer choices were slightly more plentiful. Everyone decided on iced teas with the idea that they might stop in a pub later in the afternoon during their tour of Gastown. The vintage jukebox was playing a rock and roll tune, and the lunch crowd was starting to wander in.

"It sure was a great cruise, you guys," Susan said. "I know I already mentioned this, but Hunter and I are so glad we were able to join you two on one of your wine lovers cruises."

"Yeah," Hunter said, "wine and glaciers—not a bad combination."

"Yes, it was a great cruise," Scott said, "but with one big mishap—two people died—and I probably could have prevented it."

"Well, like I said before," Hunter reiterated, "you don't know that. The motive behind their deaths is not totally clear, but with Duke's help, we're going to find out what was behind the whole thing—the attempts to get your wine, your abduction, the cease and desist messages, and the death of your friends, Ed and Joyce Cooling. Duke and I feel there is something more sinister behind it all than we presently realize."

"We hope you do find out more about what prompted the whole thing," Catalina said. "We'd hate to think this could happen again."

"If Duke's good friend, Lieutenant Blackhorn of the Ketchikan PD, can turn one of the three men they arrested—get him to confess—that would help a lot," Hunter said. A few seconds later, "Ah, here comes our food already. It looks good."

"It does," Scott said. "I'm hungrier than I thought."

The four long-time friends enjoyed their meal and their iced tea and the music from the jukebox and the atmosphere and the Canadian and Aussie accents. When they were finished, they left a very nice tip and headed back to the hotel. They checked in, went to their rooms, freshened up, and met in the lobby for their sojourn into Gastown.

They first walked to the famous steam clock, waited for it to do its tune on the quarter hour, then walked all over Gastown browsing the shops and boutiques with a mid-afternoon break at the Prospector's pub for a libation. They later had a great dinner at the Poorhouse restaurant on Water Street. It was in a hundred-year-old building and featured a thirty-eight-foot-long bar handcrafted from 120-year-old planks of Douglas fir, along with antiques from that era. The food was also interesting and tasty.

The next morning, the Kingsleys and the Poncetrans rode to

the Vancouver International Airport together. Hunter and Sue had a direct flight back to Phoenix. Scott and Catalina flew home to Albuquerque via Seattle. Both couples picked up their pets soon after arriving home. They were all glad to be home, and their canine friends were glad to see them.

CHAPTER 62

Wednesday, May 10, 12:30 p.m.
Phoenix, Arizona

Duke and Kimberly walked off the plane at Sky Harbor and headed for the baggage claim. "Where is your car parked?" Kimberly asked Duke.

"I didn't bring my car. I got a ride to the airport."

"Is someone picking you up?"

"No, not until I call Uber."

"You know, you can arrange for an Uber driver to be waiting for you ahead of time so you don't have to wait."

"I know, but it's all part of the way I like to do things. I like to stay flexible—keep my options open."

"Well, you don't have to call Uber. I'll give you a ride home."

"No, you don't have to do that. I'm fine. This is the way I do things."

"Don't be silly. I'd be happy to drop you off at your place. You said you live in Scottsdale. I live just past Apache Junction in Gold Canyon. Maybe a bit out of the way for me, but you're worth it."

"Okay then, I'll take you up on your ride offer. And, if you've got time, I'd like to take you out to lunch if you know a good place along the way."

"I know an excellent place we can sit outdoors under a giant tree, and it's just up the road."

"What's the name of it?"

"The restaurant is called Lon's. It's at the Hermosa Inn, which has been a desert getaway for people—a lot of famous people—since the 1930s. I think you'll like it."

"Sounds familiar. I think Hunter Kingsley mentioned it for some reason."

Kimberly and Duke retrieved her azure gray metallic Ford Bronco from the East Economy parking garage and drove to Lon's on Palo Cristi Road in Paradise Valley. It was a perfect May day in the Phoenix area, with a temperature of 78 degrees, 12 percent humidity, and a light breeze. Some of the best weather in the country occurs in the greater Phoenix area in March, April, and May and again in September, October, and November. The winters aren't bad either, but the summers can be brutal if you're not used to the routine, that is, perform all outdoor activities early in the morning, then mostly stay in air conditioning until mid-evening.

Duke and Kimberly were seated at a table for four under the big tree and near the giant fountain. They each ordered a glass of local Arizona wine and the Lon's Louie salad. Even though the waiter assured Duke that the Louie salad was enough for most people, Duke also ordered the seared salmon salad enhancement just in case.

The conversation was light, mostly revolving around Kimberly's love of horses and horseback riding and Duke's curiosity about that and about Kimberly personally. Duke again wondered how such a beautiful, wholesome lady had escaped marriage thus far.

After a very tasty, relaxed lunch, Kimberly fired up the Bronco and asked Duke, "Where to?" Duke told her his address on East Quartz Rock Road, and she punched it into her navigation system and headed to Scottsdale. Thirty-five minutes later, Kimberly drove the Bronco up the drive to one jaw-dropping, awesome house. It was not only the four-bedroom, four-and-a-half-bath house itself that was eye-catching, but the landscaping and the views were spectacular. The property had a gorgeous pool and spa, with an elaborate waterfall, and sat on the sixth fairway of Troon Country Club's private course with views of Troon Mountain and Pinnacle Peak.

Kimberly popped the door to the cargo compartment, and she and Duke got out of the SUV. "This is one ooh la la place," Kimberly said. "I guess you've done all right for yourself."

"I can't complain, but this place is a little above my pay grade. I'm leasing the place from a friend of my friend and golf buddy, Hector Perez, back in Golden, Colorado. I'm essentially babysitting this guy's property. It's a deal I just couldn't pass up. I'll get my bag and give you a tour."

"Okay. A quick tour, then I want to get going and see my horses."

"Rex and Rowdy, right?"

"Yes, Rex and Rowdy, my good buddies."

Duke gave Kimberly the tour, which didn't take all that long. It was not the size of the house, four thousand six hundred and forty-three square feet, but the features, the windows, and the views. It had walls of windows that opened to the extended covered patio, including an elaborate bar that opened to the outside as well. The pool and spa and built-in barbeque all helped make it the perfect entertainment house and pool party setup.

Kimberly gave Duke a generous hug and drove off in her Bronco, anxious to see Rex and Rowdy—something a cowgirl would understand. Duke raised his arm in a goodbye as she left. Duke wondered why some girls loved horses so much. He snagged a Golden Colorado Coors from the ice box and sat down by the pool to think about it.

CHAPTER 63

Friday, May 12
Home of Hunter and Susan Kingsley
Ridgeline Road, Carefree, Arizona

"Hey, Hunter, we just received an email from Catalina and Scott."

"Oh, yeah? What's it say?"

"It says, 'Hi kiddos, how's it going? Wasn't that a great trip? We sure had fun with you guys. And we thank you two so much for all your help in assuring that our grand finale wine taste testing went off so smoothly—that it even went off at all. We can never thank you enough.

"'We are still unwinding, and I'm sure you are too. We just received an advance copy of Stephen Bullon's article, which he said will be published in the June edition of the Wine Spectator magazine. You'll recall that he was one of the two freelance wine reporters on board the ship. I copied the article and sent it as an attachment. I hope you enjoy it. We'll talk soon.'"

Sue pulled up the attachment and started reading. "'What three words go together and make us come running? Wine, taste, and test. Sure, not everyone loves wine, but for wine enthusiasts, comparing different wines excites us. And this is what I was recently privileged to witness—a blind wine taste testing of wines from four different states: California, New Mexico, Arizona, and Nebraska.

"'The taste test was performed on the beautiful Alaskan Princess cruise ship and was hosted by Scott and Catalina Poncetran. The Poncetrans sponsor a yearly wine lovers cruise with usually one or two different winemakers on board presenting and sharing their wines. This year, which is their fourteenth year, the Poncetrans went all out with four winemakers on board. The four vintners not only presented their wines by themselves on separate occasions, but they also participated in a grand finale blind taste test pitting their wines against the other three winemakers.

"'This taste test was reminiscent of the famous Judgement of Paris blind taste test in 1976 in which California wines were compared with some of the best French wines. To the surprise of everyone, California won in two of the categories, and California wines were suddenly on par with French and European wines.

"'Well, I don't think it's much of a stretch to say that a similar thing happened here. Of the five categories or groups of wines tested, New Mexico and Arizona won best taste test in two of those groups, with California winning the other three. And Nebraska—don't discount the Corn Husker state—came in a very close second in two of the five groups of similar wines from each state.

"'Here are the wines in each of the five categories and how they fared, and any medals they won.'"

"I won't go through the listing of how they came out," Sue said. "We pretty much remember all of that. But the article goes on to say, 'Now you know. As a few have suspected for years, there are very good wines from a number of states that can go head-to-head with our beloved California wines. So, the next time you are at your favorite wine and beverage store, look for something other than your favorite California wine. Expand your horizons. Surprise your dinner guests. Look for a Leaping Merlot from Leapfrog Vineyards in Camp Verde, Arizona. Or, a Smugglers Tempranillo from Black's Smuggler Winery in Bosque, New Mexico. But if you really want to wow your dinner guests, treat them to a bottle of Nebraska Red, a blend of three varietals, somewhat unique to the area, from Silver Leaf Vineyards near Lincoln, Nebraska.

"'Now, it's not always easy to get some of the lesser known non-California wines. Most of them are not the big production wines California is known for. You're not likely to find them in your local supermarket. You may not find them in your local beverage store either, although you have a much better chance of doing so. You may have to order them directly from the winery, which, nowadays, is often the better way to go anyway.

"'So, move over, California, make room for wines from other states. And don't laugh at Nebraska or Arizona or New Mexico or other states that produce wine the way France laughed at you prior to May 24, 1976, and the Judgement of Paris.

"'Until next time, folks, this is your roving wine aficionado, Stephen Bullon, saying, if it weren't for wine, what would we do with all those grapes.'"

"That's a pretty good article," Hunter said. "I think that's exactly what Scott and Catalina were hoping for—an article that gives credence to non-California wines while, at the same time, recognizing the prominence of the California wine industry."

"Yes, and in a subtle way, the article, I think, called for an end to the aloofness some Californians and California vintners have about their wines."

"Yes, I picked up on that too. Hopefully, it doesn't go unnoticed. But that's one of the age-old problems with human beings. Give us a little success, and it goes right to our heads. However, you are a rare exception to that."

"How's that?" Sue asked.

"Even though you're the most beautiful girl in the world, it hasn't gone to your head."

Susan put on a Southern accent. "Oh, Hunter, you say the nicest things."

Hunter smiled and marked an imaginary point for him in the air.

CHAPTER 64

Friday, May 12
East Quartz Rock Road, Scottsdale

Duke answered the phone.

"Duke Rawlings, this is Bob Blackhorn."

"Hey, Bob, how's it going?"

"Things are fine up here. A cold rainy day, but nothing unusual about that. I thought I'd give you an update on the four perpetrators you and your buddy Hunter Kingsley helped arrest."

"Yeah, great. Fire away."

"As you know, the woman, Arleen Simpson, told us all she knew, which wasn't much, so probably no charges are going to be filed against her for her cooperation. Her husband, Ralph Simpson, was uncooperative at first, but when first-degree murder charges for the deaths of the couple pulled out of Glacier Bay were mentioned, he was suddenly more than happy to start talking.

"The male Simpson told us how he and a guy named Grady Flanigan hired the other two guys, Antone Gillespie and Wit Kraske—two thugs out of Vegas—to put a scare into Scott and Catalina Poncetran, the wine lovers cruise couple, so that they wouldn't have this big wine event on the cruise ship."

"Did he say why they didn't want the Poncetrans to have this wine event?"

"He and Flanigan, and some other wine growers in California, were afraid the Poncetrans were going to somehow set up this wine taste test so that California wines looked bad, and it would hurt the California wine industry. He said the wine industry in California is a very big deal and needs to be protected. Anyway, he said Gillespie and Kraske tried different little dirty tricks to dissuade the Poncetrans from having their event, but nothing worked. They were then going to really give the Poncetrans a strong message, rough them up a little, but they couldn't get to them. They were never alone.

"They couldn't get to the Poncetrans, so they went after Ed and Joyce Cooling—the California wine people who were going to be a part of the taste test. Eliminate the California wines from the competition, and then the California wines couldn't be made to look bad.

"So, they were stalking out the Coolings, got the opportunity to grab them, chloroformed them, put life jackets on them so they would look like little fishing bobbers bouncing up and down, and threw them into Glacier Bay—unconscious. The original intent wasn't to kill them, but, at that point, Simpson said Gillespie and Kraske didn't care. They said that if the Coolings died—well, that was just a stronger message."

"Are Gillespie and Kraske tied in with the Vegas mafia?"

"We don't know yet. Probably, in some way. But they are going to be charged with first-degree murder. I mean, come on! You render someone unconscious and throw them in freezing water; what do you expect? Plus, thanks to Simpson, who told us where they hid the mixture of chloroform and some other fast-acting knockout chemical, and the rags, we recovered those with Gillespie and Kraske's fingerprints."

"That helps quite a bit, doesn't it?"

"Yes. And regarding the abduction attempt at Annabell's restaurant, Simpson said that all he and Gillespie and Kraske were trying to do was to take the Poncetrans a little ways out of town, tie them up, and leave them. By the time they got free and found a way back to town, the ship would have been long gone by then. Thus, no big wine taste test the next day as the Poncentrans wouldn't have been there to put it on. Also, I think I mentioned before that the FBI is going to be talking to Gillespie and Kraske about some other shenanigans in which they are suspects."

"Good. Sounds like these two guys are definitely looking at some time."

"Speaking of shenanigans, Simpson also told us that this somewhat clandestine group of California wine owners and operators he and Flanigan belong to—I mean, they use code names and a secret rendezvous and so forth—are planning dirty tricks against other wineries they think might be a threat to their well-being. We are looking into who—what authorities we should contact in California about this.

"And, that's it. That's all I have. You got anything?"

"Hunter Kingsley and I are going to be partners. He's going to become a PI, and I'm going to help him out when needed."

"Good for you guys. Hunter seems like a trustworthy, squared-away guy. I hope that works out well. Anything else?"

"I met a lady on the ship. She lives in the area. We're going to be seeing each other."

"There you go. Move cautiously."

"I am. Give my regards to Sharon."

"You got it."

CHAPTER 65

Saturday, May 13
Troon North Golf Course

At 7:20 a.m., Hunter sat down on a bench just outside the Troon North clubhouse near the practice green. A few minutes later, Duke drove up in a golf cart and said, "Hey, Hunter, you ready for some golf?"

"I am. I haven't checked in yet."

"Me neither. Load your clubs on the cart, and we'll go check in. They have two courses here—the Pinnacle and the Monument. I thought we'd play the Pinnacle."

"Fine with me, Duke. I've never played either one. Is your golf partner you mentioned playing?"

"No. He couldn't make it today. It's just you and me, and maybe another twosome they might put with us."

Duke and Hunter checked in with the starter. He told them if they wanted to tee off now, they could play as a twosome as he had no one to pair them up with.

"Do you need to practice, Hunter?"

"I'm good."

"Then, let's do it."

They pulled up to the number one tee. "Which tee boxes do you like to play?" Duke asked.

"I usually play the mid-range—the silvers. What about you?"

"The silvers are fine."

"I bet you usually play the blacks."

"I play the blacks sometimes, but on this course, I've been playing the silvers. Some of these holes have a good amount of dessert between the tee box and the beginning of the fairway. If you don't make the fairway, you're usually in a lot of trouble."

"Why don't you go first?" Hunter said. "Show me the way."

"My pleasure. It's a par four, and it's 369 yards to the center of the green. It doglegs left at about 270 yards out. That's where I'm going to try to put it."

"Two hundred and seventy yards, huh? I can dream of a two-hundred-and-seventy-yard drive."

Duke teed up and hit the ball with a gentle fade about two hundred and seventy-five yards out onto the left side of the fairway. Hunter hit his ball two hundred and fifty yards onto the center of the fairway.

"A good start," Hunter said, "we're both in the fairway."

"I'm happy," Duke said.

Duke drove up to Hunter's ball, and Hunter jumped out. Duke said, "One hundred and fifty-eight to the pin. It's a blue flag."

Hunter pulled out a seven iron and swung. The ball landed short and to the right of the pin, about eight yards away.

They drove up to Duke's ball, and Duke pulled out a pitching wedge and swung. His ball landed pin high and to the left on the upslope about seven yards from the pin.

Hunter yelled, "Look at that! We're both on the green with birdie attempts."

Duke said, "Yeah, how about that."

They drove the cart over to the cart path, up to the green, and parked across from the flag. They pulled out their putters and walked over to their balls.

Hunter sized up his putt and read a slight break to the left. He putted, played the break, but it didn't. It didn't break. Hunter went ahead and tapped it in for par.

Duke had a slight downslope and break to the right. His ball broke to the right, but not enough, and it rolled two feet past the hole. He made the putt and also parred the hole.

They high-fived each other, and Duke said, "Hey, I think I have myself a golf buddy."

Hunter said, "Yeah, I think maybe I can keep up with you."

On the par-five hole, number eleven, Duke played his fade, but it didn't fade enough, and he wound up in the rocks in the desert. It took him two shots to get back into the fairway. He momentarily lost his cool and hit the ground with his club. Hunter also had some bad shots, but it never seemed to bother him. Both golfers shot in the eighties. Duke could power the ball out there with his drives, but Hunter had a more accurate short game. They were pretty evenly matched.

After they putted out on number eighteen, they shook hands, got in their golf cart, and drove over to the clubhouse. Duke said, "I'll buy you a beer here at the clubhouse if you want, but I'd really like to show you my house. I have beer, and I can make us sandwiches. It's not really my house—I rent it—but I think you'll give it at least one wow."

"Yeah. That will be great. Want me to follow you over?"

"Yeah, that will be best."

Duke drove the golf cart into the parking lot and over to their respective vehicles to drop off their clubs. Duke then turned the cart in and walked back to his Kelly green Expedition. As he pulled out of the lot, he made sure Hunter was following.

CHAPTER 66

Duke turned left onto East Dynamite Boulevard with Hunter following in his pearl white Ford Edge. Three-point four miles later, Hunter followed Duke into his driveway on East Quartz Rock Road in the Windy Walk estates of Troon Village.

The two climbed out of their vehicles at the same time, and Hunter said, "Wow, I am impressed already."

"Well, there's one wow. That's all I asked for."

Hunter continued, "The desert landscape and the views of the mountains—just from the driveway—spectacular!"

"Wait until you see the inside and the backyard and the views from there."

Duke opened the front door with Hunter following. As they stepped into the foyer, Hunter stopped and took it all in. Everything was mostly black and white. White marble flooring and white walls with black built-in shelves and a black wall where the wall-mounted TV was with the elongated quartz rock fireplace below. The living room also had a long white leather couch with a black coffee table and end tables sitting on a plush white carpet with black streaks. Past the living room area was a wall of windows that made the outside seem to be just a continuation of the house.

From that first step into the entry, Hunter could tell that the whole house was going to be like this throughout—simply stated elegance. There were objects of art on the shelves here and there, with ample space in between. Nothing was crowded. Nothing was overstated. It was simplistic beauty.

The kitchen was also particularly spectacular. Virtually the whole back wall above the sink and countertop was glass that looked out beyond the patio and pool to the sixth fairway of the Troon Country Club's private course.

Duke gave Hunter a quick tour of the rest of the house, but Duke was anxious to ask Hunter something—to discuss something that had been increasingly bothering him. Duke quickly made two Dagwood-size cold meat sandwiches, retrieved two Coors Light beers, and he and Hunter went outside to sit and eat under the patio shade and gaze out at the golf course and mountain views, with the signature deep blue Arizona sky as a backdrop. If it got too hot, Duke could turn on the misters, but it was only mid-May. They weren't needed.

"You know," Hunter said, "I've seen the outside of your Golden, Colorado, home when I helped arrest your wife, Vivian, around two years ago. But this house has the Golden house beat by a mile."

"You helped arrest my wife?"

"Yeah, the FBI let me tag along."

"I never knew that. You know, my ex-wife Vivian is something I'd like to talk to you about. I'm going to tell you something that is strictly between you and me. You can't tell anyone—not even your wife."

"Well, I'm not sure I can agree to that. What are you going to tell me? That you murdered your wife?"

"That's exactly right. I didn't physically do it, but I paid someone to make it happen."

"I thought your wife, Vivian, was killed in a car accident, skidded off an icy mountain road."

"That's right. Arranged by me. I paid a guy who knows how to arrange accidents like that."

Hunter couldn't believe it! Here, he was making a joke—being facetious—about Duke murdering his wife, and Duke told him that's exactly what he had done. "Why are you telling me this?"

"I'm telling you this because it has been bothering me ever since I had it done. I'm confessing it to you. I want God to forgive me. I've done some bad things, but I figure having my wife killed is about the worst of them. If I want to become a Christian, I know I have to confess my sins. So, that's what I'm doing."

Hunter didn't know what to think. Here's his friend, Duke, bearing his soul, confessing his worst sin, believing, as Hunter and others have been telling him, that there is no sin except the sin of unbelief that God won't forgive. Hunter didn't know how to react. He didn't know how he should react.

The joy he felt that his newfound friend was apparently coming to Christ was diminished by the weight of the sin his friend had just confessed. Hunter had questions about Duke's sincerity, and now he had questions about his own sincerity. Was he sincere when he told Duke that there was no sin so egregious that God wouldn't forgive? That was the Christian part of Hunter's thinking and questioning. The law enforcement side of Hunter was telling him he had to tell the authorities about a murder he had just become privy to.

Hunter decided it was all too much to ponder at the moment. He would need to sort it all out—soon—but not right now. His newfound friend, who, in a short time, he'd grown to really like and care for, was seemingly on the verge of becoming a Christian, of accepting Jesus Christ as his Lord and Savior. Should he dare diminish the joy of such an occasion?

"Well, good, okay. You know, you don't have to confess your sins to a person. Just to God."

"I understand that, but I feel I should tell a person also. You're a Christian. You are close to God. Plus, where two or more are gathered, there God is also. So, there you have it. I confessed to you and God at the same time."

"You're sincere about this? I mean, are you really sorry about arranging your wife's death and all the other terrible things you say you've done?"

"I am. Some of the people I took care of got what they deserved—I'm talking about some very bad people—but I'm sorry I had to do it."

"Well, I know God heard your confession, and I'm sure He has forgiven you. That's the first step in becoming a Christian. The second step is to ask Jesus Christ into your life. That is, ask Him to be your Lord and Savior. Let Him control your life. Let Him lord over your life and save you from the consequences of your sins—spiritual death."

Duke slipped out of his seat and knelt down. "Jesus, I want You to be my Lord and Savior. I want Your guidance for my life. I want to live for You and not for myself."

After a pause, Hunter said, "Amen."

"Amen. Amen—what does that really mean?"

"Something like, 'So be it.'"

"So, am I a Christian?"

"You are. You are a Christian."

"Fantastic! Hallelujah!"

"So, brand new Christian, do you feel any different? You don't have to. Many people don't, at least not at first."

"Actually, I think I do. I feel happy. I feel good. I feel like a great weight has been lifted off of me."

Duke had a big grin on his face, and Hunter did also. Hunter stood up and said, "I have to give you a big hug, my Christian brother." Duke stood up, and the two gave each other a sincere man hug—that is, they hugged each other, held it for two or three seconds, then released and patted each other on the back. They sat back down, and Hunter said, "Now we're double brothers. We're fraternity brothers and Christian brothers—brothers in the faith."

"Wow," Duke said. "I feel such a sense of relief. I feel like tension that I didn't know I even had is gone—disappeared. I just feel so free and happy."

"Not to get technical, but what you're actually probably feeling is joy more than happiness. Happiness is temporary. Joy is permanent and comes from the Lord."

"Yeah, that is more like what I'm feeling, I think. It's deeper than happiness. It feels permanent, like you said. It feels like it's not going to go away. So, what now? What do I need to do next? Anything?"

"Yes, plenty of things. But it's not a rush job. It's all part of growing in the faith. You're a baby Christian now. Over time, you should mature into an adult Christian. The great thing is you have your salvation right now. You have a place in heaven. You're not going to hell. So that's worth another hallelujah."

"Hallelujah!" Duke exclaimed. "Okay, what are the next couple of things I should do?"

"You should get plugged into a church. I was already going to invite you to our church—Calvary Chapel 14:6, in Surprise. It's a little out of the way for us, but Susan and I really like it. It's an excellent church, and like all Calvary Chapels, the pastor goes right through the Bible in his sermons. Therefore, it's a good church in which to learn the Bible in an understandable way."

"Okay. I'll check out your church. What else?"

"You can start reading the Bible. Start with one of the four Gospels—Matthew, Mark, Luke, or John. Do you have a Bible?"

"No."

"I'll get you one before I leave. I always carry two or three in the car, just in case. And this is one of those just-in-case occasions."

"What else?"

"Well, when you're ready, you'll want to get baptized. Your salvation is already assured with your repentance and acceptance of Jesus as your Lord and Savior. Baptism is just a public demonstration of your confession of faith and allegiance to the Lord. It symbolically demonstrates that you're a new creature—a new man. You are dipped under water, and when you come up out of the water, that represents the new you. A person now dedicated to God rather than himself."

"I'm ready. Can I be baptized right now? There's a body of water right over there—my pool. You're a Christian—and a Chaplain—you can baptize me."

Hunter started laughing. He started laughing uncontrollably. He got to laughing so hard that Duke, in spite of the fact that he thought maybe Hunter was laughing at him, started laughing also. Finally, after Hunter had calmed down, Duke asked what was so funny.

Hunter said, "The eunuch—the Ethiopian eunuch—Philip and the Ethiopian eunuch. In Acts chapter 8 in the Bible, after hearing the gospel explained, the Ethiopian eunuch wanted to be baptized then and there. He didn't want to wait. They were near a body of water, so Philip baptized him."

"Will you baptize me then?" Duke asked. "I have an extra swimming suit I can loan you."

"Yes, absolutely. I'd almost say let's get you baptized in the clothes we have on, but better to use swimming suits."

The two men quickly changed, and Hunter dipped Duke into the water and back out and baptized Duke in the name of the Father, the Son, and the Holy Spirit. The two men climbed out of the water, refreshed and renewed, and sat back down in their chairs. They hadn't touched their beers or their sandwiches, and Duke said, "I don't feel like drinking my beer now. I think I'll get a soda instead."

"Me too," Hunter said. "I'll take a soda—whatever you have."

Duke came back with two diet sodas and said, "Thanks for baptizing me."

"You're welcome, bro."

The two looked at each other, clinked their sodas together, and started laughing again. As the laughter subsided, Duke said, "What a day."

"I'll second that," Hunter said.

CHAPTER 67

The drive home from Duke's place in Scottsdale to Hunter and Susan's house on Ridgeline Road in Carefree was about thirteen miles and took about twenty minutes. Hunter walked in the door, and Susan said, "I was just going to call you. How was the golf game?"

"It was great. Duke and I are pretty evenly matched. His drives are longer, but my short game is a little better, more accurate."

"I take it you had lunch."

"Yes, but I almost didn't. Duke suggested we go to his place for lunch and a beer as he wanted me to check out his house."

"How is it?"

"It's drop-dead gorgeous inside and out. It's on the sixth fairway of the Troon Country Club's private course. It has a pool and spa with great views of the mountains and fairway."

"So you almost didn't have lunch. What happened? Did Duke discover he had no food in the house?"

"No, nothing like that. We were sidetracked. We started talking about things, and, well, Duke became a Christian right then and there. He accepted Jesus Christ into his life. He accepted Jesus as his Lord and Savior."

"No lie? I'm shocked. I didn't think he would come around—at least this quickly and so abruptly. That is great news. Praise the Lord!"

"It is an awesome thing. He and I are now double brothers. Fraternity brothers, and now also brothers in Christ. And another thing, he was baptized too, all in the same afternoon. He did almost the same thing as the Ethiopian eunuch did in Acts chapter 8 with Philip when the eunuch said something to the effect of, 'Why not baptize me now, there is water nearby.' So I baptized Duke in his pool."

"We need to follow up with him. Did you offer to take him to church? Tomorrow is Sunday."

"No, I didn't. I was so excited at the moment that I didn't think about it. I'll call him right now." A few minutes later, Hunter said, "He's going to meet us at the front entrance of the church at 7:45 for the eight o'clock service."

"Did you tell him there are two later services?"

"Yes, but he wanted to go to the eight o'clock. He's either anxious or an early riser."

"Or both."

Hunter thought, Great, I can't tell you this, Sue, but we're going to church with my brother in Christ, the wife murderer.

CHAPTER 68

Sunday, May 14
Surprise, Arizona

At 7:45 a.m., Susan and Hunter Kingsley walked up to the front entrance of their church, Calvary Chapel 14:6, in the town of Surprise, Arizona. Duke Rawlings was there waiting for them. The three of them walked in, shook hands with the greeters, and found three seats toward the front. At exactly eight o'clock, the worship and praise team leader welcomed everyone, and the band began with a lively worship song. The words to the song were projected on the TV screens, and most everyone stood and started singing. At times, some people raised their hands in praise and adoration to God.

Twenty minutes or so later, the praise music ended, and the worship team left the stage. One of the associate pastors walked on stage and prayed for the offering. When the offering had been collected, the congregation was asked to take a couple of minutes to say hello and greet the people around them. As this was winding down, Pastor Marks walked over to his small podium and said in a loud and enthusiastic voice, "Hello, Calvary Chapel 14:6. How are you?

"For those of you who are new here, I am Pastor Patrick Marks, the senior pastor here, and we at Calvary Chapel 14:6 sometimes use the biblical pronunciation for things, such as Yeshua for Jesus. It's not that we think we're better than anyone else—because we're not. It's because we think it's officially cool." And the whole congregation helped him say "officially cool."

"Again, if any of you are not familiar with Calvary Chapel churches, we go through the books of the Bible chapter by chapter and verse by verse. We don't leave anything out. We like to preach the whole council of God. We're not saying that topical preaching is wrong. It is not. We just want to make sure we don't miss anything God has to say to us."

Duke looked over at Hunter and nudged him. "I like this guy already."

"We're in the Book of Isaiah, and this last week, we finished up chapter 8. This morning, we'll see how far we get into chapter 9."

As Pastor Marks fleshed out the first part of Isaiah 9 with references to Revelation 19, verses 11 through 16, he said that right now, Jesus offers His right to rule as a choice. You can submit to His rulership voluntarily, but you don't have to. But Jesus is coming again, and this time, He will take His rightful rulership over everything. You will not have a choice. Every knee will bow. Everyone will submit to His rulership. So, it is better to choose to have Jesus rule over your life. Better to choose Him while you have a choice." Duke nudged Hunter again and smiled and gave him a big thumbs up.

After the service, Hunter and Susan introduced Duke to Pastor Marks. Hunter, Susan, and Duke then drove a short distance to a local after-church breakfast place called the Broken Putter. It is located on one of the golf courses in Sun City West.

While waiting for their order, the three discussed Pastor Mark's sermon. Duke said, "I guess Jesus is not going to be patient forever. He is eventually going to take charge."

"That's true," Susan said. "We're so glad you chose to have Jesus be the Lord of your life."

"Oh," Duke said, "me too. I really messed up big time while I was running my life all by myself."

In short order, breakfast showed up. The three prayed over the meals, and Duke thanked Hunter and Susan for inviting him to church. Susan told Duke that she believes Kimberly goes to Calvary Chapel Fountain Hills, which is a lot closer to him than Fourteen Six. Duke said that if Kimberly invites him, he may have to go to church with her. Susan told Duke that she was sure he would like Calvary Chapel Fountain Hills just as much as Fourteen Six.

Duke asked what the 14:6 meant. Susan told him that the 14:6 refers to the Book of John in the Bible, chapter 14, verse 6, where Jesus said, "I am the way and the truth and the life. No one comes to the Father except through me."

"That's a pretty straightforward statement," Duke said.

"That it is," Hunter said.

The three concentrated on eating for a couple of minutes, then Duke said, "Something I was going to tell you yesterday, Hunter, was that I got a call on Friday from my friend in Ketchikan, Detective Bob Blackhorn."

"Yeah?"

"He said that Arleen Simpson was cooperative but didn't know much. They could have charged her with something like conspiracy to kidnap or abduct, but there was so little evidence against her that they released her. Her husband, Ralph Simpson, was not cooperative until he was told he could be charged with first-degree murder. That changed his mind, and he told the detectives that he is part of a secret group in California that takes an active role in protecting the California wine industry.

"He and the guy who heads up this group, Grady Flanigan, hired Antone Gillespie and Wit Kraske, the other two people you and I helped arrest who were trying to stop your friends, the Poncetrans, from having their wine-tasting contest. Simpson said Gillespie and Kraske tried different things to encourage the Poncetrans to cancel their big wine event on the ship, but nothing worked. So, Simpson decided he would help them, and the three of them grabbed the Coolings, rendered them unconscious with liquid knock-out stuff, put life jackets on them, and tossed them into Glacier Bay. He said it was the perfect time to send a message, as just about everyone was out watching the glacier.

"Simpson claims they didn't mean for the Coolings to die, but, unfortunately, they did. He said, with the Coolings out of the picture, they were sure there was now not going to be any contest with California wines being compared with wines from other states. But when they learned that your friends were going to have the contest anyway with the Cooling's California wines, they realized that they had to really do something drastic to the Poncetrans. So, they planned an abduction of Scott and Catalina Poncetran. The plan was to chloroform them real good, drive them to a remote place, and leave them there without transportation back to the ship. The ship would leave without them and, bingo, no wine event."

"Thank God you guys were able to help stop them from carrying out their abduction plan," Susan said.

"Yeah, they could have murdered Scott and Catalina," Hunter said. "Too much chloroform can be fatal."

"It sure worked out," Duke said. "I guess we'll never know if God intervened in this in any way or not."

"Probably not on this side of heaven," Hunter said.

"And another thing," Duke said, "Simpson said that their secret little group was planning some big-time dirty tricks on some competing wineries, including wineries in other states.

"Is Blackhorn and his fellow detectives following up on this?"

"Yes, they're going to try."

"Well, good," Hunter said. "That may give the authorities the opportunity to stop something sinister before it even starts."

"Yes," Duke said. "Blackhorn may call me with an update tomorrow or Tuesday. If he does, I'll let you know."

"Yes. Absolutely."

The three finished their breakfast and headed home—the Kingsleys to Carefree and Duke to Scottsdale. It was a beautiful sunny day in the Phoenix area. It was 11:15 a.m., and the temperature was 83 degrees and the humidity 6 percent. The sky was that gorgeous deep dark blue that low humidity renders.

CHAPTER 69

Sunday, May 14, Afternoon

"Hello."

"Hi, Kimberly. It's Duke Rawlings."

"What a pleasant surprise. How are you doing this beautiful Sunday afternoon?"

"I'm just fine. In fact, I'm super fine."

"Great! I sense a joy in your voice that I haven't heard from you before."

"Yeah. I did it. I became a Christian. I'm a brand new Christian."

"Praise God! That is fantastic news. Hallelujah! I just want to crawl through the phone and come give you a big hug."

"You could come over if you want and give me that hug."

"What if you come over here? I'll give you that hug, then I'll take you riding, and when we get back, I'll cook you a big ol' cowboy steak with baked beans, coleslaw, and corn on the cob."

"I love it. I'm not so sure about the horse riding, but the dinner you're talking about is making me hungry. Give me your address, and I'll be right over."

"Okay. I'll text you the address and directions. And Duke…"

"Yes?"

"This is not an invitation to spend the night. I told you I'm an old-fashioned girl."

"I remember you said that, and I respect that. Don't you worry."

"Well, get on over here. Meantime, I'll get Rex and Rowdy saddled up and ready to go."

***

A little while later, Duke pulled up to Kimberly's ranch house on Palermo Avenue in Gold Canyon. Kimberly came out to meet him. "Here's your big hug," Kimberly said as she gave Duke a big squeeze.

"Oh, I like that," Duke said.

Kimberly released her hug and said, "You know, the horses are saddled up and ready, but first, I want to hear all about you coming into the fold—the faith. I thought it might happen eventually—I was praying it would—but wow, praise God!"

"Yeah, crazy. It just sort of happened—yesterday—after golf with Hunter and over at my house. We got to talking about God. I told Hunter and God about some of the things in the past I have done that I am sorry for. I asked God to forgive me, and I asked Jesus to come into my life and be my Lord and Savior. Then, I even got baptized. Hunter baptized me in my pool."

"Oh, that makes me so happy. I am so filled with joy for you. I hope and pray this is genuine and you just didn't get caught up in the moment. You know, here today and gone tomorrow."

"No. I really feel it is genuine. I think I've been yearning in the back of my mind, in the back of my heart, for God for quite some time."

Suddenly, Kimberly started crying—a lot.

"Are you all right?" Duke asked.

"Yes, I'm fine. I'm just overwhelmed with joy. With joy for you. Now, no matter what happens with us, we will both be in heaven forever." Kimberly found a tissue and dried her eyes and said, "You ready to go riding, cowboy?"

Kimberly had Duke ride Rex, and she rode Rowdy. Duke did well for a first-time rider and seemed to enjoy it. Dinner was great, and after a little post-dinner conversation, Kimberly walked Duke to his Expedition. There, they kissed for the first time. It was a great kiss.

CHAPTER 70

Monday, May 15, 9:00 a.m.
Hunter Kingsley's Accountability Group
Calvary Chapel 14:6

Hunter is in an accountability group of seven men from Calvary Chapel 14:6 who meet every Monday morning at 9:00 a.m. at the church. They usually sit outdoors under a big sissoo tree in the back of the church unless the weather makes the indoors the better choice. To encourage complete openness, one of the strict rules of the group is that nothing of a personal nature that is discussed in the group goes outside the group. Dave is the leader or moderator of the group, and the normal routine is for each man to do a one or two-minute check-in. Then, if anyone has any burning issues or anything else they want to bring up, those items are discussed. If no issues are brought up, then Dave usually goes through a prepared spiritual lesson. The group adjourns promptly at 10:30, if not before.

Hunter had a burning issue.

"Greetings, brothers," leader Dave said. "Welcome to another great Monday morning. Lord, we ask you to bless our time together this morning, and we pray for wisdom and discernment to prevail in our discussions.

"Okay, let's go around the circle and do our one or two-minute check-in. Tell us how it's going with you spiritually, physically, relationally, and personally." Each man, in turn, checked in. When they were finished, Dave prayed. "Lord, we ask that You continue to help and watch over each one of us as we strive to grow and become the man You want us to be. Amen.

"Hunter here told me he is struggling with a situation or dilemma he would like to present to the group. That's all I know. So, Hunter, go ahead."

"In a nutshell, there is a person I encouraged to become a Christian, and I told him that to do so, he needed to repent of his sins and accept Jesus Christ into his life. His hang-up about becoming a Christian was that he had done some terrible things in his life, and he didn't think God would forgive him. I told him there was no sin—except the sin of unbelief—that God wouldn't forgive. He promptly told me, in confidence and before God, that one of the most egregious sins he had committed was that he had paid a person to arrange for his wife to be killed in a car accident. I knew his wife, and I know for a fact that she was killed in a car accident, and no foul play was suspected by the police or anyone else.

"So now I know a person who committed a very serious crime, and the law enforcement part of me feels obligated to report this to the authorities. On the other hand, this person just told God, in my presence, that he repented of his sins, including arranging for the murder of his wife, and he accepted Christ into his life. And I don't think he would have done this had I not told him that there is no sin God wouldn't forgive.

"My first inclination in pondering this situation was that, legally, I have an obligation to report this to the authorities. However, after looking into it, there apparently is no legal requirement to report a crime confessed to me. There is not even a requirement to report a crime that I am a witness to. Now, there are exceptions, like if you're a mandatory reporter and you witness or are told of sexual abuse, child abuse, or elder abuse, and so forth.

"So, I am now privy to a murder for hire, and I know who did the hiring, but under the law, I don't have to report it. Good. That prevents what could have been a real dilemma for me. However, morally, the issue is still not settled in my mind. There's something in me that says there should be some sort of consequence for such an act. King David had Uriah killed, and God forgave him for that, but God still meted out a consequence or punishment for that heinous act.

"I know God has forgiven this person, but do I tell the authorities even though I'm not obligated to? Do I need to try to help God measure out a consequence for this act, if He is so inclined, by alerting law enforcement authorities about this? Or should I hold this secret inside of me, like the person asked me to, and go on my merry way and let God deal with it however He wants?"

"It's a no-brainer to me," Jamal said. "Let God handle it. He will hand out a punishment or a consequence if He wants."

"Maybe God already has given your friend a consequence," Phillip said.

"That's possible," Brad said. "Possibly, God has already allowed some sort of consequence to befall your friend. Maybe the anguish he has gone through in realizing the terrible thing he has done is consequence enough."

"Wait a minute," Jamal said, "we might be thinking too much in Old Testament terms, an eye for an eye mentality. God is a forgiving God. He forgives the sins of the repentant. I'm not sure there is any requirement of a consequence or punishment for every one of our sins. If there were, I'd be receiving consequences on a daily basis."

"I'm looking on my phone," Juan said, "and I just pulled this up from a Christian website. Romans 6:23 says, 'for the wages of sin is death.' So that's definitely a punishment for sin. But the second part of 6:23 says, 'but the gift of God is eternal life in Christ Jesus our Lord.' So, paraphrasing, this article says that God poured out the punishment for sin upon Jesus. And it says that, therefore, for those who accept Jesus as Lord and Savior, the punishment for sin is taken care of."

"Amen," Brad and Dave both said.

"And," Juan continued, "the article goes on to say that even though we Christians no longer receive punishment for sin, God still sometimes disciplines us as a correction, as a parent would correct a child. Also, the article says there are also societal or earthly consequences of sin which may result in jail time and so forth."

"Yeah," John said, "as an attorney, although not a criminal attorney, I can confirm what you, Hunter, found out from the internet: there is no legal requirement for you to report the crime, as heinous as it is, to any government authority. And, as a Christian, I personally don't think I'd repeat something told in confidence. It would be considered hearsay anyway, not direct evidence. In Christian circles, it might also be considered telling or spreading a rumor. At least that's the way I see it."

"This is not the same dilemma as a person telling you they are going to kill someone," Phillip said. "In that case, you could possibly prevent a murder by alerting the authorities. In your case, Hunter, the killing has already taken place, and it sounds like your confessor is not likely to do that again."

"You know, guys," Hunter said, "I think I have a good idea of what I should do, thanks to our discussion here. I think the best thing for me to do is to talk to the person in question and suggest that he consider going to the authorities on his own recognizance."

"Out of all of the things you could do," Jamal said, "besides doing nothing, I also think that is the best thing for you to do."

"What do the rest of you guys think?" Hunter asked.

The rest of the men responded in the affirmative. John suggested that Hunter make sure he doesn't come across as condemning when he brings up the idea of his friend turning himself in. Hunter agreed. The group discussed another minor situation one of the gentlemen brought up, prayed for each other, and adjourned.

CHAPTER 71

Monday, May 15, Afternoon
East Ridgeline Road, Carefree, Arizona

"Hello."

"Hey, Hunter, it's Duke."

"Hey, what's up, my brother?"

"Three things. One—how about golf Wednesday morning? I was checking around and was able to get a tee time of 9:06 at Boulders Golf Club South Course. That's near you."

"Okay, yeah, I can play Wednesday."

"Good. I took a chance and went ahead and booked it. Since I'm new to the Phoenix area, I'm checking out all the different golf courses around here. There are a lot of golf courses. Phoenix is like golf heaven."

"It is."

"Since the course is near your house, why don't I pick you up? Say 8:15."

"That's fine. Zero eight fifteen it is."

"That takes care of number one. Number two is—we haven't discussed our partnership yet with you as a PI and me helping whenever you need me. We were going to Saturday after golf, but something else happened instead."

"That's right. An awesome and fantastic event took place. You became a believer."

"So, maybe we can talk about your private eye business after golf this time."

"Let's do."

"And thirdly, I just got a call from Bob Blackhorn—my buddy in the Ketchikan Police Department. He said our little four-person arrest the other day is getting national attention."

"Yeah, bad boys Gillespie and Kraske are persons of interest with the FBI."

"Yes, that, but also now the Park Police are involved. The National Park Service just sent two Special Agents of the National Park Service Investigative Services Branch to investigate the murders of Ed and Joyce Cooling in Glacier Bay. Glacier Bay is a National Park, and, therefore, the feds have concurrent jurisdiction regarding any crimes committed in a National Park."

"I'm not surprised. I've run into overlapping jurisdictional issues before, and that's not necessarily a bad thing."

"No. Blackhorn thinks it is mostly a good thing. He said their investigation is essentially done, and even though the feds might try to take some of the credit, a little national attention to the case may shine a good light on the Ketchikan Police Department."

"That would be all right. They're good people. They deserve a little notoriety."

"Bob said that Ralph Simpson, once he realized he was in deep kimchi, gave them enough information to make a decent case against Gillespie and Kraske. He also gave them enough information—names and so forth—to have someone take a serious look at this secret militant protect California wine group he is a part of."

"Excellent."

"The bummer is that Blackhorn contacted the Napa Police Department in California with the information, and they basically weren't interested. Well, more correctly, it wasn't that they weren't interested—the lieutenant that Bob talked to said that the Attorney General in California has severely restricted some of the things that

California police departments can do—like investigating or making inquiries into something like this might be considered harassment and performing undo diligence."

"What? That's crazy!"

"Yeah, Bob couldn't believe it either. Bob said he then called the California Department of Consumer Affairs as he knew that they had a fraud unit and had jurisdiction over such things. They weren't interested either."

"I'm afraid California is becoming a crime-friendly state. That's part of why Susan and I left. It's still a beautiful state, but very sad things are happening there."

"Yeah, I know you said you and your wife hated to leave, but things were just getting too looney tunes."

"Exactly."

"So, that's all I have. You got anything?"

"Not prying—just curious—have you seen Kimberly since Saturday?

"Yep."

"Things good?"

"Yep, very good."

"That's all I have then. See you at 0815 hours on Wednesday. Do you know how to get here?"

"I've got your address. I'll find it."

"I know you will."

CHAPTER 72

Wednesday, May 17
Boulders Golf Club
Carefree, Arizona

Hunter and Duke walked off the 18th green at Boulders South course a few minutes past one o'clock in the afternoon.

"Great game, Hunter," Duke said as they climbed in their golf cart to drop their clubs off at Duke's Expedition.

"The two gentlemen they paired us up with were interesting."

"Yes, I don't think they are Christians, though."

"You're right. And you do start to notice things like that. Nothing has to be said—you don't have to ask—but you know. Not judging or condemning. Just an observation."

"Yeah, I never noticed before, but now I do. Unless they cuss up a storm or get mad and go off in a tirade, it's just little things that indicate they're probably not a believer."

"When I figure someone's not a believer, I usually say a little silent prayer for an opportunity to uplift God and share the gospel. If that doesn't happen, then, later, I usually pray for their salvation."

"I like that. I think I'll start doing that, although I don't feel I'm equipped to start sharing the gospel yet."

"You might be pleasantly surprised. The gospel might just naturally come flowing out of your mouth. But I'd say, don't push it. Remember how you probably felt around an overzealous Christian."

"Got it. Hey, you want to grab a beer and some lunch?"

"Sounds like a plan."

Duke and Hunter turned their golf cart in and walked over to the Grill Restaurant and Bar and snagged an outside table by the railing overlooking the 18th fairway. They each ordered a Coors Light—a no-brainer for Duke. Duke also ordered the prime rib dip, and Hunter asked for the Sonoran fish tacos.

"So, Hunter, let's talk about your PI business. I'm excited about it."

"Me too. I've been researching it more. I think I want to make it official—get my license and whatever else is necessary—but I don't want it to be a full-time job. I don't see the need to have a commercial office as I have a computer and office at home. That should suffice. I don't see the need for a lot of advertising, either. Actually, none, just word of mouth. Just like you do, Mr. Available, right? Word of mouth?"

"Right. I already have contacts and a reputation in certain circles that generates occasional jobs for me. Some of the types of jobs that come up are better done with a reliable partner."

"Good. I know you're probably never going to tell me the whole story of just exactly what all 'Mr. Available' does."

"Mostly the 'Mr. Available' thing is a bluff. To some people, it might imply that I operate like the mafia and break kneecaps and eliminate people, but other than my mercenary days in Afghanistan and other places where it was kill or be killed, I don't use those methods. I do occasionally use intimidation techniques to get the desired results for my clients, but no mafia-type methods, except the one time with my wife, who turned out to be a murderer. Having her set up to be killed in an auto accident was, I admit, a mafia-type operation. That was way out of bounds for me, believe it or not, and I am truly sorry I resorted to such a terrible thing.

"If I could undo it, I would, in a heartbeat. I truly believe God has forgiven me for that and all my sins. But, nevertheless, I'm starting to feel I need to go to the Colorado State Patrol and set the record straight on what really caused the vehicle accident my wife died in."

"Are you talking about turning yourself in?"

"Well, yes, maybe. At least, I'm thinking about it."

"Doing that, I think, would help free yourself of this lingering remorse you say you have. If you do decide to turn yourself in, which I think would be a good thing, I would go with you if you want."

"Thanks, Hunter, I appreciate that. I'm not sure I'm going to do it. I'm concerned about the consequence—prison time."

"Yes. That's a real possibility."

"I may have to do this to get totally right with God."

"You're already totally right with God. You're talking about getting right with your fellow man and his laws."

"Yeah, you're right. Thanks for the clarity."

"Well, anyway, getting back to PI work and operating above board, you're a Christian, and now I'm a Christian. You're concerned about ethics and morals and operating in a way that would, hopefully, be pleasing to God."

"Exactly. And you have brought up an interesting dilemma. How do you get certain worthy things accomplished in a fallen world? A world that exerts strong pressure on you to compromise certain of your moral mandates.

"Telling a lie is a sin. God hates lying. He doesn't hate the liar. He hates the lie—the sin. During World War II, in Germany and the occupied countries, many Christians—many devout Christians—hid Jews in their homes. A lot of these Christians would rather die than tell a lie. But when the Gestapo came to their door and asked if they were harboring any Jews, they said 'no,' and they had to say 'no' with conviction.

"And, that's the point—under the circumstances, in a fallen world—sometimes you have to choose which is the greater good, which is the higher moral consideration. These World War II Christians realized that saving the life of a human being is a higher moral calling than not telling a lie, as bad as lying is, and as much as God abhors it."

"Yeah, absolutely," Duke replied.

"The Gideons and other Christian groups smuggle Bibles into countries that forbid Bibles under penalty of death. They obviously feel that helping save a few people for eternity in heaven is a higher good—a higher calling—than not breaking smuggling laws. In the Secret Service, as in other law enforcement agencies, undercover operations in order to get the evidence on and arrest bad guys so they wouldn't harm or kill people always involved lying—representing yourself as someone you are not—and so forth."

"I understand," Duke said. "One of the things I have done is to go into Afghanistan and help extract Christians, who, if found out and located, would be executed on the spot. That involved a lot of compromising of who I was and what I was doing, and so forth—big-time lying."

"Well, there you go. And I applaud you for your Afghanistan incursions to rescue those people."

"Yeah, thanks. But now that I'm a Christian, I'm going to be taking this lying situation a little more seriously."

"And well you should."

"So, when does the Kingsley Detective Agency officially start?"

"I'm thinking this Monday, May 22."

"Really. You've got something in the works already?"

"Some unfinished business. I thought about what your friend, Lieutenant Blackhorn, said about trying to alert the Napa Valley Police Department to the dirty tricks Simpson's secret wine group apparently has planned. They already used a number of dirty tricks to try to stop my friends, the Poncetrans, from having their big wine-tasting event. Two people were murdered as a result. Something has to be done to stop any further dirty tricks."

"You have something in mind?"

"Yes, I do. I think we call in the United States Rangers."

"The United States Rangers?"

"Yes, the U.S. Rangers."

"I know about the U.S. Marshalls. I know about the U.S. Army Rangers. And I know about the Texas Rangers of the Texas Department of Public Safety. But I've never heard of the U.S. Rangers. Is there such an outfit?"

"There is if you're willing to do something a little daring—a little bizarre—in the name of justice."

"You and I are the U.S. Rangers?"

"That's right. If it were only me, I'd be the lone ranger. But with the two of us, we're the United States Rangers."

"Okay. I guess I can go along with that."

"You gotta be all in," Hunter said. "You gotta play it to the hilt."

"Yeah, I got ya. Let's do it. But what about the PI work?"

"This is a division of the PI work. Once in a while, the U.S. Rangers may have to be called into action."

"So, what's the plan?"

"Thanks to Simpson singing like a canary, we have the names and wineries of all the people in that secret Napa Valley wine group from your buddy Bob Blackhorn. So, Monday, the U.S. Rangers take a drive to these wineries and put a little pressure on these secret wine group members. But first, we'll have to go shopping at some tactical and military surplus stores. How about tomorrow morning I pick you up and we get our U.S. Rangers uniforms and equipment? You open for that?"

"Listen, whatever we have to do, if I have anything going, I'll cancel it. I'm looking forward to this. I'm all in. This is my kind of mission."

CHAPTER 73

Thursday, May 18

At 0945 hours, Hunter picked up Duke, and they drove to 5.11 Tactical on East Thomas Road in Phoenix. Sanctuary Tactical in Cave Creek was closer to home, but 5.11 Tactical was close to Tombstone Tactical on North Metro Parkway. So, if one store didn't have what they needed or the right size, they could go to the other store. Plus, Tombstone Tactical also had guns and ammo, as did Shooters World, which was also close by.

Hunter drove to 5.11 Tactical first. He was a big fan of 5.11 clothes, especially the cargo pants. Hunter had decided that the best color in outerwear for what they were going to do was black. Black everything.

On the way over, Hunter gave Duke the low down on everything he figured they needed. He said they should have similar-looking uniforms and equipment so it looks like everything was issued, like the military and some police departments do. "Do you happen to have a black Glock 17?" Hunter asked Duke.

"I do. It's one of my better handguns."

"Good. We're on the same page there. Neither of us will have to purchase a gun."

Between the 5.11 and Tombstone Tactical stores, Hunter and Duke acquired everything they needed. That included 5.11 Stryke Point cargo pants, police-type short-sleeve button-up shirts, tactical Kevlar vests, pants, belts, and duty belts and keepers to keep the duty belt attached to the pants belt. They also purchased Glock 17 Hi Ride duty belt holsters, magazine pouches, Peerless black handcuffs and cases and keys, pepper sprays and holders, 5.11 Tactical 8-inch side zip duty boots, and Gatorz Spector Model high-performance black sunglasses.

The entire shopping spree took a little over three hours. As Hunter and Duke were loading up Hunter's Ford Edge with their newly purchased equipment, Duke said, "Something we don't have that would make us look more official are badges. We would be more believable if we had some sort of badges."

"We should have them tomorrow. After I talked to you Monday, I went online and ordered two silver badges that look similar to the Texas Rangers badges, known as the star-in-the-wheel badges. On the wheel, ours will read, 'UNITED STATES RANGERS,' and on the banners at the top and the bottom of the star, they will read, 'SPECIAL AGENT.' I designed them myself. I also ordered black baseball caps for us that read, 'U.S. RANGERS.'"

"That should top us off just fine."

"Literally."

On the way back to Duke's house, Hunter and Duke stopped at the Citizen Public House on 5th Avenue in Old Town Scottsdale. After lunch, they drove to Duke's house, and Duke invited Hunter in for a Coors. They sat down in the shade on the back patio.

"So, Hunter, how well have you planned out our little sojourn into deepest, darkest California?"

"I've got the basics and the logistics planned." Hunter pulled out his day-timer and referred to it. We leave here on Monday, May 22, at 1155 hours on Southwest flight 3619 nonstop to Sacramento. Our Glocks will be unloaded in a locked case in our checked baggage—ammo separate. Upon arrival in Sacramento, we walk over to Hertz and rent a black Chevrolet Suburban that's reserved for us and drive four miles to the Hyatt House in Natomas, the suburb in which I used to live. We relax for the rest of the day.

"We get up very early the next day, put on our U.S. Rangers uniform, but without the badge and the duty belt and the Rangers ball cap. We are still civilians until we get to Napa Valley. We also have to have our handguns still in the locked cases, unloaded, and separate from the ammunition. That's California law.

"When we get to Napa, we'll have breakfast, after which we will become Rangers by putting on our duty belts and equipment and pinning on our badges."

"Where?"

"I don't know yet. I still have to work on that, along with who we see first and second and so forth. This is also where we switch plates on our SUV. I have old inactive U.S. Government license plates to put on. We also load our magazines and Glocks to capacity. I don't know if you know this, but California has a law that you are only allowed to have a total of ten rounds in your magazines and weapons."

"Are you serious? That doesn't make any sense. That's about the silliest thing I've ever heard of."

"I know. The bad guys aren't going to comply with this, so it puts the good guys, who comply with the law, at a serious disadvantage."

"That is just so crazy."

"It's California. What can I say? We won't comply with it, of course. In the remote possibility that we have to defend ourselves, we want to have all seventeen rounds in our mags with one round in the chamber."

"For sure."

"Besides, if we get arrested for something, we're already going to be in trouble for impersonating law enforcement officers."

"Right."

"So, anyway, as soon as we're all set, we go visit our customers. As soon as we're done, we take off our badges, unload our weapons and put them back in the cases and lock them, switch the license plates back, and become civilians again in full compliance with the law."

"What are we going to say to these yahoos—these customers?"

"It probably doesn't matter that much what we tell or say to them. It probably doesn't even matter that much if they believe we are legit law enforcement agents or not. Just by showing up and confronting them will let them know that we are on to them and are going to be keeping an eye on them. I think that will stop them from trying any more shenanigans."

"I think they are going to believe that we are some kind of legit government law enforcement agency."

"I do, too. If they try to inquire about our legitimacy, they, of course, won't find anyone to confirm that we are legit, and that will probably add to their concern and fear. The fact that other government agencies deny our existence may make us even more mysterious and believable.

"So, we go to Napa Valley, talk to a few people, and come home."

"Right. I booked us on a Southwest flight leaving Sacramento at 0930 on Wednesday, May 24th. We could try to come back Tuesday, but it is probably better to spend another night in Sacramento. I think Tuesday is going to turn out to be a long day, so why push it."

"Yeah, I'm sure. I'm looking forward to it. Like you said, it's a little daring, but that makes life interesting."

"Well, I'll take my last sip of beer to that—making life interesting." With that, Hunter left Duke's house and drove home.

Susan was by the pool and was talking to friends of theirs from Sacramento. She put her hand over the phone and said, "Honey, it's Fran and Bill from Sacramento. Should I tell them you're going to be in their neck of the woods next week?"

"No. It's black ops."

CHAPTER 74

Hunter went into the house, changed into his swimming trunks, came back out, and started swimming laps. When he was done, he plopped down in one of the lounge chairs and popped open the zero-sugar cherry Dr.Pepper he had brought out from the kitchen. A few minutes later, Susan finished her chat with Fran in Sacramento and put the phone down. She looked at Hunter and said, "What do you mean 'black ops'? I thought you were just going to talk to the people in the secret wine group and let them know that the authorities are on to them."

"That's exactly what we're going to do."

"So why do you say it's a black operation? What's the black part about it that I don't think you mentioned?"

"The only black part is that when Duke and I talk to these people, we're going to do it in uniform as law enforcement officers."

"But you're not a law enforcement officer anymore, and Duke is not one either."

"That's the black part."

"Did you pray about this?"

"You and I both prayed about it."

"I know, but the black ops part was not mentioned."

"I prayed about that part later."

"So, what did God say?"

"He said, 'You're on your own.'"

"God said, 'You're on your own'? He said that?"

"No, no. I'm kidding. It was a joke."

"What did He say? What did God tell you?"

"He didn't say anything in particular. He gave me a peace about it. It's sort of like Charlie and Stephanie. When they went to Vietnam for those five years with Wycliffe, they did some black ops and unauthorized things in order to get Bibles translated and into the hands of people who didn't have Bibles in their native language. They said that God gave them a peace about the whole thing."

"I remember. I just don't want you to get in any trouble."

"I know. Thanks. It could happen, but I think we'll be all right."

"Yes. You're trying to do a good thing. I feel the Lord will be with you."

"I think so. I pray so... It's about time to be thinking about dinner. I'm thinking it's time for salmon on the grill, some steamed or grilled Brussels sprouts, and baked potatoes with sour cream and chives."

"That sounds good," Susan said. And that's what they had—outdoors on the patio as they watched the sunset over the mountains.

CHAPTER 75

Sunday, May 21

Kimberly did invite Duke to her church. Duke picked her up at her house and drove to Calvary Chapel Fountain Hills for the ten o'clock service. They arrived about ten minutes before service time and found two seats on the right near the front. Duke looked around, and Kimberly said, "This church isn't near as big as Calvary Chapel 14:6, but it's a good group, and I think you'll like the pastor."

"I really liked the pastor at 14:6."

"Calvary 14:6 is a good solid church with a good solid pastor. I've been there a few times. Calvary Fountain Hills hasn't been around as long. It was started in 2011 by our pastor, Pastor Rick Ponzo. The important thing is that you go to a church which preaches the word of God, as there are a few so-called churches that don't."

At ten o'clock, the praise and worship music started. About twenty minutes later, there was prayer, an offering, announcements, and a quick meet and greet with the people nearby. Pastor Rick then walked up, prayed again, and began the sermon.

Pastor Rick had just started a new series in the Book of Romans two weeks before. Today's message would cover Romans chapter 1, verses 18 to 23. At the end of the service, Kimberly introduced Duke to Pastor Rick and a few other people. They then jumped into Duke's Expedition and drove a little less than two miles to the

Saddle Bronc Grill on Saguaro Boulevard.

It was immediately apparent to Duke why Kimberly liked the Saddle Bronc. It was a heavily themed cowboy and cowgirl eatery. The full-sized metal statue of a cowboy on a bucking bronco near the entrance was a clue. More and more, Duke was realizing that Kimberly was a cowgirl at heart.

The restaurant was crowded, but they managed to find a barstool table near a window. They each ordered a craft beer and barbeque lunch. The conversation began with a discussion of Pastor Rick's sermon. "'So that men are without excuse,'" Duke said. "Boy, that statement really got to me. All the time I was not a believer, I was without excuse."

"Yes," Kimberly said. "Eye-opening, isn't it? 'The wrath of God is being revealed from heaven against all the godlessness and wickedness of men who suppress the truth by their wickedness, since what may be known about God is plain to them, because God has made it plain to them. For since the creation of the world God's invisible qualities—his eternal power and divine nature—have been clearly seen, being understood from what has been made, so that men are without excuse.'"

"You memorized that word for word, didn't you?"

"Yes, Romans chapter 1, verses 18, 19, and 20. I'm not that well versed in the Bible, but I have memorized certain passages over the years that have really spoken to me."

"'So that men are without excuse.' Is that the part that spoke to you, like it did to me?" Duke asked.

"Yes, it is."

"Tell me about it."

"Okay, but not the long version. Maybe another time for the long version. But the short version is something like what happened to you. One day, something just hit me, and I realized I was on the wrong horse."

Duke started laughing and couldn't stop. Kimberly started

laughing at Duke's inability to stop laughing. Eventually, they got their laughter under control, and Kimberly asked Duke what he was laughing at.

"I was laughing at the way you sometimes put things. You said you realized you were on the wrong horse. Only a cowgirl like you would have put it that way. Most people would have said they realized they were on the wrong road or something like that. But you—you realized you were on the wrong horse. It just hit me as very funny—cute and very funny."

"I guess I'm just a horse-minded person."

"You are, and I love it. It's cute—charming in a Western sort of way."

"Thanks. You know, with a name like Duke, I think you need to have more Western in you. John Wayne was called 'the Duke.' You're a John Wayne type. I'm surprised you had never ridden a horse until the other day."

Duke feigned a Western drawl. "Well, ma'am, I sure did like riding your horse."

"Good. I'm going to teach you everything I know about horse riding if you're game."

"Oh, yes, ma'am. I'd be much obliged."

"Speaking of the West, you're heading west tomorrow—you and Hunter—on some kind of mission that you won't say much about. Sounds exciting."

"When we get back, I'll tell you all about it."

"Good. I'll look forward to it. I'll have you over for another Western-style cookout."

"Ma'am, you got a deal."

CHAPTER 76

Monday, May 22

At 0915 hours, Hunter picked up Duke, and they drove to Sky Harbor Airport in Phoenix. Hunter parked his SUV in the East Economy parking garage just east of terminal four. They retrieved their bags, walked a short distance to the tram, got off at terminal four, then walked over to the Southwest Airlines counter and handed off their bags with the properly stowed handguns and ammo.

Hunter and Duke then went through the security screening. Duke made it through just fine. Hunter's carry-on was pulled aside and checked. Hunter stood as close as he could and watched. The TSA lady looked at the duty belt, equipment, and the U.S. Rangers badge, looked up at Hunter, and said, "You should have told us you were law enforcement."

"You're right," Hunter said, "I should have, but I just wanted to feel totally off duty."

"I understand. Have a good day."

As Hunter and Duke sat waiting for their flight, Duke said, "I hope our pieces don't get lifted. I know that's how we have to transport our weapons—in our checked bags—but I've heard of firearms being stolen out of checked bags by not-so-honest baggage handlers."

"Yeah, I know that has happened. We did the best we could. Our pieces are locked in their cases, and we put stickers on them warning that there are tracking devices inside. If they do get lifted, our backup is a buddy of mine in Sacramento who has a handgun collection. He'll loan us whatever he's got."

"Good to have a backup plan."

"It is. I have thought up backup plans for some of the things we're going to do, but not for everything."

Hunter and Duke boarded the plane and had an uneventful flight to Sacramento. As is not unusual with Southwest Airlines, one of the flight attendants had some particularly good comments and jokes at the beginning and end of the flight. After landing, Hunter and Duke hurried directly to the baggage claim area and waited at the beginning of the conveyor belt for their bags. They grabbed the bags right away and took them to the side and opened them to make sure their weapons and equipment were still there. They were.

The two then went over to Hertz and rented their reserved black Chevrolet Suburban. They drove to the Hyatt House, checked in, unpacked, and readied their stuff for tomorrow.

Since they didn't have a chance to have a real lunch, they were hungry early. Hunter took Duke to the Grange restaurant in downtown Sacramento, near the state capital building. They were seated, and a friend of Hunter's came over to their table to wait on them.

"Duke, this is a friend of mine, Clint Hostetler. Clint, meet Duke Rawlings, a more recent friend. The two shook hands, and Duke sat back down. "Clint and I used to go to the same church, Calvary Chapel Natomas, until I moved to Arizona. Clint, Duke here is a new Christian."

Clint smiled and said, "Welcome to the fold, Duke. There's always room for one more."

Duke smiled and said, "Thanks."

"Hey," Clint said, "you were just on that wine cruise our sommelier, Reggi Narito, was on, weren't you?"

"Yes," Hunter said, "in fact, both of us were, except Duke wasn't part of the wine lovers group."

"So, what brings you back to your old stomping grounds?" Clint asked Hunter.

"We're on a mission. We're operating incognito," Hunter said as he stared straight at Clint.

"Okay. I've got you, man."

"Are there any assemblymen or senators here tonight?" Hunter asked.

"There's a few that I recognize. Do you want me to introduce you to some of them?"

"No, not if you don't want to cause a ruckus."

Clint looked at Duke and said, "Rumor has it that some of the silly laws that California enacts are the result of what has become known as the three-martini lunch by some of the senators and assemblymen. Have you ever had the privilege of living in California, Duke?"

"No, I can't say that I have. Have I missed anything?"

"Insanity."

"I'm beginning to get that impression."

"So, Clint, why don't you move—get out of the insanity like Susan and I did?"

"Dannielle and I are seriously looking into it. We've been looking at Idaho."

"Why don't you move to Arizona like Duke and I did? You're welcome there."

"Too hot."

"Too hot? It's only hot nine months out of the year."

"I thought it was just three months."

"It is. I was just kidding about the nine months."

"I'd better get going. I see my boss looking this way. Here are your menus. Do you want me to send Reggie over to suggest some wines?"

"Yes, mainly to say 'hello.' We have an early get-up tomorrow, so we may not even order any."

Hunter and Duke had a great meal, each with a four-ounce glass of excellent wine, and then they went back to the hotel and turned in. It was only 2100 hours.

CHAPTER 77

Tuesday, May 23

At 0400 hours, Hunter woke up and shut off his alarm, which was set for 0415. For some reason, Hunter thought and talked in military time when he first started thinking about the mission. It seemed like the natural thing to do. Duke fell right in line with it, too.

Hunter shaved and showered, after which Duke did the same. They dressed in their black uniforms, which didn't look much like uniforms without any rank or badge or patches. They loaded the black monster SUV with everything in case they didn't come back to the hotel that night. One of Hunter's axioms: keep your options open.

They jumped in the black monster and headed for Highway 80 toward San Francisco. (When Hunter was in the Secret Service, the agents got to calling the presidential limo the beast or black beast. Duke called their rented SUV the black monster, so Hunter went with it. Same idea, he thought, mean and bad.) Duke was at the wheel, and it was only 0515 when they merged onto the freeway, but rush hour traffic was already building.

After not quite fifty miles, they took exit 39 B onto Highway 12 toward Napa. A few miles later, they took a right onto 221, then left onto 121, which is also called West Imola Avenue. They stopped at the Chevron station there at the intersection and topped off their gas-guzzling SUV. They went on down the road a few blocks and turned into the parking area for Emmy Lou's Dinner at 1429 West Imola Avenue and parked near the entrance.

They were now officially hungry. They waited a few minutes until they saw someone unlock the front door, then walked in. They were seated, ordered, ate, and paid with cash, as they had at the gas station, and left.

They pulled around to the back of the shopping area the restaurant was part of and found a secluded spot and parked. First, they put their Kevlar vests on under their shirts, tucked their shirts back in, and attached their silver U.S. Rangers badges in the proper place on their shirts. Next, they buckled their duty belts with all their equipment around their waists and secured them to their pants belts with the keepers. After that, they loaded their magazines with seventeen rounds of 9-millimeter jacketed hollow point ammunition. They inserted one of their loaded magazines into their Glock 17s and racked the slides back to chamber a round. They then took the magazines back out of their weapons, replaced the round now in the chamber of their Glocks with a new round in the magazine, and then reinserted the magazine into the hand grip of their handguns. As Hunter always liked to say, "No sense in having a seventeen-round magazine with only sixteen rounds." Finally, they each donned their black baseball caps that read "U.S. Rangers" and looked each other over.

"What else?" Duke asked.

"I think that's it. Can you think of anything else?"

"Maybe, in hindsight, some arm patches would have been nice."

"Maybe, but I think we're good. We have a good, clean, mean, no-frills look that says we mean business."

"All right then. Let's do this thing. Where to first?"

"Let's get in—or should I say, mount up. I have to look at my list and directions."

Duke mounted the driver's seat again so Hunter could navigate. "I've got the visits laid out here in the order that we'll come to them. First off, we go to the Winemeister Winery off Road 121. I've got a map and directions, and as a backup, I'll have my phone give us directions also. I'd rather not use the vehicle's navigation system."

"Right, just in case. Winemeister is obviously German. What's the low down on this guy?"

"The owner's name is Hans Schumacher."

"Now, it doesn't get any more German than that."

"You got that right. The code name he used in the secret group was Dingo. It looks like he has a fairly small winery. A midget among the big boys. He may not even have a tasting room. Not all wineries are open to the public."

A few minutes later, Siri, the lady who lives in Hunter's iPhone, had them turn off the paved road and drive up a dusty dirt road. There was a small sign at the turnoff, which indicated the Winemeister Winery was up ahead. The road ended at a clapboard two-story house that was in need of a paint job. To the right of the house, about a hundred yards, was a yellow metal building, in far better shape than the house, with a sign over the slider door that read "Winemeister Winery."

Duke drove over to the yellow metal building and parked a few yards from the door. A long-haired man, thinning on top, about five feet six inches tall, in a plaid shirt, emerged from inside the building. He stopped and stared at the black monster while wiping his hands on some sort of shop apron.

Hunter and Duke opened their doors at the same time and walked over to the man while staying four or five feet apart from each other. They stopped a little more than arms-length in front of the man while maintaining their separation from each other. The man said, "Can I help you officers with something?"

Hunter spoke. "Are you Hans Schumacher?"

"I am. Yes, sir, I am."

"Are you the owner of this winery?"

"Yes. I—I don't do a lot of business. I supply a few local stores with wine, bottle some for friends, and so forth, and sell some to the few customers that drive up. We're not on the wine maps. It's mainly a hobby with us—with me and my wife."

"Do you belong to the PCW—the Protect California Wine organization?"

"Yes, I do—we do. Is there a problem?"

"Do you participate with a few others from the PCW in a secret little group who want to take action to discredit other wineries—local wineries and wineries from out of state?"

Schumacher looked down at the ground, shuffled his feet, looked back up, and said, "No, I don't belong to any such group. I've never even heard of such a group."

"Are you sure about that, Dingo?"

Schumacher's face dropped. In fact, his whole body lost countenance. "I'm not going to be a part of that group anymore. They started out with good intentions but then started talking about doing some things that I thought were out of line. I know they hired a guy to keep some wine cruiser dude from having a taste test to undermine our California wines. I went along with it, but then I understand that things got out of hand, and some people drowned in the ocean—actually, in Glacier Bay up in Alaska. Yeah, I want no part of that. I'm done with that group."

"Well, that's good to hear," Hunter said. "Accessory to murder is not a charge to be taken lightly." Hunter nodded his head and said, "You take care now. We, or some of the locals, may come back and talk to you down the road."

Hunter turned and walked back to the SUV. Duke stayed, facing Schumacher. When Hunter had reached the passenger door of the black monster, he turned back and faced Schumacher from behind the door. Duke then gave Hans a double-fingered salute from the bill of his cap, turned and walked back to the Suburban, climbed into the driver's seat, and started the engine. Hunter climbed in, and they drove off in a cloud of dust. Duke stopped just short of the paved road. The two looked at each other—high-fived—and started laughing.

"That was just too easy," Duke said.

"It couldn't have gone any better."

"Where to now?"

"Turn left. When you get back to 121, turn right. When you get to Silverado, turn right. We're going up the Silverado Trail to the Pickford Family Winery."

CHAPTER 78

On the Silverado Trail

"There's a sign for the famous Stags Leap Winery," Hunter said, "one mile ahead."

"Famous in what way?" Duke asked.

"It was the California winery that won the blind taste test in two different flights over the French wines in 1976 in Paris."

"The Judgement of Paris, you told me about that."

"Yes. If we weren't on a mission, I wouldn't mind stopping and checking the place out."

"Maybe we can come back later if we finish early enough."

"Maybe. I wouldn't mind getting a bottle for Scott and Catalina and a bottle for Susan and me. Now, the Pickford Family Winery, according to the map, is the next winery past Stags Leap. It will be off to the right."

"It looks like another sign up ahead."

"I see it. That's probably going to be it. Yep, Pickford Family Winery. Looks like a right turn onto the road just past the sign."

"Got it."

"You want to do the talking this time, Duke?"

"Naw. You do it. You're good at it."

Duke and Hunter followed the paved road up and around to a small parking lot next to a one-story building with a sign that read, "Pickford Family Winery Tasting Room and Store." Duke parked the black monster and said, "Now, this is more like it. Compared to old Schumacher's operation, this looks first class."

"That it does. Let's get out and look for someone. It's still a little early, and it looks like the store and tasting room haven't opened for business yet."

Nearby the tasting room and store was a large metal warehouse-looking building with large slider doors. The doors were open, and two men in jeans and work shirts were just inside, talking to a lady wearing a blue denim skirt and red blouse. As Hunter and Duke approached, the three people stopped talking and looked up. "May I help you?" the lady asked.

"We're looking for Chuck Pickford," Hunter said. The lady said something to the two workers, and they went further inside the warehouse.

The lady came closer to Hunter and Duke and said, "Chuck Pickford is my husband, but he's not here. He had to go into town. I'm Mary Pickford. Can I help you?"

"Mary Pickford—that name sounds familiar," Hunter said.

"Yes. She was an old movie star. My mother named me after her. What is it you need to see my husband about, officers?"

"Well, it seems that your husband, also known as Ted Bundy…"

Upon hearing her husband's code name with 'the group,' Mary's countenance sank. "Listen, I don't really know anything about that group. My husband wouldn't tell me anything. The only thing I know is his silly secret name, Ted Bundy. He said he picked that name because someone once told him that he was as charming as Ted Bundy. Stupid."

"Not a name I would have picked," Hunter said.

"My husband won't be back for a while. Do you want to wait, or is there something you want me to tell him?"

"This secret little group your husband is in was involved in the murder of two people from here in Napa Valley."

"Oh no. That's terrible. I knew that group was up to no good. I don't think my husband could be directly involved in anything like that—not murder. Who were the people who were murdered?"

"Ed and Joyce Cooling. They had the Los Amigos Cellars Winery here in Napa Valley."

"I know who they are—not personally—but I know—we know of them or knew them. That's so terrible. I know Chuck had nothing to do with this. And I assure you, as of this moment, he is no longer involved with that group."

"That's good to hear, ma'am. We still may need to come back at some point and talk to your husband—us, or possibly the FBI."

"I hope not, but I'll tell him. He'll cooperate any way he can."

"That's good to know. Well, you take care, Mary Pickford." Duke gave Hunter the nod that it looked safe to walk away, so they both turned and started back toward their vehicle.

Mary called out to them, "Hey, you didn't tell me your names."

Hunter turned back and said, "Just tell your husband that the United States came for a visit."

CHAPTER 79

Hunter and Duke left Mary Pickford and the Pickford Family Winery and headed north again on the Silverado Trail. They came to the Yountville Cross and, a little further north, the Oakville Cross, where they turned left. There were several other crosses or crossroads further up. These crossroads crossed over a series of hills that separated the Silverado Trail from Highway 29 and were scenic, windy, twisty roads that weren't always in the best of repair. Their next customer, Doug Betterman, aka Dog Bite, owned and operated the Oak Leaf Cellars Winery on twisty, windy Oakville Cross.

The winery was a hidden gem in the hills and seemed to be quite the going operation. The tasting room, gift shop, and restaurant were in an impressive and modern two-story stone building. It was a little past ten o'clock, and there were a number of customers milling around.

Hunter asked the female greeter at the main entrance to the stone building where they might find the owner, Doug Betterman. The cheerful greeter asked them to wait on the front patio near the entrance and said Mr. Betterman would come by shortly. The two pretend lawmen had a seat on a big wooden bench and waited.

A few minutes later, a six-foot-tall middle-aged man with sandy hair and a limp walked up to them and said, "I'm Doug Betterman. What can I do for the Rangers?"

"Is there someplace we can talk?" Hunter asked.

"Yeah, I reckon. Follow me to that building over there." Betterman nodded toward the smaller and older-looking stone building about fifty yards away. "That used to be the tasting room and so forth until we built this bigger building. Now, we use the smaller building for private gatherings, wedding parties, and so forth. There's a deck in the back where we can talk with a view that looks out at the rolling hills and some of the vineyard. No one should try to disturb us there until the first tour, which isn't for a while yet."

Hunter and Duke followed Betterman to the back side of the building and to the wooden deck with about a dozen or so metal tables with chairs. As they neared the deck, Betterman turned and said, "You boys aren't going to arrest me or rough me up, are you?"

"No sir, we don't plan to," Hunter said.

"Well, that's good. In that case, gentlemen, let me offer you a glass of our signature cab. It's what we're famous for. It has a ninety-nine point rating."

Hunter and Duke looked at each other and then back at Betterman. "We're on duty," Hunter said, "but it would be a shame to pass on your hospitality and on a really good wine. How about a taste—about a one-ounce pour?"

"Coming right up." Betterman opened the back door and went inside. A minute or so later, he came back out with a bottle of the signature Cabernet with a one-ounce pour spout and three etched Oak Leaf long-stemmed wine glasses. Betterman poured an ounce in each glass, then raised his glass and said, "Gentlemen, to the Rangers."

Hunter and Duke raised their glasses and repeated, "To the Rangers."

Each took a sip and then put the glass down.

"Superb," Hunter said.

"I second that," Duke said.

"We'll have to get a bottle to take back," Hunter said.

"You know," Betterman said, "I've never heard of the United States Rangers. I've heard of the Texas Rangers, but I've never heard of the U.S. Rangers. Are you guys legit?"

"Oh, we're legit, all right," Hunter said. "We're the latest entry from Homeland Security. In fact, we're so new we don't even have name tags or arm patches yet."

"I see that. So what is the occasion of your visit? What did you come to see me about?"

"It's about this offshoot clandestine group of the PCW—the Protect California Wine organization. It seems they have gotten involved in something that has turned nasty. We're looking into the group's involvement in a double murder that took place the other day in Glacier Bay on an Alaskan pleasure cruise. That is, we, the FBI, and the National Park Investigators, along with the ABI, the Alaska Bureau of Investigation. There are multiple jurisdictions involved here."

"Look, I went to two or three meetings of that offshoot PCW group you're talking about. I went along with the plan to try to stop the couple who put on wine cruises from having a Judgement of California taste test, but I have thought better of it since, and I quit that group. They don't know it yet, but I already went to my last meeting. I think the guy that started that group is a conspiracy nut."

"Jeep?"

"That's right. Grady Flanigan—code name Jeep. That should have been a clue to me right off the bat when he said we needed to use code names. Mine was Dog Bite. I know we were trying to do something away from public scrutiny, but no one was supposed to get harmed by what we were doing. When I found out there was a physical abduction of that cruise guy, I decided to quit."

"Good for you," Hunter said. "More often than not, when people get involved in something that starts going in a direction they don't approve of, they still stick with it. They don't get out. So, kudos to you for getting out. I can't say for sure that we, or one of the other agencies, won't come and talk to you further about this matter, but I wouldn't be overly concerned."

Hunter and Duke scooted their chairs back and stood up to leave. "That's all? That's all you wanted to talk to me about?" Betterman asked.

"That's it for now," Hunter said.

"Before you go, let me get you something. Wait right here." Betterman went inside and came back out with two bottles of Oak Leaf signature Cabernet Sauvignon. "For you, gentlemen."

"Oh, thanks," Hunter said, "but we can't accept that. We're not allowed to accept favors." Duke turned his head and looked at Hunter. "But we'd be happy to purchase two bottles of that very fine wine."

"That will be one dollar each." Hunter gave Betterman a questioning look. "I'm one of the owners here. I'm allowed to set the price of my wines."

"We'll, thank you, Mr. Betterman," Hunter said as both he and Duke each pulled a dollar bill out of their wallets and handed it to Betterman.

Hunter and Duke turned to leave. Hunter suddenly turned back as Duke kept on walking. "Which branch of the Service were you in, Doug?"

"Army. Afghanistan. What about you?"

"Air Force. Afghanistan and Iraq. I can usually tell a vet. I guess you can, too."

"Most of the time."

Hunter turned back and followed Duke to the monster. As they were driving away, Duke imitated Betterman and said, "The U.S. Rangers? I've never heard of them." Duke then imitated Hunter, "Yeah, we're a brand new outfit from Homeland Security. We're so new we don't even have name tags or arm patches yet." Duke, in his own voice, then said, "Yeah, we're so new we didn't even exist until this morning." Duke and Hunter had a good chuckle as they drove away.

CHAPTER 80

"Where to now, Kemosabe?" Duke asked.

"Turn left back onto Oakville Cross, and when you get to Highway 29, turn left again. We're going to visit the big guy, Grady Flanigan, aka Jeep. He's the infamous leader of the secret group and, according to Betterman, maybe a little wacky."

"Maybe a little extra precaution is in order."

"Check. He's the caretaker of Dominic Hills Winery. Apparently, the owner is an absentee landlord."

Duke and Hunter turned left onto Highway 29 and, after a short distance, turned right onto Oakville Grade. They drove a little ways, then turned left at the Dominic Hills sign onto a paved road that was in less than pristine condition with weeds growing in the cracks and a few potholes. The Dominic Hills sign was also a little weather-beaten.

"Looks like Mr. Caretaker is not doing the best of jobs on the upkeep," Duke said.

"Yeah, I'm getting that creepy feeling. Keep your eyes peeled."

After a few back-and-forth turns up the driveway, Duke and Hunter came to a sign that indicated that a parking lot and a picnic area was to the left, and the tasting room was straight ahead. The parking lot was about a third full, and Duke found a spot at the far end of the lot, away from most of the other vehicles. As Duke and Hunter dismounted the black monster, they got a glimpse of a fairly large picnic area a short distance from the parking lot and tasting room.

The two U.S. Rangers walked up the railroad tie-reinforced crushed granite steps to the tasting room and gift shop. They asked the young girl at the check-out stand near the front door if they could speak with Mr. Grady Flanigan. She told them that Mr. Flanigan was over at the picnic area refurbishing the picnic tables. They thanked her and turned to leave as a hard-looking middle-aged woman approached.

"What can I do for you, deputies?"

"Nothing, ma'am," Hunter said. "We're headed over to the picnic area to talk to Grady Flanigan."

"Well, he ain't there."

"We heard he was over there working on some picnic tables."

"You heard wrong. He ain't there. He went into Yountville for some varnish or something. Probably won't be back right away."

"Are you Mrs. Flanigan?" Hunter asked.

"Yes, I am. If you got a message for my husband, I'll tell him when he gets back."

"No, Ma'am, no message. We just need to talk to him about a particular matter."

"You'll have to come back when he's here."

"Yes, ma'am, that makes sense. We'll just have to come back a little later. Before we leave, though, we might just take a look around. Looks like a pretty nice spread you got up here."

"Ain't ours. Owner lives at his other winery. Pays us to run the place."

"Some people got all the money. Just don't hardly seem fair, does it? Well, we'll be running along. You take care now."

Duke and Hunter walked out the door and turned right to go down the main pathway to the picnic area. Hunter had read that the picnic area at this winery had a great view and was one of the special features of the winery. As they started down the path, they came to a barricade across the path with a sign that said the picnic area was closed for repairs. They walked around the barricade and continued on.

As soon as Hunter and Duke had walked out of the door of the tasting room and gift shop, Silvia Flanigan turned and gave the young check-out girl a look of displeasure, then she high-tailed it past the sandwich and gift shop proper, and the wine tasting counter, to a back room where she pulled out her cell phone and called Grady. "There's two law enforcement dudes coming your way."

Hunter and Duke continued down the crushed granite pathway toward the picnic area, spread apart as much as the path would allow. Suddenly, a shot rang out, and a nine-millimeter slug whizzed past Hunter's ear. Hunter yelled, "Shots fired, take cover!"

At the same time, Duke yelled, "Duck and cover!" Both men immediately dove to the ground and rolled over to whatever cover they could find. Hunter rolled over to a granite boulder and crouched behind it on the far side of where the shot came from. Duke came up behind the start of a stone half-wall that surrounded part of the picnic area.

Safely behind cover, Hunter and Duke both tried to spot the shooter. After a few seconds, Hunter caught a glimpse of a man behind a stone fireplace on the far side of the picnic area. Duke and Hunter had visual contact, and Hunter signaled to Duke that the shooter was behind the fireplace.

Hunter then signaled that he was going to try to talk to the fireplace man, who was very likely Flanigan. Duke signaled that he was going to try to circle around and come up behind Flanigan—so, check your fire.

Hunter acknowledged, then started to try to reason with Flanigan and, at the same time, distract him. Hunter used his best authoritative command voice. "Grady Flanigan, hold your fire. We are not the police. We only want to talk to you about a group of wine growers you may be involved with."

"I won't go back," Flanigan yelled as he fired another round and hit the boulder that Hunter was safely behind. Hunter had a flash. Could Flanigan possibly be Johnny Belinda, the inmate who escaped from San Quentin about a year ago and was never apprehended? There was quite the manhunt for him at the time, and he had told someone that he would never go back. Maybe, Hunter thought. Maybe this is the guy. At least this guy apparently has done time and really doesn't want to do any more.

"Listen, Grady, we mean you no harm. We're here to get some information on that wine group you're in. That's all."

"I told you. I'm not going back." He fired again.

"We didn't come here about that. We are only interested in the wine group you head up. We already talked to Hans Schumacher and Doug Betterman. Betterman said he thought you were a good leader for the group."

"Yeah, I'll bet. Then why is he quitting the group?"

"You know, that's a good question. You should ask him."

"What'd you guys do with the Simpsons? I heard they got arrested in Alaska."

"Yeah, we don't..." Just then, Duke jumped over the stone half-wall directly behind Flanigan and, with his full body weight, slammed him against the back of the stone fireplace he was hiding behind. A split second later, Duke used both hands to grab Flanigan's right wrist and peal the weapon cleanly out of his hand. Duke continued with his maneuver and brought Flanigan's right hand around behind his back using a wrist lock. At this point, Grady Flanigan had slithered down the back side of the fireplace and found himself sprawled out face down on the ground. Applying a little wrist lock pain, Duke then had Flanigan bring his left arm around and behind his back, allowing Duke to apply the handcuffs. Duke double-locked the black Peerless cuffs and brought Flanigan to his feet. Duke then called to Hunter, "All clear."

Hunter acknowledged and called back, "Ten-four, all clear." Hunter stood up, holstered his weapon, and walked toward Duke and Flanigan. Duke held Flanigan by the chain that connected the two cuffs in case he tried to run. Hunter performed a field pat down for weapons and then walked back to the stone fireplace and retrieved Flanigan's handgun. Duke and Hunter then walked Grady up the stone path to the black monster.

Flanigan had a bloody face and was clearly in some pain. Hunter pulled out a handy wipe from one of his pockets, and Duke stopped Flanigan for a second while Hunter wiped Grady's face.

Flanigan looked at Hunter and said, "Why did you send this monster after me? I think he broke a rib or two."

"I doubt it," Hunter said. "If you have any broken ribs, you'd know it."

"Well, you didn't have to do all this. I would've talked to you guys."

"You shot at us," Hunter said.

"Well, sure. I didn't hit ya, did I? And why didn't you fire back, anyway?"

"Because if I did, we wouldn't be having this conversation. I don't fire unless I have a target. If I have a target, I usually score. Besides, Johnny, you still have some time to do."

"What do you mean, Johnny?"

"You're Johnny Belinda, aren't you? Escaped from San Quentin a while back."

Flanigan didn't say another word. Duke strapped Grady into the car seat the second row back and then walked around, climbed in the Suburban, and sat in the seat next to Flanigan, right behind Hunter in the driver's seat. The parking lot was virtually empty. No doubt, people had been scared off by the sound of gunfire.

Hunter drove back down the Dominic Hills Winery drive, turned right on Oakville Grade, then right on Highway 29, and headed for Yountville.

CHAPTER 81

It was close to one o'clock when Hunter pulled up to the Yountville Police Substation on Mulberry Street. The Yountville Police was run by the Sheriff's Office, which provided contracted police services to the town. The contingent at the substation was one sergeant and three deputies. They wore Sheriff's Office uniforms that bore special insignia, which indicated they were assigned to Yountville.

Hunter climbed out of their SUV and covered Duke as he got out and went around to the other side and unbuckled Flanigan's seat belt. Duke then grabbed Flanigan's upper arm and helped him out of the vehicle. They walked Flanigan to the front door of the police station, and Duke sat him down in one of the chairs in the small lobby area. Hunter walked up to the counter. A deputy arose from behind his desk and walked up to the back side of the counter. His brass name tag read "J. Combs." "Yes, sir, what can I do for you, Ranger?"

"We have an individual here who might just turn out to be Johnny Belinda, the man who escaped from San Quentin a little while back. Since we're federal and you're local California, we're turning him over to you."

Deputy Combs turned and yelled back toward the rear of the station, "Hey, Lester, get on up here. We have a customer."

Deputy Lester Barns immediately appeared from a back room and came alongside Deputy Combs. "They think this guy they have in custody over there might be Johnny Belinda, who escaped from San Quentin about a year ago."

"Well, let's get him fingerprinted, and we'll run him through the system and see."

"Should we call the sarge?"

"Na. They're doing some PR work. Let's not bother them. We'll surprise them."

"Ten-four."

"Now, officers," Barns said, "if you'll bring the suspect through the gate here and over to our live scan, we'll see if he is in the system. Did you guys do a pat down?"

"A field pat down for weapons," Hunter said.

Duke maintained control of Flanigan as Deputy Combs performed the fingerprinting. Flanigan wasn't a big guy—certainly not Duke's size, but you never know. While Combs fingerprinted one hand, Duke had Flanigan's other hand handcuffed to the backside of his leather belt.

When the fingerprinting was done, Deputy Barns started the run-through of the system of Flanigan's prints. In the meantime, the two deputies performed a more thorough search of Flanigan—not a full-blown prison search—but they emptied his pockets and checked his shoes and socks and squeezed and checked everywhere else. They put him in their jail cell and removed his handcuffs through the handcuff removal portal in the bars.

Deputy Barns went over and checked his computer. "Bingo. You guys were right. You brought in Johnny Belinda—escapee from San Quentin. There are several outstanding warrants for his arrest. Good job, Rangers. Now, there's some transfer paperwork we need to fill out and have you sign. I'm not sure what all has to be done. The Sergeant should know. I'll give him a call."

"I'm sorry, deputies," Hunter said, "but we really can't stick around. We're on a mission, and we got sidetracked with old Johnny boy here. It's been nice meeting you two. You take care now." With that, Hunter and Duke walked out the door.

"You driving or you want me to take up the reins again?" Duke asked.

"You drive unless you're tired of it."

"No, never. So, what now?"

"Well, I think we have mission accomplishment. I think we probably have successfully curtailed the shenanigans of this secret little wine group. The leader is going back to prison. His number two guy is going to serve some kind of time for helping in the abduction attempt of Scott and Catalina Poncetran. And, the other members of the group who we talked to don't seem to want to carry on. So, I think it's a wrap."

"No, you don't. I think I'm starting to be able to read you, Hunter. We didn't complete what we set out to do. We didn't talk to everybody we planned on talking to. You still want to pay a visit to those other two wineries and talk to Darth and Forklift—just to make sure they're clued in—just to make sure they know firsthand they've been found out."

"You good with that?"

"You bet."

"Okay, then. When you get back to Highway 29, turn left."

Duke cranked up the monster and drove off. After a minute or so, Duke said, "By the way, Hunter, what did you leave on the counter back there? You left something on the counter as we were walking out."

"Just a little something to remember us by."

CHAPTER 82

A short time after Hunter and Duke left, Sergeant Toliver and Deputy Nunez returned to the Yountville Police Station from their PR mission.

"Now, tell me this again," Sergeant Toliver said. "You say two men dressed in black—two big men—with U.S. Rangers badges and ball caps came in here with Mr. Belinda, a wanted felon fugitive, a person who has evaded capture for over a year, and they just handed him over to you two and left?"

"Yes," Deputy Barns said, "that's essentially it. They stayed for a spell while we fingerprinted him and ran the prints through the system, and then they left. They said they were on a mission and had to leave."

"And you didn't get their names or badge numbers or any information about them—what office they were out of, contact information—nothing?"

"No, Sarge," Barns said. "I thought there would be time for that later, but suddenly, they just up and left."

"And what is this that you say they left on the counter?" Sergeant Toliver held up a small object.

"Well, it's a silver bullet, Sarge."

"Do you expect me to believe the Lone Ranger was here?"

"No, Sarge, there were two of them."

CHAPTER 83

Hunter and Duke visited the remaining two wineries and encouraged Darth and Forklift not to participate in any wine shenanigans. They both seemed to get the message. Since Duke and Hunter had not had lunch, they were hungry and decided to have an early dinner somewhere on the way back to Sacramento.

On the way out of Napa Valley, they found a park with an out-of-the-way section where they turned back into civilians. They took off their badges, duty belts, and ball caps. They unloaded their Glocks, took rounds out of the magazines so they only had ten rounds in each mag, put the empty Glocks back in their locked cases, and stowed the weapons and the ammo in separate areas of the vehicle.

Duke looked at Hunter and shook his head. "Remind me to never even think of moving to California."

"Pretty country. Decent weather a good part of the time."

"Oh, for sure, but I couldn't stand the stupidity. Ten rounds in a seventeen-round mag. And you can't even have a loaded weapon to protect yourself. So, they relax or eliminate the laws against criminal activity, which encourages even more criminal activity yet won't allow the law-abiding citizen to protect himself. It's insane."

"I hear you. I guess I better not tell you some of the other insane things California has done in recent years."

"Please don't. It will just upset me even more."

"It's a shame. California used to be the place to be, but something terrible has happened to it in the last few years. Its soul is rotten. Maybe it doesn't even have a soul anymore. Well, I'm glad I got to live there during its better times, and I'm glad I got out when I did. Have you ever eaten at an Air Force Officers Club?"

"Not since Afghanistan. Sometimes, we were allowed in."

"It used to be that only active duty and retired military could eat at the Officer and NCO Clubs. Now, veterans can eat there, too. I feel like celebrating our sterling mission accomplishment—we had a clean sweep, to put it in a submariner's vernacular, and somehow an Officers Club seems like the appropriate place."

"I'm game for it. Where's the nearest one?"

"Travis Air Force Base. It's in Fairfield, right off Highway 80. We're going to go right by it."

The two civilians climbed back into the black monster and continued the drive out of beautiful Napa Valley and onto Highway 80 toward Sacramento. A few miles up the road, they took the Air Base Parkway exit off the freeway to Travis Air Force Base main gate. Hunter showed the guard his veteran card and asked for directions to the Officers Club. The guard seemed a little confused but said he could give directions to "The Club." Hunter told him that was exactly what they wanted—directions to "The Club." As they followed the directions to "The Club," it dawned on Hunter that he had read quite a few years ago that Officers Clubs and NCO (Noncommissioned Officer) Clubs had fallen on hard times. Many of them were eliminated and replaced with just one club for Officers and NCOs alike. So be it, Hunter thought. Times, they are a changing.

Upon arrival at "The Club," the two hungry civilians checked in at the front and were shown to a table. Hunter and Duke perused the menus and ordered their dinners, along with a small glass of wine each. Hunter excused himself for a minute and took a look around. When he returned to the table, the two wines were sitting there. "I waited for you so we could toast," Duke said.

"Good. You make the toast."

"Here's to successful mission completion—with the Lord's help, I'm sure."

They raised their glasses, and Hunter said, "Hear, hear, and Amen."

"How was your little tour of 'The Club'?"

"Well, I'm a little disappointed—actually, a lot disappointed. There are families here, with kids, which is all right; they seem to be having an enjoyable time. But it's not the same. When I was still in the service, the Officers Club was a lively place. The bar was filled with guys having a drink and telling war stories. There was music, usually live bands, on Friday nights. It was a place to unwind. There was camaraderie. It was fun. It was the place to be. This—this is just a family restaurant.

"Well, anyway, I'm disappointed. I miss the way it used to be. I wonder if people in the military nowadays even have a place to unwind, let loose a little, and foster camaraderie. I hope they do, but it's certainly not at 'The Club.'"

"Yeah, I agree with you, Hunter. This is certainly not how Officer and NCO Clubs used to be—especially overseas."

Hunter took another sip of his wine. "And, this may not have been the best idea—having a glass of non-descript wine after having that most excellent Cabernet at the Oak Leaf Cellars with Dog Bite."

"Yeah," Duke said, "Dog Bite—I liked him. He was down-to-earth and honest. He seemed like the kind of guy who would always try to do the right thing. And I've been thinking. I think I want to do it. I think I want to take a trip to Colorado, to Golden, present myself to local authorities, and tell them the truth about Vivian's death."

"Really? Well, I think that's the right thing to do despite the consequence of possible prison time."

"Yeah. That part has been holding me back."

"If you do, I'd like to go with you if you want me to."

"Yes, definitely. I would like you to go with me. I also need to tell Kimberly. I don't know if she would go with me, but I do need to tell her. Heck, if she goes with me, you ought to bring Susan, and we can make a fun road trip out of it."

"Right. The only thing is, it might be a lot of fun on the way up but a sad trip back for the three of us if you don't get to come back with us."

"I can see that. I think my next step is to see Kimberly and tell her and go from there."

"I think you're right. I think that's your next move."

Duke and Hunter enjoyed a decent and filling meal at "The Club," drove back to Sacramento and their hotel, and hit the hay. The next morning, they got up, threw everything in their bags, drove to the airport, dropped off the black monster, had an expensive airport breakfast, and boarded their Southwest flight back to Phoenix.

After arrival at Sky Harbor airport, they jumped into Hunter's car and headed for Scottsdale. Hunter parked in Duke's driveway, and the two men got out and just looked at each other as they shook their heads.

"Hey, man," Hunter said, "it was sure great working with you."

"Likewise, brother."

"We should get together in the next couple of days and debrief. As successful as the operation was, there may be things we could improve upon, just in case we have occasion to do something like this again."

"Absolutely."

"I'll call you."

"Yes."

"I hope things go well with seeing Kimberly."

"Yes, me too."

Hunter didn't know what else to say. He got back in his Edge and drove home.

CHAPTER 84

Hunter parked in the circular drive of their Carefree home on Ridgeline Road. Susan bounded out of the front door to greet him. She had a big smile, and her blond hair was up in a ponytail. She ran over to Hunter and gave him the biggest hug he had had in a long time.

"Welcome back, big boy. I made you lunch. One of your favorites. Cobb salad."

"What kind of dressing?"

"It's a love dressing—a dressing with lots of love in it."

"I guess that means you like me a little bit."

Susan's eyes welled up, and a tear rolled down her cheek. "Very much so, Hunter, very much."

CHAPTER 85

After being home not even five minutes, Duke telephoned Kimberly.

"Hello, Duke, I was hoping that was you. Welcome home."

"Thanks, yeah, Hunter dropped me off just a few minutes ago."

"I know you must be tired. I made you lunch. I can bring it over if you like. It's all ready to go. It's a salad with crab and scallops and all kinds of different things. It's guaranteed to fill you up."

"That sounds great. You sure you don't mind coming over."

"Not at all."

Forty-five minutes later, Kimberly rang Duke's doorbell while holding a large bowl covered with plastic wrap. Duke opened the door, and immediately, a giant smile appeared on his face.

"Do come in. Let me take that." Duke carried the salad bowl to the kitchen and placed it on the counter. He turned around to get a good look at Kimberly, and before he could say anything, she grabbed him in a giant hug with her head pressed against his chest and wouldn't let go.

"I guess you're glad to see me."

Kimberly released him, looked up with tears in her eyes, and said, "Yes, I am." After a few more minutes of holding hands, looking at each other, and a couple more hugs, Kimberly said, "Let me dish you out a big guy portion of salad. Do you want it on a plate or in a bowl?"

"A big bowl. I'll get us two big bowls. Since I live here, I know where they are."

"That's helpful. With all the cabinets in this marvelous kitchen, it would probably take me a while to find them."

"What would you like to drink?"

"Do you have iced tea?"

"I do. Iced tea sounds good. I'll get us two glasses of iced tea. And do you want to eat outside?"

"Oh, absolutely. It's such a beautiful day."

"Good."

Duke and Kimberly carried their salad and iced tea out the back slider to the round table under the white pergola and sat down. They enjoyed the beauty of the day while eating an absolutely delicious seafood salad. When they had finished, Kimberly took the empty salad bowls inside and put them in the dishwasher. She came back out with the container of iced tea, refilled their glasses, stood behind Duke's chair, and started massaging his neck and shoulders. After two or three minutes, Duke reached back, grabbed Kimberly's hands, and brought her around to where she was to the front and side of him.

"You don't like my massage?"

"I love your massage. It was fantastic. But there is something I need to tell you, and there seems to be no easy way to do it."

"You're leading a double life. You're married and have a family in another town."

"No. Nothing like that, or maybe it is something like that. Maybe it is that devastating. Maybe even more devastating."

"Duke, you're serious. What is it? I don't know if I want to hear it."

"I think I have to tell you."

"Well, okay. What is it that you have to tell me that is so terrible? I know you've had a checkered past. You told me that."

"Yes, well, I've done some stuff to some very bad people that I don't care to speak about, but those were evil people, and I stopped them from doing even more evil. What I did that I never should have done—and I'm very, very sorry for—is arrange for my wife to be killed. I paid a guy to fix the brakes on her vehicle so that she would have a terrible accident and die. I found out that she had murdered her previous husband, but that didn't give me the right to, in turn, murder her. She was going to trial for murdering her husband, so no doubt justice would have been served.

"But the cost of her high-priced defense attorney, and the appeals and so forth, would have drained our savings dry. I did it for the money. I had her killed so she wouldn't deplete our money—our nest egg. My motive was greed. And the ironic thing is, the money I was trying to protect was the insurance money she had acquired by killing her previous husband."

Tears were streaming down Kimberly's face. She was sobbing so hard it looked like she was convulsing. Between sobs, she managed to cry out, "Oh, Duke, how could you!"

Tears started rolling down big guy Duke's cheeks, but nothing like what Kimberly was experiencing. Nothing else was said for a while. Kimberly finally calmed down enough to say, "Duke, I don't think I can see you anymore." A few seconds later, she grabbed her purse and said, "I have to go," and went into the house through the slider and headed for the front door.

Duke followed her and said, "Your salad bowl is here."

As she walked out the front door, she said, "You keep it." She climbed into her Bronco, backed out of the driveway, and drove off.

Duke was so devastated that he started to punch his fist through the drywall by the door but thought better of it and stopped short. With tears still rolling down his cheeks, he stomped through the house, looking for something to hit. He finally grabbed a Coors can of beer out of the refrigerator and squeezed it with all of his might. It popped open, and beer squirted everywhere.

CHAPTER 86

Duke looked at the mess he just made in the kitchen by squeezing the beer can so hard that it burst open. He thought, Well, that didn't help. I guess I do have to punch something. He went into the guest room, pulled the spread and top sheet off the bed, set the mattress up against the wall, and started punching. He punched and jabbed for several minutes and worked up the beginning of a good sweat.

He went back out to the kitchen and pulled two Coors cans out of the refrigerator. He walked out to the backyard, sat down, and popped open the first beer. He chugged that one down and popped open the second. As he brought beer number two up to his lips, he thought, What am I doing? This is old school. This is how I used to handle bad news. I'm supposed to be a new man. I'm supposed to be different now. I'm a Christian. So, how does this new man handle what just happened with Kimberly?

I pray. That's one thing for sure. I pray. The old man never prayed. But now I pray. Okay, God, here goes. "God, I thank You for being able to talk to You anytime. I thank You for letting me be one of Your believers. I thank You for Hunter and Kimberly, who helped me see your truth. They encouraged me to turn from my old ways and ask for Your forgiveness. And God, I know You forgave me of all my sins, including my terrible sin of having my wife, Vivian, killed—murdered.

"So You forgave me of that. Kimberly is a Christian. It doesn't seem like she can forgive me. Yeah, I know she's a human. It's probably harder for her. It really seemed like our relationship was going somewhere—somewhere good.

"Yes, I know God. I once asked the question, 'How do you live with a person who murdered their previous mate?' and I concluded: you can't. So, I murdered Vivian. Maybe Kimberly asked herself the same question a little bit ago and concluded she couldn't either. Maybe if I had been a Christian at the time, I would have forgiven Vivian instead of having her murdered. Boy, that's something to think about. Maybe Kimberly overreacted and will find it in her heart to forgive me after all. I don't know.

"Maybe I should have never told Kimberly about having Vivian killed. But I know that's not true. If Kimberly and I did get married, then I would have a wife I was never fully honest with.

"Lord, I don't know what You want to do with this situation, if anything, but I'm glad I talked to You about this. And I pray for Kimberly. Please help her. I just laid a big heavy on her—out of the blue. She certainly wasn't expecting that.

"Well, Lord, I guess that's it. I thank You for Your Son Jesus and that He died for our sins. And I thank You for being available twenty-four seven. In the name of Jesus, Amen."

Duke opened his eyes and was surprised to find himself on his knees by his chair. He stood up and looked around. It was early evening, and the sun was setting behind the mountains. It was still warm, but there was a ting of coolness creeping into the air, and the slight breeze had the smell of gardenia mixed with jasmine.

Duke stretched, did a few shoulder exercises and arm circles, then walked around his backyard checking things out. He particularly checked out his bushes and plants, including the gardenia, jasmine, and bougainvillea. He felt good and alive. He felt a peace he could not explain, especially in light of being so upset just a little bit ago. He felt that, no matter what happened, everything was going to be all right. Then, he thought, This must be the peace that surpasses all understanding mentioned in the Bible.

CHAPTER 87

Thursday, May 25, Morning
Windy Walk Estates of Troon Village

The phone rang at Duke's house. "Hello."

"Hello, Duke. It's Kimberly. Can you talk for a second? I can call another time if you're busy right now."

"I'm not busy. I can talk. By the way, your salad bowl is clean. I washed it."

"Duke, dog gone you, I don't care about the salad bowl. I called to apologize. I shouldn't have reacted the way I did. I'm sorry. But I don't know if I can date you anymore—probably not. Well, that's all I wanted to say."

"Maybe I'll see you at church Sunday."

"Sure. That would be all right. I don't think I want to sit with you, though."

"Well, okay."

"Don't take that personally—it's just me."

"Okay. I think I understand. Thanks for calling, Kimberly. Goodbye."

"Goodbye, Duke."

Well, that was interesting, Duke thought. He put his partially eaten bacon, eggs, and toast in the microwave for a warm-up, then took them back outside to finish them off. It was another beautiful morning in the desert. Later in the day, it would be in the low nineties. With the low humidity, temperatures in the low and mid-nineties were quite nice. However, the days with the highs in the one hundreds were just around the corner. June, July, and August were the hot months in the Phoenix area, which Duke was sure kept some people from moving to the valley. And it occurred to Duke that maybe that was a blessing. Maybe that has kept Phoenix from becoming even bigger than it already is.

Duke finished his breakfast and sat there for another minute. Then, he abruptly stood up and said out loud, "That's it, I'm doing it. I'm turning myself in. Monday morning." He grabbed his phone and called Hunter.

"Hey, Duke, what's up?"

"I've decided. I'm turning myself in Monday morning. I wanted to see if you're available to go with me—just you and me."

"You bet. I know I don't have anything going on, but if I did, I'd cancel it."

"Good. Excellent. What are you going to tell Susan about our trip—our mission?"

"I don't know, I'll think of something."

"I think you should tell her the truth. You should tell her the real reason for the trip."

"Well, if you want me to tell her what you told me in confidence, I'll tell her. But you give me the go-ahead."

"Better yet, what if I tell her? Are you guys busy right now? I could come over to your house and tell her in person. I could be there in half an hour if that's all right."

"Come ahead."

"You sure it's all right with Susan? It's still a little early."

"Just to put your mind at ease, I'll ask her." A few seconds later, Hunter got back on the phone and said, "Yeah, no problem, come on over."

"Okay. See you in a bit."

CHAPTER 88

Ridgeline Road
Carefree, Arizona

Duke parked his Kelly green Expedition in Hunter and Susan's half-circle driveway and rang the doorbell. After greeting each other, the three of them went to the back patio and sat together in the shade of a sissoo tree. After a few minutes of small talk, Duke looked at Susan and said, "The reason I came over is I wanted to tell you something that I told Hunter the other day—actually, the day I surrendered my life to the Lord Jesus and Hunter baptized me in the pool. I asked God to forgive me of my sins that day, and I confessed what I believe was my worst sin. I confessed it to God and, actually, to Hunter also. So now I've asked your husband to take a trip to Colorado with me, and it has to do with that terrible sin I confessed to God in Hunter's presence.

"I feel I need to tell you the terrible thing I did so you know the reason for our trip to Colorado if you're okay with Hunter going with me."

"You don't have to explain things, Duke. Whatever it is, I trust Hunter."

"I think your trust in Hunter is well placed, but I still want to explain. You probably remember my ex-wife Vivian from a couple of years ago on that cruise across the Atlantic we all were on. I understand you two helped uncover the fact that she murdered her husband on that cruise, but I didn't know it at the time. Vivian and I married, and months after that, I realized she had killed her previous husband. Well, with the way my mind worked back then, I decided I needed to have her killed in case she ever thought of doing the same to me. I could have divorced her, of course, but then I wouldn't get to keep all our money and our house. So, I hired a guy to tamper with the brakes of her car so that she would have an accident and be killed."

"Oh," Susan said, "I remember. We were living in California then, but we learned that your wife had been killed in an accident going down an icy mountain road near where you lived in Colorado. She was going too fast and hit a patch of ice at a curve in the road. She lost control of the vehicle and crashed down the mountainside. It smashed into a boulder or something, and she died instantly." Susan's eyes became moist as she finished recalling the incident.

"That's right, but it was my doing. She did drive too fast most of the time, but it's very unlikely the accident would have happened had the brakes not been fixed so that they would fail."

"Well," Susan said as she found a tissue and dabbed her eyes, "that is a horrendous thing. Purposely causing the death of another person. I guess that's murder. God looks at all sin as an abomination. I don't know if He grades sins as not so bad, bad, or really bad, like we do. But when you surrender to Him, like you did, He forgives it all. And like He said to the woman caught in the act of adultery, 'Go now and leave your life of sin.'"

"Yeah, I've read that story. 'If any one of you is without sin, let him be the first to throw a stone at her.'"

"So, what does what you just told me have to do with you and Hunter going to Colorado?"

"I want to go to the authorities and set the record straight. I want to tell the Colorado State Patrol, who investigated Vivian's accident, what actually happened—that I paid someone to tamper with the brakes so they would fail."

"Wow, that's pretty brave of you. You are really sorry for doing that."

"I am."

"Do you think they will arrest you?"

"I think there's a good chance they will."

"Are you prepared for that?"

"I believe so, as much as I can be."

"So, you've been forgiven by God for this, but you still don't feel right about it and want some sort of punishment or consequence for it?"

"I think so. I think that's it. I think that's why I feel I should do this. I think then I will be released from this lingering guilt I've been carrying around."

"Well, Duke, I commend you for wanting to, as much as you can, right your wrongs. I'm not sure many people would do what you want to do. I'm glad my husband wants to go with you and support you."

"Me too."

"It's creeping up on lunchtime," Susan said. "I can make some sandwiches. Anyone interested?"

Both men said yes. "But before you do," Duke said, "I might as well tell both of you this. Yesterday, I told Kimberly about this, and she didn't take it well. In fact, she doesn't want to date me anymore. So, it looks like our relationship has gone by the wayside."

"You know," Susan said, "if I knew her better, I would talk to her about it. I understand how she could react that way. That was a pretty heavy thing you dumped in her lap. But, well, we can hope that maybe she'll come around to realizing she reacted to the old Duke, not the new Duke."

"Maybe. Like you say, I can hope. But I'm at peace with it—with the whole thing. I talked to God about it, and He gave me this peace that I guess the Bible says surpasses all understanding."

"That's excellent," Susan said. "You seem to be really coming along in your walk with the Lord..."

"Yeah," Hunter said, "as another friend of mine, Mike Harms, sometimes says, 'You really got it going on!'"

"Okay, Hunter, but I think I like what Susan said better, that I'm really coming along with my walk with the Lord."

"I have to agree," Hunter said.

With that, the three of them adjourned to the kitchen, where Hunter and Duke watched Susan make tuna fish salad sandwiches. The conversation continued with much lighter subject matter, and today helped Susan become Duke's friend rather than just Hunter's wife.

CHAPTER 89

After lunch at Hunter and Susan's house, Duke drove home. He no sooner arrived home than he thought, Why not tomorrow? Why not fly to Denver tomorrow and turn myself in?

Duke telephoned Hunter.

"Hey, Duke, what's up? Hungry for another tuna salad sandwich?"

"I'd like to fly to Denver tomorrow and turn myself in. I just want to get it done. I want to do it before I chicken out. I know that's pretty short notice, so if you can't go, I understand."

"Tomorrow? Wow. No, I can go. Like I said, I'll make myself available for whenever you want. So, make the reservations, and I'll start packing."

"Good."

"And I'll come pick you up and drive us to the airport. That will make it one less thing you will have to concern yourself with."

"Okay. Thanks, man. And it's better that way anyway because I might not be coming back."

"Good point. Let me know the flight time as soon as you find out. And let me know if there's anything else I can do to help."

"Will do. And Hunter, thanks."

"No problem, my friend."

CHAPTER 90

Friday, May 26

Hunter and Duke drove to Phoenix Sky Harbor airport, parked in the East Economy parking garage, and boarded Southwest flight 402 for Denver. They arrived at Denver International at 6:50 a.m. and rented a car in Hunter's name.

They headed for the Colorado State Patrol office at 15055 S Golden Road in the town of Golden after stopping at an IHOP for breakfast. They walked up to the counter, and Duke asked for the Desk Sergeant. Sergeant Delany came over and said, "What may I do for you, gentlemen?"

"I would like to talk to someone," Duke said, "preferably the investigating officer, about an accident that took place two Christmas Eves ago on Lookout Mountain Road. I have new evidence regarding that accident."

"Very well. If you'll have a seat, I'll see if I can pull up that file and see who the lead investigator was." Sergeant Delany disappeared as Duke and Hunter sat down in the reception area.

Approximately fifteen minutes later, Lieutenant Wilcox walked into the reception area and greeted Duke and Hunter. "I understand one or both of you have some information on the Christmas Eve one-vehicle accident on Lookout Mountain Road a couple of years ago."

"Yes, I do," Duke said.

"It's a closed case. I'm not sure what you could add to it of any significance, but come on back and tell me what you have." Hunter started to follow Lieutenant Wilcox and Duke. Wilcox turned and said, "You can wait here if you don't mind."

Duke turned to Hunter and said, "It's cool. I'm fine." Hunter nodded and turned around and grabbed his seat back. He then said a prayer for his friend.

Lieutenant Wilcox led Duke to an interview room where they each had a seat at opposite sides of a four-foot by six-foot metal table. Wilcox pulled out a recording device and put it on the table. "If you don't mind, I'd like to record what you have to say. It helps with the accuracy, and it keeps me from having to take notes."

"That's fine. Were you involved in the investigation of the accident?"

"Yes, I was. I was the lead investigator. Sergeant Delany printed out the report here, but I remember it well. It was a real tragedy. An apparent nice-looking middle-aged woman in a red Jeep Grand Cherokee, in a hurry to get somewhere on Christmas Eve. She lost it on icy Lookout Mountain Road, careened down the steep mountain sloop, and crashed head-on into a large boulder. Died instantly."

"That lady was my wife."

Wilcox looked at Duke and said, "Rawlings?" He then scanned the report and said, "Yes, Vivian Rawlings—victim. I'm sorry, I didn't remember her name, only the tragedy of the whole thing. That must have really been devastating for you."

"No, to be honest, it wasn't. That is, it wasn't a surprise. You see, that's why I'm here. I'm here to set the record straight. I'm responsible for my wife Vivian's death. I..."

"Hold on here," Wilcox said, "it sounds like you're about to make a confession. I'd better read you your rights before you go any further."

"I know my rights, and I do want to talk, and I don't want a lawyer present."

"Nevertheless, let me Mirandize you for the record."

"Fire away."

Lieutenant Wilcox gave Duke the Miranda warning from memory, and again, Duke said he understood his rights and didn't want an attorney present. Wilcox reminded Duke that he was being recorded and told him to go ahead with what he wanted to say.

"Okay," Duke said. "My wife, Vivian Rawlings... her death on Christmas Eve two plus years ago in that auto accident on Lookout Mountain Road was due to brake failure. I paid a guy who was good at arranging 'accidents' to fix the brakes so that the brake fluid would totally drain out after a few pumps on the brake pedal. My wife died in that car accident because the brakes failed."

"Who did you pay to tamper with your wife's brakes?"

"Oh no, I'm not going to say. He stays out of this. I'm the one responsible for my wife's death. He only did what I paid him to do."

"Very well. Have it your way. Do you have any more to add to what you told me?"

"Not much. That's it in a nutshell. You probably know this already, but Vivian was in the process of going to trial for murdering her previous husband. She was no angel. When I found out for sure that she had murdered her husband, I knew I couldn't trust her anymore. She could try to murder me for who knows what. I could have divorced her, but then we would have had to sell the house and split our nest egg. I didn't want to do that, so I had her killed, and I got to keep everything.

"So, there you have it. I've done a number of things I'm not proud of, but I think this was the worst. If I had it to do over again, I definitely would not have had my wife killed. I might have divorced her, or I might have stuck it out with her. I don't know. That's a tough one. I was pretty certain she was going to go down for killing her previous husband and spend most or all of the rest of her life in prison.

"That's it. That's my confession. You can type that up if you want, and I'll sign it."

"That's what I'd like to do. It won't take long. Wait here if you would."

"Sure."

"Would you like a cup of coffee while you wait?"

"I would—black—no cream, no sugar."

"I'll have someone bring it to you."

"Oh, and my friend, out in the lobby, might like something. He doesn't drink coffee, but I know he'd like a cup of tea if you have it."

"We'll take care of it."

"Thanks."

Duke sat there in the interview room and wondered what would happen next. Would they arrest him right away and put him in jail? Maybe they would release him on his own recognizance. After all, he showed up on his own. One thing was for sure, Duke thought. He was relieved. He was glad to finally get this off his chest. A female trooper brought him his black coffee, and he wondered if the coffee in prison would be any good. He wondered if anyone would come see him in prison. Probably Hunter, once in a while. Kimberly—no. Maybe Yvonne, his wife after Vivian, the wife who tried to poison him—maybe she would pay a visit if she found out he was in prison. But, he made a mental note: don't eat any baked goods she might bring.

While Duke was alone with his thoughts in the interview room, Lieutenant Wilcox had one of the secretaries busy transcribing Duke's confession, which didn't take long. Wilcox then saw his captain, Captain Donaldson. After cluing him in on the situation and the fact that Duke was sitting in the interview room, he showed him the accident report and Duke's transcribed confession.

"What's your impression of this guy?" Donaldson asked.

"He seems pretty squared away. I didn't detect any kookiness at all. I think he may well have paid some guy to mess with the brakes on his wife's car, but for whatever reason, the guy didn't come through. As you can see in the accident report, we did our typical thorough investigation. There was no sign of the brakes on the vehicle having been tampered with. The brake fluid reservoir was intact and full. And there was no trail of any kind of fluid on the road just prior to the vehicle's departure from the pavement. I think Mr. Rawlings got scammed."

"Yeah. This is one for the books. Guy comes in, confesses to having paid someone to kill his wife—he's remorseful about it—wants to get it off his chest, confesses, and it turns out the guy he paid to off his wife stood him up and didn't follow through, took the money, and ran. The ironic thing about all of this, to me, is that the wife was killed anyway—by her own doing—going too fast for the road conditions."

"That is ironic. Crazy things do happen sometimes. So, what do you think, Captain? We cut him loose, right?"

"Well, we still have him on intent, or, more specifically, solicitation. He still intended to kill his wife, and he solicited someone to carry that out, but you said he's not going to give the individual up he paid to do it, so we're dead in the water. The district attorney is not going to go with a confession alone, especially when what he confessed to having happened didn't happen. So, yeah, cut him loose. Send him on his merry way."

"Okay, Captain, you got it."

As Lieutenant Wilcox got up to leave, Captain Donaldson said, "And tell him not to come back."

Lieutenant Wilcox went to his office, took a swig of the lukewarm coffee he had left there, and shook his head as he muttered, "One for the books, all right." He left his office, went to the interview room, knocked on the door, and entered. He sat down and pushed the transcribed confession over to Duke. "Go ahead and read it over. Make sure it's how you want it. If it's okay, go ahead and sign it."

Duke read his confession over and said, "That's it." He signed it and handed it back to Lieutenant Wilcox.

Wilcox looked across the table at Duke and said, "You know, on rare occasion, we have had people come in here and confess to something they didn't do. These people usually have some parts missing, if you know what I mean."

"That's not me."

"Oh, I know. I believe your confession. I believe you believe your wife's accident happened the way you said it did. However, we here at the CPS did a thorough investigation of the accident at the time and found no evidence whatsoever of mechanical failure, including the brakes. Sure, the vehicle was smashed in pretty bad, but the brake reservoir was intact and full of fluid, and there was no sign the lines had been tampered with. We can tell the difference between deliberate man-made damage and crash damage."

"Well, then, I didn't cause her accident. It truly was an accident?"

"That's right. It was determined that your wife was going at least ten miles an hour faster than what was deemed a safe speed for that particular curve in the road—and that's in ideal weather conditions without ice. There were patches of ice where she entered the curve, and with her speed, the result was inevitable."

"She did tend to drive a little faster than she should. But I wonder what happened to Hack…"

"What's that?"

"Oh, nothing. But I honestly did pay a guy to sabotage my wife's brakes."

"Your guy obviously took the money and ran."

"Apparently so." Duke sat there for a spell and processed. Wilcox let him process and didn't say anything. Finally, Duke said, "What's next, then?"

CHAPTER 91

"'What's next?' What's next is you get up and walk out of here and let me get some work done. I enjoyed chatting with you, but I have some paperwork to finish, and then I can get out on the street and help my men keep the roads safe."

"Well, I'm no lawyer, but I know what I did, even though it wasn't carried out, is a crime—an arrestable offense. I had intent. The fact remains that I intended to kill my wife."

"Yes. We could arrest you for solicitation to murder. We have your confession that you solicited a person to sabotage your wife's vehicle brakes so she would have a serious accident. But our district attorney would not try to prosecute on your confession alone. She would at least require the guy you solicited to testify that you enticed him—paid him—to carry out the plan. The fact that he didn't actually tamper with the brakes doesn't really matter. All we need him to say is that you asked him to do it. We don't even need him to confirm that you paid him, but we do need you to identify him and for him to testify."

"No. I won't do that. I absolutely won't give him up. He's saved my life more than once in war zones. He stays out of it."

"And, a guy like that, I bet he would still not testify against you even if you did give him up. I've heard about wartime loyalty. So, there you have it. We're not going to arrest you for something our district attorney is not going to prosecute. She would scold our butts if we did."

"Call her. Just run it by her and see what she says about my specific case."

Wilcox thought for a moment, then said, "All right, I'll do it on one condition—that if she's not there for some reason, you'll leave."

"Okay."

"And, you know what, I'm even going to let you listen in, so follow me to my office."

"Thank you. I really appreciate this."

"I'm doing this because I know your type. If I left you in this room and came back a few minutes later and told you she said no go, you might not buy into it one hundred percent. You would always wonder, 'Did he really call?'"

Duke followed Lieutenant Wilcox into his office and took a seat in front of his desk. Wilcox looked at his quick reference phone list and punched in a number. The phone rang, and a female voice said, "District attorney's office, how may I direct your call?"

Wilcox punched the speaker button and said, "This is Lieutenant Wilcox over at Colorado State Patrol. I'd like to speak with district attorney Marsha Mason, please."

"One moment, sir. I'll ring that number." Duke and the Lieutenant could hear the phone ringing.

"Marsha Mason."

"Yes, ma'am. I have a Lieutenant Wilcox from Colorado State Patrol on the line for you."

"Okay, put him on."

"Go ahead, sir."

"District Attorney Mason, this is Lieutenant Steven Wilcox from CSP, and I am sitting in my office with a gentleman by the name of Duke Rawlings. I have put the phone on speaker so he can hear our conversation."

"Do tell. Hello, Mr. Rawlings."

"Hello."

"So, what have you got, Lieutenant?"

"I'll make it as brief as possible."

"Please do."

"Mr. Rawlings came into our office this morning and voluntarily confessed to having paid an individual to tamper with the brakes of his wife's vehicle so that she would most probably have an accident on Lookout Mountain Road and be killed. The accident did take place on Christmas Eve a little over two years ago. However, the department's very thorough investigation showed no brake tampering and no mechanical failure of the vehicle.

"It was determined that the one-vehicle accident was caused by the vehicle traveling at a rate in excess of ten miles more than what is deemed safe for that section of roadway in ideal conditions. Unfortunately, the road conditions were much less than ideal at the time. The road was icy, and there was a large patch of ice at the point where the vehicle left the road, careened down the slope, and ran head-on into a large boulder."

"Dear me, I remember that tragic accident. So, what does Mr. Rawlings want us to do?"

"He wants justice to be done. He wants to pay in some way for his intent to have his wife killed. We have his written confession, but he said he absolutely will not give us any information on the person he paid to tamper with his wife's brakes. And, obviously, the gentleman he paid to interfere with his wife's brakes didn't follow through."

"I see. Well, as we've discussed before, Lieutenant, I won't try to prosecute anything based on a confession alone. There has to be some corroborating evidence. Even the most inept court-appointed defense attorney could come up with five or six reasons the confession is invalid. To go forward with this would be an exercise in futility. It's commendable that Mr. Rawlings wants to receive some sort of punishment for his lapse of good judgment regarding his wife, but I cannot waste the court's time and expense on a ninety-nine point nine percent for sure acquittal. Is there anything else, Lieutenant?"

"One second." Wilcox looked at Duke, and Duke shook his head. "No, that's it, District Attorney Mason. I felt Mr. Rawlings was sincere and worthy of hearing it from the horse's mouth."

"If I weren't familiar with you, Lieutenant, I would resent the implication. But since I know you to be a conscious law enforcement officer, I take that possibly unintended implication with a sense of humor. I'll get back to my task at hand now. Good day, Lieutenant."

"Thanks."

"There you are, Mr. Rawlings. You did the right thing by coming forward and confessing. But, as you heard firsthand, the district attorney is not going to go forward with your confession as the only evidence. I think we all have some things we regret—things we would like to change or do over, but we can't—so I think we just move on. Learn our lesson and do better next time."

"Are you a Christian, Lieutenant?"

"I like to think so."

"I'm a new believer. I try to do the right thing now."

"Good for you. I wish you well. Keep up the good work. Now get out of here and let me catch some people who never have any remorse for their wrongdoings."

"Nice meeting you, Lieutenant."

"Same here, Duke Rawlings."

CHAPTER 92

Duke walked out of Lieutenant Wilcox's office, down the hallway, and out to the reception area as the Lieutenant watched him go. Duke walked over to Hunter and said, "Let's go have lunch."

"You're free to go?" Hunter asked.

"Yes, I am."

The two walked out of the CSP office and walked over to their Ford Explorer rental. "Let me drive," Duke said, "I know just the place to go."

"So, what happened?" Hunter asked. "Did they reject you because you're too ugly?"

Duke started the Explorer and headed for a particular well-known restaurant in downtown Golden. "Essentially, I confessed, the Lieutenant recorded it, had it transcribed, and I signed it. Then he told me the department had done a thorough investigation of Vivian's accident and determined there was no mechanical failure of the vehicle, including the brakes. There was no tampering of the brakes or brake lines, and the reservoir was intact and full of brake fluid. The conclusion was my wife was going too fast for the curve and the icy road conditions, and that was the cause of the accident. Vivian was responsible for her own death."

"Are you serious? Then you're not in any way responsible for her death. The guy you paid to make her brakes fail apparently reneged on the deal."

"Yes, but I still intended to have her killed, and I solicited someone to do it, so I could have been arrested and prosecuted for that, but their district attorney wouldn't touch it with only a confession."

"Yeah, if the guy you contracted with to jimmy the brakes testified against you, they might go for it then, but I know you won't give him up, and I wouldn't either if I were in your situation. So, you're free! Hallelujah!"

"Physically free, yes."

"I hear ya. So, where are we going?"

"The Buffalo Rose. It's one of Vivian and my last wife, Yvonne's old haunts. I don't know—I guess I just feel like revisiting."

A minute or so later, Duke pulled into the Buffalo Rose parking lot. "Here we are." The two gentlemen walked in and, despite the crowd, were shown a table for two. A waitress named Jojo took their orders, and Duke and Hunter sat back and waited. Duke looked around and said, "I took a little bit of a risk coming here, as Yvonne, the wife I recently divorced, may still come here on occasion. She is not a person I care to run into. If I do spot her, I'm going to throw some money on the table, and we can try to slip out unobserved."

"I'll keep my eyes peeled also. I remember what she looks like as I saw her at your wife Vivian's Grand Jury proceeding a couple of years ago…"

"That's right. You both testified against Vivian."

"So, picking up on what you said a bit ago, you're physically free from any obligation or consequence of trying to have Vivian killed, but maybe not emotionally?"

"Well, yes. The new man in me still can't believe the old man of my past would even try to do such a thing."

"It is an amazing thing that God forgives all of that junk—every bit of it—when you turn your life over to Him."

"Amen to that. I am still truly amazed."

"Uh oh."

"What, Hunter?"

"Hard to believe. Don't look, but I think that is Yvonne who just entered the restaurant with four other ladies."

"Of all things. I mean, what are the odds?"

"I could be wrong. I need you to confirm. I'll tell you when to look. She's in a red top. Okay, hold on—hold on—okay, look toward the entrance now. They're all looking away."

Duke turned his head toward the entrance and looked. One or two seconds later, he turned back toward Hunter. "Unbelievable. That's her all right. And she's with the same girlfriends she and Vivian used to pal around with. They all know me. We've got to get out of here."

"Yeah," Hunter said as he pulled his ball cap bill a little lower to help hide his face. "Do whatever you can with your shirt and hat to make it not look like how you usually wear them."

Duke turned his shirt collar up and pulled the bill of his cap down to also help hide his face. "That's about all I can do, bro."

"Yeah, it's not much, but it's something." Hunter put his hand up to his face like he was scratching it and kept it there. "I think we have to wait and see where they get seated before we make a move."

"Ten-four."

A few moments later. "Okay, the maître d' grabbed some menus, and it looks like she is going to lead them somewhere... yep. She is leading them off to the left of the entrance to the right of us. I see an empty table over by the wall. I think she is leading them there. Yeah...that's it. They are being seated about as far from the entrance as they could get in that section."

"Good," Duke said with relief. "That certainly helps."

"Okay. As soon as Yvonne and friends are preoccupied with looking at the menus, we'll make our escape. I'll let you know. When we do get up to leave, stay on my left side, opposite the ladies, and bend your knees and scrunch down so you look shorter than me."

"Got ya. I'm putting fifty dollars on the table for our meals and tips."

"Good thinking. They're sitting and chitchatting, no menu perusing yet. Yvonne is toying with her menu…now she has picked it up and is starting to look at it. A couple of the other girls have done the same. Let's go, slowly and carefully."

Hunter and Duke got up from their table and slowly walked toward the doors. Duke was scrunched down on Hunter's left and looking away from the ladies perusing their menus. As they passed by the maître d' stand, Duke said, "Have to go—emergency—the money's on the table."

As they approached their rental car, Hunter looked back and said, "No one is following us." They jumped in the Explorer, and Duke drove out of the parking lot and headed toward Denver International.

"Well, so much for reminiscing," Duke said. "I think we head for home."

"Fine with me."

After driving for a minute or two, Duke said, "We don't have plane reservations. What say we check in with the rental agency and see if they will let us drive back to Phoenix and turn the car in at Sky Harbor? When I moved to Arizona a few months ago, I drove straight through and didn't stop to see any sights. I told myself I would have to take another trip at some point and stop and see the sights I missed. I know it's mostly open country, but there were some intriguing things I just drove on by when I moved."

"I'm game. I love road trips."

"Good," Duke said as he pulled over to the curb. There's a place I passed by in Utah during my move to Arizona that intrigued me. It's a little hole-in-the-wall place called Mexican Hat. I don't think more than a hundred people live there, and it's one of the gateways to Monument Valley—a place I've always wanted to visit. A lot of Western movies were filmed there."

"Let's do it. I've always wanted to visit that place, too. The pictures I've seen of it are awesome."

"Excellent. I'll punch in Mexican Hat into the navigation system if you'll square it with the rental car company."

A few minutes later, Duke was following the navigation lady to get onto Interstate 70 toward Utah. Hunter was on the phone with the rental car agency.

"Yes, sir. Instead of turning the Ford Explorer we rented in at Denver International, we'd like to drive it to Phoenix and turn it in at Sky Harbor airport."

"Would you be turning it in on the same date of your contract—Saturday, May 29?"

"Aw—that day, or maybe the day before."

"Hold on while I see if there will be an extra charge for the change to a one-way rental. Sometimes there is, and sometimes there isn't, depending on if we can use another vehicle at your destination, among other factors."

"Okay."

A minute or so later, "You're in luck—no extra charge."

"Good. Thanks a lot." Hunter ended the call with the rental car guy and said to Duke, "That was painless."

"We're set then. The open road is before us, beckoning us onward." A few seconds later, Duke said, "You know, I'm beginning to like commercial flying less and less. Unless you can pay the big bucks for first class, they cram you into small seats with no legroom, won't feed you or entertain you, and cancel your flight if it's not full enough."

"I hear you, man. I'm looking at the navigation readouts here, and it estimates we pull into Mexican Hat at 7:52 this evening. That's without any stops. I know we don't want to get there much later than that. How about we stop at a fast food place and grab some food to go, and how about we switch the driving back and forth so we can take turns with some shut-eye if we're so inclined?"

"Sounds like a plan. Also, there are not many hotels around Mexican Hat, but one I remember seeing a sign for was called the Hat Rock Inn. Maybe we'd better call them and see if we can get a room for tonight."

"Good idea. I'll give that a shot right now."

Hunter and Duke arrived at the Hat Rock Inn at about 7:45 in the evening, checked in, then went over to the recommended Mexican restaurant for some awesome Mexican food. They turned in right after dinner. It had been a long day.

CHAPTER 93

Saturday, May 27

As the first rays of the sun were peeking over the rock formation by the hotel, Duke woke up, shaved, showered, and dressed. He grabbed a Styrofoam cup of coffee from the lobby coffee maker and walked down to the sitting area around the firepit next to the San Juan River.

Hunter arose, shaved, showered, and dressed and joined Duke by the river but without coffee. "What's up, my friend?" Hunter asked.

"I love it out here," Duke said. "I love the desert, the rock formations, the feeling of unlimited space."

"Me too. The Southwest U.S. is the place for me."

"I think we spend the day exploring around here. What do you think, Hunter?"

"I'd love it. We're celebrating your freedom, so whatever you'd like to do, I'm for it."

"That's what I'd like to do. Let's check at the hotel desk and see if we can stay another night, then go have some breakfast."

"You got it."

Even though they were able to book another night at the hotel, they took everything with them—something that Hunter and Duke both lived by: stay flexible—keep your options open. At breakfast, they had a couple of sandwiches made up to take with them for lunch. They heard that there were two decent restaurants in Monument Valley, but again, their mantra was "stay flexible."

First off, they had to go see Mexican Hat, the rock formation, which was only a few miles up the road from town. They checked out the hat and took some photos. And, yes, from certain angles, in particular, the rock formation did look like a Mexican sombrero sitting on top of a man's head.

They then went to Goosenecks State Park and checked out the rock formations that looked like goosenecks. They also saw the deeply cut San Juan River canyon. From there, they got back on Highway 163 South and headed for the Monument Valley visitor center, where the seventeen-mile drive dirt and gravel scenic loop road begins and ends. On the way, of course, they had to stop and take a photo from Forrest Gump point of the iconic view of Highway 163 stretching forever across the open land and seemingly disappearing in the massive rock formations far, far away.

Just a little ways across the state border into Arizona, they reached the visitor center. Hunter purchased a souvenir for Susan, and Duke bought one for either Kimberly, himself, or who knows who. They paid the twenty dollar fee to drive the seventeen-mile loop road and set out to see the sights of Monument Valley. All the sights of Monument Valley are not visible from the loop road, but most of the well-known rock formations are.

As Hunter and Duke drove the seventeen-mile drive, they both were in awe of the vastness and openness of the landscape, along with the enormity of the buttes, mesas, and spires. At one point, they pulled off the road, brought their sandwiches and chips and drinks, climbed up onto a kind of outcropping mesa, dangled their legs over the edge, and had lunch.

"Just look out there, Duke. Look at this whole vast expanse of red dirt and rock formations. Look at how massive the buttes are and the sheer height of the spires and pillars. Does any of that talk to you—say anything to you?"

"I don't know."

"Gaze out there for a minute. Empty your head of any other thoughts. Clear your mind and gaze and listen."

Duke put his sandwich down and tried what Hunter had suggested. A couple of minutes later, Duke said, "Stand strong. That's what just popped into my mind: stand strong."

"I can see that."

"What's it say to you, Hunter?"

"Almost the same thing: stand firm—don't waiver. When you contemplate certain parts or aspects of God's creation—parts that haven't been cluttered by man—I think God can really speak to you. I believe God can more readily answer your questions. Or, maybe we're just more open to what God has to say. Try it. Gaze out there and ask a question. Ask a question that maybe has been bothering you for a time."

"Okay. So, Kimberly, I'm pretty sure, is done with me as a potential marriage prospect. If I start dating other women, should I tell them that I tried to have my wife killed, or should I forever keep it to myself?"

Several minutes of silence went by. "I'm not getting anything, Hunter."

"Stand strong."

"Yeah, that's what I got before." Thirty seconds later, Duke said, "Stand true. Stand strong and stand true. If I'm to stand true, I must be honest and transparent. Like those pillars and monoliths. They are not hiding behind anything. They are forthright. They are out there for everyone to see. If I have more than two or three dates with a girl, I'll tell her. I'll tell her what the old man in me tried to do. I stand tall, I stand strong, I stand true."

Hunter stared at Duke for a second, then said, "That's good. That's really good."

"Wow, Hunter. Do you do this sort of thing often?"

"I've never done it before. Well, maybe I've sort of done it before, like gazing up at the stars at night. But not like this, not in broad daylight, at least not expecting God's handiwork to speak to me."

"Well, I take it that God Himself was speaking to us as we were gazing at His handiwork."

"Duke, my brother, you are right on the money. We were not in any way, shape, or form worshiping the creation—expecting the creation to speak to us. We were admiring His creation and open for Him to speak to us. I believe you are rapidly becoming a mature Christian—a mature believer."

"Thank you, Hunter. I'm sure glad we became good friends."

"Me too, my brother."

Hunter and Duke finished their lunch, climbed down off the mesa, and continued their drive of the loop road and more awesome sights. They took their time getting back to the hotel in Mexican Hat and took more photos on the way. With the sun low on the horizon, it made for some awesome shots of the rock formations and the long shadows they cast.

The next morning, they headed home, going south again on Highway 163, this time all the way to Kayenta, Arizona, where they picked up Highway 160 south to the junction with Highway 89 to Flagstaff. It was scenic driving all the way. They took the 17 freeway from Flagstaff on into the greater Phoenix area and onto Sky Harbor airport. They dropped off the rental car, retrieved Hunter's SUV, and headed for Duke's home in Troon Village.

After dropping Duke off, Hunter pulled into his driveway around 6:00 p.m. Susan welcomed him home, and Hunter told her all about what had happened in Golden, Colorado, while she put the finishing touches on the dinner she was preparing.

After dinner and part of a second glass of wine, while Hunter was telling Susan about Mexican Hat and Monument Valley, he dozed off on the couch. Susan lifted his legs up onto the couch and laid him down with a pillow under his head. She looked at him and thought what a wonderful, caring husband she had.

CHAPTER 94

Monday, May 29
Windy Walk Estates of Troon Village

Duke charged up his burner phone, ate breakfast, then used their ring code and called Hacksaw. Before he called, he reminded himself that he and Hacksaw only use their old code names with each other.

Hacksaw answered his phone the second time after the appropriate rings. "Hey, Dancer. I haven't heard from you for a while. What did you do—fall off the face of the earth for a spell?"

"No, nothing like that. I just haven't needed your services."

"I understand. Say, I sure did a great job with that lady in the red Cherokee, didn't I?"

"Yeah, the objective was achieved, but I'm not sure it was because of your handiwork. Now, don't get mad and don't hang up, but according to the Colorado State Patrol, who investigated the accident, there was no brake failure or any other mechanical failure. So, I don't know what happened with your assignment of sabotaging the brakes on that lady's Jeep, but I'm not upset, and I don't want the money I paid you back. You keep it. In fact, I'm glad you didn't follow through with the brakes. I now regret that I asked you to do it. But I'm curious as to why you didn't follow through with the assignment."

After a period of silence, Hacksaw came clean. "I'm sorry, Dancer. I tried to fix the brakes on that lady's car, but I got in an accident on the way to that lady's house. Can you believe it? On the way to set up an accident, I got in an accident. It wasn't a bad accident. I was all right and all that, but it delayed me, and I couldn't make it to the lady's house on time. I didn't even try because I knew it would be way past the time you said I had to be done."

"No problem. Like I said, I'm glad you didn't follow through, but I'm not glad you were in an accident yourself. Hopefully, the money helped compensate for any damage your vehicle received."

"It did. Thanks. I was going to contact you and see if I could give it another shot at some later time, but when I saw on the news that the lady had the accident anyway and was killed, I figured, well, mission accomplished, even though I had nothing to do with it."

"Listen, that's fine. Like I said, I'm sorry I asked you to do that. I won't be asking you to do anything like that again, but who knows, I may need your services in some other capacity down the line. I'm going to be doing more investigative-type work now rather than the stuff we were doing over in the war zones. So, if something comes up I think you can help with, I'll be in touch."

"Well, all right, Dancer. Thanks. You know, I can do all sorts of things."

"I know. That's why I may have something for you down the road. So, you take care.

"I will, Dancer. You do the same."

Duke punched off the phone with Hacksaw and wondered. Did You do that, Lord? Did You cause Hacksaw to have a minor accident so he couldn't carry out that terrible task I asked him to do? If You did, Lord, thanks.

CHAPTER 95

Wednesday, May 31, Near Midnight
Ridgeline Road
Carefree, Arizona

Hunter's phone rang. "Hello."

"Is this Hunter Kingsley, Private Investigator?"

"Why, yes, it is. What's up, Duke?"

"I just got a call from my kid sister, Nadine. It seems that her daughter, Natalie, is missing. Nadine asked me if I knew any private investigator types who did missing persons. I said I did and recommended you."

"I've never done any missing persons cases."

"Me neither. It shouldn't be hard, though."

"You're right. It should be a piece of cake."

"So you'll do it? You'll take the case?"

"Yes, partner. Let's start our first PI case. Let's go find Natalie."

Milton Keynes UK
Ingram Content Group UK Ltd.
UKHW032033191024
449814UK00010B/570